FINDING HER STRENGTH

THE SONOMA SERIES
BOOK THREE

SHELBY GUNTER

For all the strong women

PROLOGUE

UNKNOWN

The flash drive is handed to me as I walk into the empty computer room. Despite having special privileges, I'm still treated as a second-rate citizen in this shithole. It's infuriating. No part of this is going to plan, but this flash drive holds one of the keys to getting my kingdom back. And I will get it back.

Opening the only file on the drive, the computer screen illuminates a hooded figure as they walk across the bus terminal, keeping their head turned away from the cameras. They load their suitcase and step onto the bus headed for Atlanta.

I don't need to see her face to confirm her identity, I'd know that body anywhere. Did she really think she could run away from me? That I wouldn't look for her the minute I was told she was gone?

I thought my lessons on respect and obedience had stuck, but apparently, I have some reteaching to do. She won't disobey again after I'm through with her.

As the bus leaves the terminal, I bring up the route map. So many places she could be hiding, but none of them are out of my reach. I will find her. I've got all the time in the world.

I rewind the footage and watch her get on the bus again.

Don't worry, little pet. I'll find you and bring you home, where you belong.

1

HOPE

A gasp escapes my throat as I quickly sit up in bed. My hand lands on my chest as I work to slow my breathing, shaking off the tendrils of fear. Images of cold, hard eyes and clenched fists try to push their way into my mind.

Another nightmare.

I haven't had one in a few weeks and was starting to get used to sleeping all the way through the night instead of waking up in a panic. Sometimes, I can pinpoint what triggers them, but this one came out of left field.

The clock on my nightstand reads four-thirty in the morning. With adrenaline still coursing through me, I know I won't be going back to sleep. I have to be at the shop in a couple of hours for a delivery anyway, so I might as well start my day.

Thinking about my flower shop, Blooming Beautiful, a smile pulls at the corners of my mouth. It's still hard to believe this dream of mine has become a reality. Even after being in business for over a year now, I still sometimes can't wrap my head around it.

I quickly shower in my tiny bathroom, then get dressed for my day. I bought a bunch of T-shirts with my business logo in different colors so that I can maintain a professional appearance while still being comfortable. It makes getting ready for my day quick and painless.

After making a cup of coffee, I grab my latest read and sit out on my baby balcony. Since I have some extra time this morning, I'm going to take advantage of it by escaping into the world of romance.

I love reading all kinds of genres, but romance novels are my favorite. There's something about seeing a couple get their happily ever after, no matter what they go through, that's comforting to me. Maybe it's because I'm still working toward my own happy ending—minus the man part of the equation. I do not need a guy to be happy. A puppy, on the other hand, might be a good option.

When I moved to Sonoma, North Carolina, I was finally taking back my life. Never again was I going to allow someone else to make decisions for me. Never again would I let fear stop me from doing what I want to do.

I found an apartment I loved, an adorable little storefront to open my shop, and every choice I've made has been mine alone. Now, all I have left to do is accept what happened in my past, and move forward.

I thought I was getting close when the nightmares stopped, but after last night, maybe that's not the case. I'm doing much better than I was this time last year, though, so, despite the dreams, I'm still in a great place.

After getting in some decent reading time, I move from my comfy patio chair and head back inside to make a to-go cup of coffee. Getting my day started on the right foot requires two things: coffee and flowers. Having one of those items in my hand, I leave my tiny apartment and head toward my shop for the second.

The town is quiet this early in the morning, blanketed in a sense of peace before the sun wakes the world with a new day. Despite having to be here before dawn, watching the sunrise through the windows of my shop brings me a joy I never knew I'd get to experience.

Owning a business has many pitfalls—having to wake up early, for one—but what makes everything worth it for me is being the one to make all the decisions. I love getting to choose what items come into the store, how it's decorated, or even who I employ. I also love being able to change my mind just because I feel like it. It's freeing.

A knock on the back door prompts the arrival of my flower delivery. When I prop the door open, Denny lugs in a long box of flowers. "Good morning, Denny."

He sets the box down on the large table in the middle of the room. "Mornin', Hope. You doing okay?"

"I'm just fine. How are you? How are the kids?" Denny works for the flower company in Westlake—the next town over—but lives here in Sonoma. We've gotten to know each other pretty well over the last year.

As Denny unloads the rest of my flowers, he tells me all about his little girl's dance recital, which prompts a story about his neighbor's daughter who use to do dance but is now, apparently, a surly teenager with an attitude problem.

I've found the people in this tiny town are the nosiest busybodies I've ever met. They are the masters of leading questions, trying to dig up more information on whatever gossip is being spread. It's quite entertaining to watch them try to one-up each other with what they know. I love it.

"How's everything going with you? The shop doing okay?" Denny asks when he's finally done with the last box. He's standing next to his truck with his hands on his hips, seeming perfectly content to chat the day away.

"The shop is doing great. I couldn't be happier."

"Good, good. You know, if you're lonely, I've got a cousin who's single. I'm sure he'd love to take out a pretty girl like you." Denny winks.

Mortification fills my face as I self-consciously laugh. "I'm not lonely, Denny, but I appreciate the offer. I should probably get these flowers put away before I have to open." Talk about a leading question, that was just bold.

Chuckling, Denny waves a hand in response before jumping into his truck to finish his deliveries. Shaking my head, I walk back inside to start putting the flowers in the large walk-in cooler.

Despite their meddling, the people here do genuinely care about me and my store. Even when I'm being cagey about my background, they still say hello or ask how I'm doing. What's more, they truly want to hear my answer. It's refreshing when I'm so used to no one paying any attention to me at all.

When I first arrived in Sonoma, I didn't want to be noticed. I wanted to blend into the background, hiding behind the flowers I created. I thought it would be an easier way to live, a simpler way. Instead, these people took me in and showed me I didn't have to hide away anymore. I could finally live my life exactly how I wanted without having to hold back who I truly was on the inside.

It's been a liberating experience, allowing me to slowly uncover the person I was always supposed to be instead of who I was forced to be.

The alarm on my phone blares, telling me it's time to open, so I step toward the front doors, twist the deadbolt, and flip over the *Open* sign. Turning, I take in my shop as the morning sun shines through the windows.

Around the outside edges of the store are dozens of leafy plants, creating a secret garden vibe. Interspersed are pre-potted plants people are encouraged to buy. I have a couple of tables in the middle of the room with multi-tiered displays holding an array of succulents, garden-themed trinkets, as well as items to help your garden thrive.

A long counter lines the back wall, where the cash register sits on one end, while the other is used for my worktop. Four glass refrigerators are lined up behind the counter holding several options for flower arrangements that people can either buy or use as inspiration for their own arrangements.

My obsession with flowers started when I was a little girl, creating arrangements for my grandmother using flowers from her garden. Even though I was little, I knew I wanted to do it as my career. Then I worked in a flower shop in high school. Working long hours every day, I learned a lot about the business in the hopes I could keep my job after I graduated. Then my life turned upside down, and I was never able to follow my dreams.

Memories from my past start to creep into my mind, and I shake my head, focusing on my to-do list for the day instead. I don't need or want the negative energy from my past in my shop, so I make sure to never bring those memories here.

Standing behind my counter, feeling like I'm back in charge of my life, I look at my list of customer orders. It's going to be a busy day if I'm to get everything done. When the door chimes, ushering in one of my regulars, any lingering negativity from my past is quickly replaced with flowers, greenery, and beautiful arrangements for the rest of the day.

Exactly how I prefer it to go.

2

LEVI

I swing for the fences, the vibrations moving through my arms as the drywall smashes into pieces. God, that feels good. I take another swing at the wall in front of me, working to open the space of the house we're renovating.

Some of my guys hate demolition day, and I can understand why. It's a shit ton of work to tear out countertops and take down walls. For me, it's the best therapy I could ever get. Plus, I've gotten ripped from wielding a sledgehammer, which makes every ounce of effort worth it.

It also helps to ease the constant energy buzzing through my system. Ever since I can remember, I've been on the move. Which means I wreaked a lot of havoc growing up. My mom still gives me shit about being a terror. Sitting still has always been a struggle for me, so having a job where I can expend a lot of energy has been a saving grace.

Max Miller and I started JM Construction almost five years ago. His wife, Lucy, and I have been friends since we were little. When they moved back to Sonoma after college, Max and I grew close, realizing we had many of the same interests. He has an architectural degree, and I've been doing construction since I was legally able to be on a site. Between my contacts and Max's talent at design, our business has taken off.

A whistle grabs my attention from tearing out the wall in front of me, and I glance over my shoulder as Harley nods her head toward the front yard. The new guy, Michael, is parking his truck, getting ready to come back inside from lunch.

I grin at Harley as I set down my sledgehammer. Moving quickly, I squeeze into a small alcove in the main living room. Michael comes striding back into the room, completely oblivious to me being there. I jump out of the alcove, scaring the shit out of him.

"Fuck, man!"

Harley's laugh echoes through the room, along with mine, as Michael rubs his chest.

"I'd say sorry, but I wouldn't mean it." I grin at him.

"I hate you all," Michael says, shaking his head.

"Yo, Levi, can you come look at this?" Jared calls down from the second floor.

I slap Michael on the shoulder, then head to the stairs, my boots thumping on each step. Even though I'm the general contractor, I have a hard time being super professional on-site. Around the homeowners, you'd never know I enjoy pranking my guys, but when they're not around, I gotta do something to make the long workdays fun. Especially when something major goes wrong. Based on Jared's tone, I have a feeling I'm not going to like what he found.

I walk into the room and immediately know my hunch was right. Random electrical cords are coming out of the wall we were planning on tearing down.

"Well, fuck me sideways."

"I'd rather not," Jared says unhelpfully.

"Until we know what those go to, we can't keep going with the demo up here." I sigh. "Can you finish tearing out the wall downstairs while I call the homeowners?"

"On it."

I turn to walk out of the room. Calling the homeowners when something goes wrong is one of the worst parts of my job. It's always a gamble as to how they'll react. Every so often, they'll be cool about it, but most of the time, they get pissed about unexpected issues.

Walking out the back door, I step onto the grass to make my call. The phone rings in my ear as dread swirls in my stomach.

"Hello?"

"Hi, Mrs. Silvey. This is Levi Jackson with JM construction. How are you doing?"

"Hi, Levi. I'm fine. What's going on?"

"Well, we've hit a bit of a snag. We found some random electrical wires in the wall that aren't supposed to be there. We're going to need to get an electrician out here to get it sorted."

I hear a sigh on the other end of the phone and brace for the barrage of anger.

"Any idea on what this will do to our budget or timeline?" she asks. I hesitate, surprised at the normal tone in her voice.

"Um, not anything official yet. We've still got plenty of stuff to do while we wait, so the demo schedule should be fine."

"Okay. Keep me updated."

"Will do. Thanks for being understanding, Mrs. Silvey." After hanging up, I stand in the backyard for a bit. The mild April air dries the sweat off my forehead while I try to calm down from the pointless nerves moving through me. I did not expect her to take the news so well. In most cases, these calls entail a lot of frustration, usually taken out on me. Despite having built up my walls to keep from getting my feelings hurt, it can still be hard to take the brunt of a person's anger.

Taking another breath, I quickly call my electrician, Neal.

He's able to squeeze me in tomorrow afternoon, so hopefully, he'll be able to get things straightened out before we get too behind schedule. I'm willing to work overtime to keep us on track, but there's only so much I can do if we're set back too far.

Shaking my head, I turn to go back inside the house. Jared is finishing the demo in the kitchen when I walk in. We're tearing out most of the inside of the house since it hadn't been updated since the seventies. If I never see another lime green kitchen again, it'll be a miracle.

Using the exertion of demolition, I expend the last bit of nerves in my body from the phone call. We clear out the outdated cabinets, as well as the countertops, chucking them into the dumpster outside.

It's dark out by the time we finish most of the kitchen. I tell Jared he can head home, but I stay behind to prepare for the next day. Some people say I work too much, which is probably true. I do work a lot of hours. I enjoy the work, though, so it doesn't feel like too much to me.

When I'm finally done at the site, I pack up my stuff and jump in my truck to head home. Living in a small town, there are only a few apartment buildings, so finding a suitable place isn't always easy. I got lucky with my apartment. They asked me to help them renovate, and in return, I get to live in one of the units at a discounted rate.

I could afford the regular rate, but with the cheaper rent, I've been able to save a hefty sum. One I hope to use on buying a fixer-upper house. After all of the places I've renovated over the years, you'd think I would want to build a brand-new house, but there's something special about taking an old, dilapidated building and making it beautiful again. Plus, it'll give me something to do in the evenings when I'm done working.

With nothing to do tonight, I call my brother, Cooper, to see what he and his wife, Quinn, are up to.

"Are you hurt?" Cooper asks when he answers, throwing me off.

"Uh, no. I'm fine. Why would you think that?"

"I just figured you'd still be at work right now, so if you're calling me, it's because you must have hurt yourself. Again."

I roll my eyes, even though Cooper can't see it. "I fell through the stairs one time. But no, I'm fine. We ran into a snag today, so I had to call it quits earlier than usual."

"Quinn's making… uh, some fancy dish I can't remember the name of if you want to come over. You know how she gets."

Quinn is constantly experimenting with food, creating new meals or overestimating how much my brother can eat. When that happens, she usually brings me a container of leftovers. And if I'm honest, she's a better cook than my mom. A thought I will never say out loud if I want to keep my life.

"That would be awesome. I'm going to shower first, then I'll be over. Does Quinn need anything?"

The muffled sound of Cooper's voice tells me he's asking. "Quinn says she needs frozen peas."

"Got it. I'll pick them up on my way."

"Thanks. We'll see ya in a bit." Cooper hangs up as I walk into my apartment.

Now that Coop is married, I am one of the last single people in our friend group, which has been a lot harder to deal with than I expected. I'm social by nature, so being by myself for extended periods of time isn't something I enjoy. With most of our friends having found their partners, I've been by myself more often than not. Luckily, I still have Sara to hang out with. She's the only other single person in our group.

For a long time, our friends tried to get us to date each other, but neither one of us feel that way about the other. She's more like a sister to me than anything else. The idea of dating her is just too weird.

I'm not even sure settling down is in the cards for me. I've tried many times over the years, with varying types of women, hoping one of them will be the right one. I'll take her out a few times, have some fun, then something usually happens, and we stop seeing each other. Sometimes, it's me losing interest, other times, she's the one to end things. But, no matter what I do, it always ends. At this point, I'm prepared to be alone forever. Stuck in an endless loop of going out with women who want nothing more than a good night.

Jesus, that's a depressing thought.

I head back to my bathroom to shower, grateful my brother is more like a best friend. Without his invitation to hang out, I would've been climbing the walls with boredom.

I could've called one of the girls I occasionally date to see if they wanted to go to dinner. The problem is they only want to go out with me to come back to my apartment for a quick fuck and a *see you later*. Which hasn't been appealing recently.

I also recognize how douchey that makes me look. The idea that I have women available anytime I text them makes me feel sleazy. The crazy part is I wasn't the one who set it up like that. It's like all I'm needed for is a good time and a happy ending. They don't want to date me, just fuck me. Which has been great up until a couple of months ago when I started to wonder if this was all I was capable of having—meaningless relationships with no substance. That's not how I thought my life would end up nor how I want it to continue.

When I'm done cleaning up, I grab my favorite navy blue baseball hat and keys to head to the store. Once I'm in my truck, I feel my shoulders relax, the tension of the day draining from my body. It's going to be a good night.

3

———

HOPE

The snip of my shears clicks through the room as the afternoon sunlight filters through the windows. The bouquet I'm making is for Mr. Shanihan, a sweet, older gentleman who brings flowers to his wife's grave every week. The white and blue lilies stand out starkly against the dark countertop as I place them into their arrangement. Apparently, they were Mrs. Shanihan's favorite.

My eyes flick up to watch him walk around my store. He's always requested his bouquet to be ready at 3:00 p.m. on the dot, but he also comes twenty minutes early to pick them up every week. I've offered many times to make them earlier, but he only wants them right at three. I think he's lonely. Coming here early gives him someone to talk to every week.

"Mr. Shanihan, you're looking very dapper today. Any particular reason you're all dressed up?" He has on a western button-down shirt—pearl buttons and all—and a nice pair of denim jeans. His gray hair is combed over, while his faded blue eyes hold a sparkle in them I haven't seen since I opened the shop. If I'm not mistaken, I think he's even blushing.

"Can I let you in on a little secret, sweet Hope?" He grins

at me, sauntering closer to my countertop as I finish up his flowers.

"Always," I say, returning his grin.

"I'm going on a date."

"Oh, my goodness." I can't help the chuckle that breaks free. "Who's the lucky lady?"

"Well since you told me *no* so many times, I asked out another pretty girl. Her name is Elizabeth."

Every time Mr. Shanihan came in to pick up his flowers, he'd ask me if this was the day I'd finally go out with him. I always told him I was flattered but was not the right girl for him.

"Are you talking about Mrs. Jensen?" I've heard she's a rather eccentric woman. Someone once told me she likes to oil paint naked on her back deck.

"Yep." He rocks back on his heels with his hands in his pockets, looking pleased as punch.

"Well, I hope you have the best time," I tell him, handing over his flowers.

"Oh, I always have a good time." He winks at me. All I can do is laugh in response. After Mr. Shanihan leaves, I clean up my shop, rearranging some of the displays sitting out on the table.

Today, I am closing a little early so I can have a virtual session with my counselor. I found her through an app when I first moved to Sonoma, and she's been an integral part of helping me heal from my past. Over the last year, I've steadily been able to decrease my sessions to only once a month. I think I'll be ready to cut back even more soon, which in and of itself is an achievement.

Walking back to my tiny office, I prepare my space for the session by lighting candles, organizing my desk, and doing what I can to remove any distractions and create an environment for healing.

When it's time, I join the meeting, seeing my counselor's face fill my computer screen. She's a cute pixie of a woman, who doesn't let me get away with anything. I really like her.

"Hello, Hope!"

"Hey, Joy. How are you doing?"

"Great. How's your week been?"

"Pretty good. The store has been busy, which has been nice."

"How far were you able to make it on the homework I gave you?"

"Um, I gave it a lot of thought. I even tried to talk to Claire. Open up a little more. I told her about my grandmother's flower garden."

"How was it to talk with her about your grandmother?"

"Hard." Emotions start rising up my chest.

"Let's talk about that."

* * *

THE MANGO MART is surprisingly quiet this evening as I shop. This is one of the worst errands I have to do as an adult. Grocery shopping. I don't have any real reason to not like the task. I just don't. The worst part is I love cooking. There's something special about being able to create foods however you like them. You can travel the world with a few special ingredients, all while staying in your kitchen. But having to take the time to find said ingredients is annoying.

I walk down the aisles, crossing things off my list as I go. Making a snap decision to check out the ice cream section, I start perusing the flavors. As I do, a man steps into the same aisle. My body goes on high alert as it always does, and I take him in out of the corner of my eye, doing my best to keep from being noticed.

His jeans are tight around his thighs, and his work boots

are covered in paint. His navy blue ball cap is covering his face, so I can't see much of it, but the way he fills out his T-shirt is… really nice.

My thoughts stop me short.

I don't notice men or how they fill out clothes. I normally make sure I'm not in their vicinity at all.

This guy, though… I noticed him.

It's probably because of what Joy brought up today during our session. She'd asked if I had thought any more about dating, and I vehemently denied the idea.

I do not need a man in my life. I'm perfectly content with the way things are. There's no reason to bring in some random person who could disrupt everything.

I turn, making sure my back stays toward the man, and run through the rest of my grocery list. After I grab the last few items I need, I head up to the checkout lane.

The man with the blue hat is a couple of people in front of me, and, for a moment, I let my eyes roam over his shoulders since I can't see his face. I didn't know guys actually worked out enough to make their shoulders that large. I've read about muscles like his in my books but have never seen them in person.

Fascinating.

"You're up, sweetheart," a lady says from behind me, startling me into motion. I'd been so distracted I didn't even realize it was my turn to check out.

"Sorry about that." I sheepishly smile at her.

"Oh, don't you worry. I was just as entranced. It would have been a shame not to stare at those fine muscles." She winks, making me laugh.

I set my groceries on the belt, then finish checking out, waving goodbye to the woman behind me. When I'm home, I put everything away, turning on some music to fill the silence of my apartment.

Most of the time, my little space feels cozy, comfortable. Tonight, it feels a little empty. My conversation with Joy swirls in my head. She's been encouraging me to start making friends, and for the first time since I moved here, I'm wondering if I might be ready.

4

———

LEVI

"What's your poison tonight, Levi?" Cheryl asks from the other side of the bar. She's got her silver-streaked blonde hair clipped back instead of in her normal ponytail. She's been the bartender at Donna's since before I can remember.

"Three of whatever's on tap." I smile.

She winks at me before turning to pour my drinks. When Cheryl slides the glasses across the bar, I head back to the table the guys scored. Finding a place to sit on a Friday night is always a gamble since this is the only place in town to grab a drink.

"There's no way!" Max shouts as I sit down, passing out beer to everyone but Cooper, who is on call tonight.

"I'm telling you, it's the truth." Todd grins at him.

"What are we talking about?" I ask, trying to catch up.

Cooper leans toward me. "Todd and Max are fighting over whether it's legal to spit on the ground."

"How the hell did they get on to that topic?"

"I found an old copy of Sonoma's founding laws the other day." Cooper is the police chief of Sonoma, and Todd is the deputy chief. They usually have some hilarious stories, but this is a new one, even for them.

"You're actually saying you could arrest me because I spit on the sidewalk before we walked into the bar?"

"Look it up! It's an actual law in the town's bylaws."

"He's right, Max. Not that we'd ever enforce it. I think it was originally created so men would spit tobacco in those pot things instead of anywhere they pleased," Cooper adds.

Max shakes his head. "So fucking weird. Now I'm not going to be able to spit if I need to."

"Is that something you have a problem with? Do you have a medical condition we need to know about?" I tease.

"No, asshole, but when I want to while I'm running or something, I'll be thinking about breaking the law. Then what will I do?"

"Swallow it?" Todd suggests.

"That's what she said." I'm barely able to get the words out before we all descend into hysterics.

Max attempts to sulk, but the grin he's fighting gives him away.

"Where's Tucker tonight?" Todd asks. He and Max could be brothers with their dark hair and dark eyes. If you didn't know them, they'd seem intimidating. Todd's personality actually matches his looks while Max's does not.

"He's got Noah this weekend, so he wanted to stay home to hang with him and Natalie," I respond. Natalie and Tucker are in the process of adopting Noah. Tucker—who's a fire-fighter—saved his life when the group home Noah lived in burned down. They've submitted all the necessary paper-work to officially adopt him. Now they have to wait on the state to approve their application.

"Speaking of adoption, Meg and I have been approved for the foster to adopt program," Todd says.

"For real?"

"No kidding?"

"Awesome, man!" we say in unison. I know they've been waiting for the right opportunity to come their way, and when Natalie and Tucker started the adoption process, Meg and Todd decided they wanted to do the same thing.

Todd grins at us, happiness shining through brighter than I've ever seen before.

"What does that mean for placements or who you can adopt?" I ask.

"Well, we're on a list for when the state needs a home for a kid. If their case is open for adoption, we can apply to adopt while we're fostering them."

"You guys will be perfect foster parents," Cooper says.

"We finally finished all the required courses and home inspections, and now we have to wait for the state to call us."

"Good for you, man. This is great." I'm truly happy for them. I know they've wanted kids for a long time, but Megan isn't able to have them biologically. I can't imagine a more perfect couple for children who need a good home.

"I'm going to grab another beer. Anyone else need another?" I ask.

When they all shake their heads no, I head to the bar, motioning at Cheryl for a refill. She nods in response while filling a different order.

"Hey, Levi."

I turn toward the voice to find Stephanie Arnold standing next to me. I took her on a couple of dates years ago, but nothing came out of it.

The straw of her drink is resting against her smiling mouth. I think the pose is supposed to come off as seductive, but I've always found it a little weird.

"Oh, hey, Steph. How's it going?" With her blonde hair, blue eyes, and long face, she's naturally pretty. Unfortunately, she ruins it with the amount of makeup she cakes on.

"Pretty great. How are you? It's been a while since I've seen you out."

"Yeah, I've been pretty busy recently with work." Cheryl passes my beer across the bar, and I take a welcome drink. "I'm here with the guys, so I'm going to head back over there. It was good to see you."

"You, too! Call me sometime." Stephanie grins, and I nod my head before walking back to the table.

When I sit down, the guys are looking at me like there's something on my face.

"What?" I ask, running my hand over my mouth in case I have a beer 'stache.

"We're surprised you came back over here," Cooper says.

"Why? We're having a guys' night."

"That's never stopped you from taking a girl home before," Max points out.

I shrug my shoulders, playing off their words, even though they're true. "Not really feeling it tonight."

"Are you sick?" Todd asks with genuine concern.

"Guys, I'm fine. Just because I'm not going home with the first woman who flirts with me doesn't mean I'm losing my mind. You act like I'm some man-whore who will go home with anyone."

"Well… it's sort of true, man. Although, now that I think about it, you haven't been... *out on the town* in a while." I know Cooper's words aren't meant to be harsh, but for some reason, they're sort of grating on my nerves.

I'm not sure why it's making me mad. What he's saying is true. I loved going out, flirting with women, maybe taking them home, or getting their number to go out another time. Things have started to change for me, though. I'm not looking for a quick release only to move on to the next one a few days later.

But I have yet to find someone who wants more from me than that.

5

———

HOPE

"Ouch, dammit." I stick my bleeding thumb into my mouth, attempting to stop the blood flow. After so many years of dethorning roses, you'd think I'd have learned to avoid them. I want to roll my eyes at myself sometimes.

"You okay, boss?" Claire, my one and only employee, asks me. She's twenty-two, insanely outgoing, and my only friend in Sonoma. She's never pushed me for information about my past, which is one of the many reasons I love her. I've slowly been sharing my past with her, but it's still incredibly difficult for me to trust others.

The bells on Claire's shoes jingle as she walks across the store to grab the first aid kit for me. Her multicolored, striped crop top under denim overalls is adorably trendy. I'm envious of her ability to wear whatever she wants with no qualms about what people think of her.

"Let me see." She holds her hand out for mine, and I reluctantly let her hold it as she doctors up my thumb. The feeling of her hand on mine sends a little shiver of nerves down my spine. I hate that I still have a reaction to physical touch.

"There, all better," she says. I look down at the pink, sparkly Band-Aid on my finger.

"Did you have to pick the sparkly one?"

"Yep, everyone needs a little sparkle in their life." Claire winks at me, then walks back to the front of the store to continue watering the plants. Her zest for life always adds a little color to mine. It's another of the many reasons I enjoy working with her.

I continue dethorning the roses for an arrangement going out this evening until the door chimes, signaling one of my favorite people entering the store.

"Hi, Mrs. Jackson!" I say, greeting the force that is Alice Jackson. Her brown hair is streaked with silver, but her thin frame makes her seem younger. When I first opened my shop, she made it her mission to learn everything she could about me, and while I did tell her a little bit about myself, I never gave in to her serious inquisition. I think she gained a new respect for me afterward.

She comes in regularly and always asks for the craziest arrangements for her house. Her requests constantly have my creative mind swirling.

"Hi, sweet Hope. How are you today?"

"Just fine, and you?"

"Wonderful, especially with one of my babies now happily married. You did such a great job on Quinn's flowers." Quinn and Cooper Jackson got married a month ago, and Alice hasn't stopped talking about it since. She was so happy to have Quinn as a daughter-in-law. It honestly made me a little bit jealous of them. To have someone in your life who cares as much as Alice does would be a dream.

"Thank you. They were some of my favorites. What can I do for you today?"

"I need one of your premade bouquets. The pink one, please."

"You got it." My cell phone rings as I turn to get the

arrangement Alice requested. I quickly answer when I see it's my landlord. I've been waiting to hear back from her about my lease renewal. Being on a month-to-month lease has been great, but since the store is doing well and I'm finally feeling settled here, I'd like to change it to a yearlong lease.

"Hello, Hope, I apologize for taking so long to get back to you," Susan starts.

"It's fine, am I approved for another year?" I ask as I wrap up the bouquet Alice picked out.

"Actually, I'm sorry to do this to you, but... we aren't able to approve your application. We need the apartment back for my son. He's moving home and needs a place to live. I'm so sorry about this, Hope."

Shit. This is not what I need right now. I was finally feeling settled in this apartment. Despite the size, it was mine. I loved it.

I work to clear the emotion from my throat before I speak. "I understand. My lease ends next week. Do you need me to move out right away, or do I have some time?

"Unfortunately, we need you to move right away. We only have two weeks before he moves home, so we'll need some time to clean it before he arrives."

A week. No one can move that fast, but what other option do I have? I avoid confrontation like the plague, and I know Susan isn't doing this to be mean. "Um... I guess I can figure something out," I say hesitantly.

"Thank you so much, Hope. Please let me know if I can help at all," she says, then quickly hangs up the phone.

A deep sigh has my shoulders drooping. I take a minute for myself before I turn back around to get Alice checked out. I dig down deep and pull my shoulders back, working to hold on to the little bit of strength I've built up over the last year.

"Sorry about the wait, Mrs. Jackson."

"Oh, that's okay, dear. Um, I couldn't help overhearing your call."

A soft laugh falls from me. I could almost guarantee she did everything in her power to overhear my conversation. Leave it to Alice Jackson to put a smile on my face when it feels like my world is falling down. *Again.*

"It sounds like you might be in need of a house. I have just the place in mind," she continues, a little gleam of excitement in her eyes.

"You don't have to worry about me. I'm sure I can find something."

"Don't you even think about it. It's Quinn's grandparents' house. She rents it out all the time, and I happen to know it's currently empty right now. I'll have her call you. What's your phone number?" Alice says all of this incredibly fast, and it takes me a minute to catch up. Is she actually offering me a place to rent right now?

I list off my phone number before I even realize what I'm doing while Alice punches it into her phone with a savviness I wouldn't have expected from her. "I feel like I should mention that I can't afford very much. I'm sure a house would probably be out of my range."

"Nonsense. We'll make it work." Alice winks at me, waving her hand in the air as if she's swatting away my words. All I can do is stand there in confused amusement. She looks down at the flowers I'm still holding, which prompts me to finish ringing up her arrangement.

Alice pays for her items, telling me I'll hear from Quinn sometime today about the rental. All I can do is nod my head as she walks out of the store. I'm not 100 percent certain, but it sounds like I may not have to freak out over the whole moving-out-in-one-week thing.

Nope... still freaking out. Who the hell is able to pack their stuff up in a week?

"Did you give Alice Jackson your phone number?"

I jump, not realizing Claire had come up next to me.

"Sorry, thought you knew I was here," she apologizes. I smile, waving away her apology. She's gotten used to my jumpiness and, thankfully, has stopped asking me about it.

"Um, yes, I guess I did give it to her."

"You know she's going to be the person to actually use it, right? Not be the one who says, *'Give me your number so we can hook up,'* and then never calls."

I sigh. "Yeah, that was probably a mistake. She was so sneaky about it, too."

"I can't wait to see what happens next." Claire laughs, her shoes tinkling as she walks away from me.

I roll my eyes at her, but she has a point. I've been cagey for a reason, and now, one of the biggest gossiping hens in town has my phone number. Things are definitely about to get interesting. I don't know if I'm more terrified or excited to see where life will take me next.

6

———

LEVI

My breakfast sizzles in the pan in ways I'm not sure are normal. I'm doing my best not to burn the bacon and eggs that are cooking at the same time. Quinn makes this look so easy when she has, like, four pans going all at once. I figured I could handle two, but this is starting to get out of hand.

My bacon pops, and the grease lands on the burner, turning the stove into a large ball of fire.

A high-pitched scream pops out of my mouth in surprise.

I throw the pan off the burner, then turn off the stove, breathing hard from the fear of burning the entire apartment complex down. With smoke blanketing the air and my detectors blaring, I open my front door along with some windows to help air the place out.

I turn back to the kitchen to salvage my eggs, but as soon as I give them a stir, I know they're a lost cause, as well. Black coats the bottom of both the pan and the eggs. All I can do is take them off the burner.

A knock on my open door has me turning around to find Cooper and Quinn standing in my small entryway. They both are grinning until Quinn's eyes go wide, and she slaps a hand across her eyes.

"Dude, why is your door open when you're dressed like that?" Cooper groans.

"Like what?" I look down at myself to find I'm only in my boxers. "Oh, sorry, guys." I laugh. "I was trying to air out the smoke. I'll go throw on some pants."

My brother guides his wife further into my apartment since she still has her eyes covered, and I walk back to my room to put on some clothes. Once I'm decent, I find Cooper and Quinn standing in my kitchen, taking in the chaos.

"Sorry about the mess. I tried to make breakfast, and it didn't go well."

"I could tell by the black remnants of food in your pans," Quinn says, her nose turned up in disgust.

"Not all of us can be five-star chefs like you!"

"Well then, I'll just take these scones back home," Quinn taunts.

I rush into the small kitchen to pluck them out of her hands. "You'll do no such thing!" Opening the box, the smell of blueberries and sugar hits my nose, making me groan. My stomach gurgles as I grab one, shoving it into my mouth.

God, that's good. "So, what's up? Why are you here so early?" My mouth is still full, so it comes out a little garbled.

Cooper rolls his eyes at me while Quinn ignores my behavior, answering the question instead. "We need your help moving a new renter into the house. She doesn't have much, so it shouldn't take long, but there are a couple of bigger pieces we'll need your help with."

"Sure, just let me know when you need me there."

"Thank you! She's moving in tomorrow. We haven't nailed down a time yet."

"Sounds good. I'm technically off work tomorrow, but I was thinking about going to the Silvey house to work on some stuff." I've got a bit of catching up to do now that the electrical wires got sorted.

"I will never understand your need to be constantly working." Cooper shakes his head at me.

I shrug my shoulders, knowing there's no explanation to fully satisfy him. I don't understand it myself sometimes. It's the way I've always been. I'm lucky my job is one of my passions. Otherwise, I'd probably be a miserable bastard.

"Thanks for helping out, Levi." Quinn smiles at me, changing the topic. We all know it's a horse long dead, but for some reason, Cooper just can't let it go.

"Text me with details about tomorrow."

Quinn nods, and they leave my apartment with a quick goodbye. The sound of the door closing has me turning back toward the kitchen. A deep sigh falls from my chest as I take in the mess. My kitchen is an absolute disaster that I have no desire to clean. At all. But, if I don't do it now, it's going to start smelling, which is worse than cleaning dishes.

I set to work, the blueberry scones sitting on the counter as a reward for when I'm done. The monotony of the chore causes my mind to wander. It's why I like my job so much. It forces me to use every ounce of concentration to make sure the job is done correctly.

Cooper has never understood my need to be busy. When we were younger, I got him in trouble regularly because of my schemes. He was always such a rule follower, too. If we did something a little rebellious, he'd tell Mom and Dad quickly after. Usually, he'd be the one to get in trouble, which was fantastic for me. Then he smartened up and stopped going along with whatever plan I came up with.

When I have something to focus on, my mind doesn't have the room to wander. Which has always been my ultimate goal. I hate when my thoughts begin spinning out of control. They go in so many different directions—usually all negative—it's hard to rein them back in once they start going.

What if something else happens at the Silvey house, and I end up losing the job? What if I get hurt? How would I survive an injury where I couldn't work for months on end? What if I get permanently injured and can't ever work construction again?

On and on the thoughts turn as I finish cleaning the kitchen. My ringing cellphone pulls me from my thoughts—thankfully. Sara's name is on the caller ID, which makes me grin. I haven't talked to her in a few days since I've been trying to get back on schedule at work.

"Hey, you."

"Hello, Levi," she returns with a little bite to her words.

"What's going on?"

"Did you happen to forget something very important?"

My brain starts scrambling over the last couple of days as I try to figure it out. All of a sudden, it hits me like a sledgehammer.

"Oh, my god. Sara, I'm so sorry. Your birthday was yesterday."

"Yes, it was."

"I'm the worst best friend in the world! How could I have forgotten?" I feel terrible. I was so caught up in making sure I was back on schedule, I lost track of time completely. Usually, I take her out to dinner at La Mensa—the best Italian place in town—and we gorge ourselves on breadsticks and pasta.

"You're not the worst, but you are on my shit list right now."

"How can I make it up to you? Dinner, obviously. Possibly a crate of wine to last you for years? Treats for your menagerie?" Sara has a very large zoo of pets she's rescued at her house. They're her babies. Getting something for them would be like getting her an expensive gift.

"You can take me to dinner tonight, then to the pet store for a shopping spree," she counters, and I laugh at her choice of birthday gifts.

"I'll pick you up at seven, then."

"Be prepared to pay out the nose, Levi Jackson. You're going to have to go big."

"You got it."

* * *

The overwhelming display of flowers has me swallowing hard. There are so many choices in this garden of greenery, I have no idea where to start. What kind of arrangement do you get your best friend for forgetting her birthday?

I roam around Blooming Beautiful, trying to find something Sara would like and potentially help ease her ire towards me. I finger the leaves of a leafy green plant. Another thing to take care of probably isn't the best choice since she already has enough to deal with every day.

"Sorry about your wait. I was fighting with a bird of paradise." A soft, melodic voice comes from the back of the room. When I turn, it's as if someone slapped me in the chest, forcing all the air out of my lungs.

The most beautiful woman I've ever seen stands behind the long counter. Her black, kinky-curled hair is pushed back with a red bandana, and her olive skin glows under the early evening sunlight shining through the windows. Her large almond-shaped eyes are dark but carry a warmth in them so inviting I could get lost if I stared too long.

"Sorry, did you say you were fighting with a bird? Do you need help?"

A gentle laugh brightens her face as she shakes her head. "No, a bird of paradise is a big, green plant."

"Oh, sure. That makes way more sense." *Jesus.* I mentally roll my eyes. A bird? Could I sound any more like an idiot?

"Can I help you find something?"

"Actually, I need help picking out a flower arrangement." I walk up to the counter, and the closer I get, the faster my heart beats. Am I nervous? This never happens. Talking to women comes naturally to me. Why would this one make me react so differently?

"Girlfriend, mom, or wife?"

I'm startled by her question. "Uh… none of the above?" I clear my throat. "She's my best friend, and I sort of forgot her birthday."

She looks at me with a raised eyebrow.

"I know, I know. I'm the worst. Can you please help me get something that says I'm really sorry?"

"I'm not sure I have the skills, but I can try. What's her favorite flower?"

I grimace.

"Right." She shakes her head. "Favorite color?"

"Yellow, maybe?"

"You're killing it tonight." Her grin is teasing.

"God, I know. I suck so bad today. Can you still help me?" I even throw in a pout for good measure.

She stares at me for a few seconds, then nods her head. "Give me a few minutes." She turns to the coolers behind her, pilfering through the many flowers. My eyes stray down her body, taking in the white T-shirt and tight, black jeans show-casing her curves. Damn, she's sexy.

She suddenly turns back around, holding several flowers I'd never be able to name. They're a multitude of colors that seem like they'd never go together.

Ten minutes go by when she holds up a paper-wrapped arrangement. "Holy shit." The words fly out of my mouth before I can stop them. There are oranges and yellows and reds all arranged in an artful spray of color. It's beautiful and exactly what Sara would love. "It's perfect."

She smiles at me, making my chest ache. "And you're

gorgeous." Yet again, my mouth is speaking before I can think. "Uh… sorry. I mean... you are pretty. I probably shouldn't have said it out loud, though. I'm going to stop talking now." *Shut up.* I snap my mouth closed.

The smile drops from her face as quickly as it came, and I feel the loss as if it were personal. She clears her throat, then steps to the cash register. "That'll be fifty dollars and thirty-five cents."

Okay, obviously blurting out compliments is not the right tactic. This woman isn't anything like the women I normally spend time with. She's sophisticated and aloof to my normal charms. Although, charming is a far cry from how I've acted today. Idiotic is a bit more like it.

I shake my head to focus back on the reason I'm here. Pulling my wallet out from my pocket, I hand over my card. I suddenly realize I don't even know her name. The desire to learn it almost overwhelms me.

"I didn't catch your name." She slides my card through the machine and looks up at me. Her piercing gaze slices through any resolve I have to ask her out.

"I didn't give it to you," she says, which throws me off for a minute. This is a new one for me. Most of the time, it takes all of a perfectly timed smile or a solid compliment to get me a number. I've never had a woman push me away quite like she is right now. Her body language is almost stiff like she's angry or something. Maybe I offended her with my comment. I meant what I said, but that doesn't necessarily mean it was welcome.

I nod my head. "I'm sorry if I offended you a minute ago. My mouth got ahead of me. I probably shouldn't have said what I did, even though I meant it. Thanks for the flowers and your help."

A little of the tension drains from her shoulders while a small smile curls her lips. "If that arrangement doesn't get you out of trouble, I'm not sure what will."

I smile at her, happy she's no longer mad at me, then nod my head. "Thanks again." Turning, I move to walk out of the store before I say anything else to keep shoving my foot in my mouth. At the last minute, I glance over my shoulder to get one more look at her. She's still standing there behind the counter, an almost ethereal look to her as the sun shines around her.

A look of confusion crosses her face as I walk out of her store. I know this won't be the last time I see her. I'll make sure of it.

7

"ROSEMARY"

SIX YEARS AGO

The beeping of machines provides a backdrop to my constantly swirling thoughts. I never thought this would be the direction my life would go. As a kid, I had all these dreams of what I wanted for my life. I was going places and knew exactly who I was. Then, those dreams went up in smoke faster than I could scream *fire*. I've been adrift since I was fifteen, and at twenty-one, that's a long freaking time to be so unsure of what your future holds.

My grandmother's voice echoes in my head, *"You're meant for greatness, my darling Rosebud."* Sitting here now, it's hard to believe she was right. All I've been able to do is survive these past few years. Even that feels like a stretch sometimes. I feel like I'm disappointing her every day, but how can I be meant for greatness when life is constantly there to push me back down when I try?

My father stirs in his hospital bed, and I sit up in my chair to see if he needs something. His old, weathered face is lined with stress, finally reflecting the monster he truly is on the inside. I hate having to be by his side through the end. It's not as if he deserves my support.

"Get me water," his scratchy voice grates out. Even while

dying, he's still harsh and angry. And like the good daughter I've strived to be since I was fifteen, I reach for his plastic cup, pressing the straw to his dry lips.

Our life has been hard. *My* life has been hard. All because he's a lazy, entitled asshole who believes I should be the one supporting him. Then, when I don't meet his ridiculous expectations, a punishment follows. Looking at him now, his body frail in the hospital bed, his punishments would probably break him before they broke me. And I've been broken plenty of times.

"I need to tell you something." His gaze meets mine, empty and soulless. I lean forward so he knows I'm there, but I don't say anything. Not talking out of turn is almost ingrained in me now despite knowing he's too weak to provide a punishment.

Before he starts speaking, Antony Malatelli, my father's close friend, comes into the room. With his salt and pepper hair, piercing blue eyes, and strong physique, he's quite handsome. His friendship with my father always baffled me. I never questioned him about it, though, knowing full well what would happen if I did.

"Good, I'm glad you're here, Antony. I was about to tell Rosemary the plan." My father pauses for a minute to catch his breath. The lung cancer has eaten away his entire body over the past couple of months. He doesn't have much time left now.

There's a small part of me that's glad he will no longer be around to use me as his punching bag. The other part of me is worried about what will happen next.

"How about I take it from here, Gerald?" Antony offers, and my father nods. "Rosemary, your father owes me a very large sum of money. At the moment of his death, all of his assets will become mine. Unfortunately, the few assets he does have will not cover the entire sum. Therefore, you will also be a part of the deal."

My stomach drops as his words begin to filter into my brain. I'm part of a deal? I didn't agree to any sort of exchange. "I don't understand. How am I a part of this?"

"As payment for his debt, you are to be my wife once his death certificate is signed."

I shake my head in both disagreement and disbelief. This can't be happening to me again. I didn't want to live with my father after my grandmother's death, but I had no choice. He was the only one who could take me, and I was still a minor.

I refuse for this to be my future.

"I'm sure this is a shock, but I have a sizable income, so you will be comfortable. You'll live a more affluent life with me than you did with your father. Plus, you have no other options. I hold ownership over all your money and assets. If you leave, you'll have nothing."

Standing, I rush to the bathroom, the contents of my stomach no longer able to stay down. I heave until there's nothing left to expel, my body shivering as dread races up my spine. This was not the outcome I envisioned when I knew my father was dying. I was supposed to finally be free. Free of the crushing weight I'd been carrying for so long. Free to live the life I'd been dreaming of since my grandmother died. I will not do something just because some bastard deems it so. I'm no longer the frightened little girl with no means to stand up for herself.

With shaking hands, I turn the faucet on at the sink. The cold water is cooling to my heated skin as I splash it on my face. The reflection in the mirror shows a person I barely recognize as myself. My olive skin looks pale and ghostly, the kinky curls of my black hair are sticking out around my face while my dark eyes show the fear radiating from my pores.

This is not me.

I'm so tired of not being myself.

Walking back out to the room, I have a renewed sense of energy. I will not marry this man. I'll run away. Find a new place to live. I don't have much in savings, but it could be enough to at least get me out of the city. I have work experience, so I'm sure I could find a decent job somewhere.

"Rosemary, I know this isn't what you expected to hear today. You have no other choice, though, I'm afraid," Antony says to me. I keep my head down, gaze fixed firmly on the floor. I refuse to look at Antony. Too afraid my partially formed plans will show in my eyes.

"She'll be obedient," my father rasps. "I've taught her what happens if she doesn't follow my instructions."

"Good. I expect full cooperation from her."

Chills run down my spine as Antony's icy words float through the room. No way will I let him have me. I'll be homeless before I go willingly with him.

I just need to be smart with my next steps.

I'll get away. No matter what it takes.

8

HOPE

I flip over from my stomach to my back for the umpteenth time this morning. I've been awake for the last two hours, unable to find my way back to sleep. Instead of a nightmare waking me up, the image of hazel-green eyes and strong muscles haunt my dreams. Now, I can't stop my thoughts from swirling.

The mystery man yesterday was a wrench in my day I was not prepared to deal with. What's worse is my thoughts sway from outright indignation to fascination in the span of a few minutes. I mean, who flirts with a girl while they're buying flowers for someone else? Seriously? I know he said they were for a friend, but there's no way a guy who looks like him is just friends with a girl. He probably has several women lined up, ready to go, whenever he wants it.

The other thing I keep getting stuck on was his apology for blurting out a compliment. He didn't take his compliment back, but he apologized for the inappropriate words. It was weird having a man apologize to me for something so small. It's never happened to me before, and now, I can't get the encounter out of my head.

Between his light brown hair, hazel eyes, and strong jaw,

he was very handsome. It also felt like I could feel his smile deep in my soul, which was weird. I'm not sure what's going on in my head at this point. Reacting to the guy at the grocery store as well as the mystery man yesterday is abnormal.

A sigh falls deep from my chest. There's no point in dwelling on these thoughts. It's not like anything will ever happen between us, even if I wanted it to. And I don't. I don't want anything to happen. The idea of having a man in my life sends a shiver down my spine, and not the good kind, either. I've never experienced a good shiver. I've read about them in romance books but have no idea what it would be like to feel one in real life.

I shake my head at the direction of my thoughts. I don't need any of that. I don't *want* any of that. I'd rather be alone with no experiences than to be beholden to another man— especially one who could be a womanizer. I came to Sonoma to build myself up, not have someone else do it for me, so it's best if I move on from this silly line of thinking.

Instead of continuing to dwell, I get out of bed to get ready for the day. I'm moving out of my apartment today. The last couple of days have been crazy. Quinn has been so helpful in getting the rental house ready for me. I'll be forever grateful for her kindness. She's providing a lot of the furniture since most of the things in this apartment aren't mine. They wouldn't fit in her house, even if they were. Quinn's rental is a beautiful three-bedroom house, whereas this apartment is barely big enough to hold one person.

The only things I'm taking are the kitchen stuff I bought and the stuff from my bedroom. Oh, and the comfy patio chair I splurged on when I first moved here. I was told there is a patio space in the backyard, which I'm looking forward to utilizing. My tiny balcony is nice, but not quite functional.

Walking out to my disaster area of a kitchen, I take in the boxes stacked on the floor. The empty countertop makes me realize I packed my coffee pot last night, which was monumentally stupid. If I have any hope of packing the remaining items or making it through the exhausting day ahead, I'm going to need caffeine.

Grabbing my keys from the counter, I head to the little café around the corner from my apartment. I'm going to miss being within walking distance of this place. I have a feeling this new house will be exactly what I've been missing, though.

* * *

A KNOCK at my door has me setting the tape dispenser down on top of the box I was about to close. I quickly open the door, and all the blood drains from my face when I see who's on the other side.

I expected it to be Quinn and Cooper, but instead, the hazel-eyed stranger from yesterday is standing there. Fear snakes down my spine, and I grip the door handle a little harder to keep from falling down.

"How do you know where I live?" I ask, barely managing to speak above a whisper. The stranger keeps looking at me with wide eyes. Through the haze of apprehension, I can see he's just as surprised as I am, which is odd since he's the one who knocked on my door.

"Um… are you Hope?" he asks, but before I can answer, another voice sounds from the bottom of the open-air stairway.

"Levi! I'm surprised you're here so early," Quinn says, coming up the stairs. I guess that answers my question. I take a deep breath to quell the rest of my anxiety and smile when Quinn's happy face finally makes it to the top of the stairs.

My stranger—whose name is Levi, apparently—clears his throat, then looks at Quinn with a smile and gives her a quick kiss on the cheek.

"Yeah, I woke up early this morning and decided to come get a jump on things. Sorry for startling you," he says, looking at me, his eyebrows furrowed. I'd imagine it's because this is the second time he's had to apologize to me in just as many days. Again, I find it odd how quickly he throws out an apology. Even for something he didn't do on purpose.

"Did I not tell you Cooper's brother was coming to help?" Quinn asks, her eyes wide in remorse.

I shake my head, a small smile pulling at my lips. I don't want her to feel bad since she's been so helpful to me. Plus, normal people don't freak out over a random person knocking on their door. "It's no big deal. Just a bit of a shock to have a hulking man outside my door when I expected a friendly woman."

Quinn grins at me. "Well, this is Levi. Levi, this is Hope. He's not always so hulk-like. He probably needs some breakfast."

"We're in luck, then. I stupidly packed my coffee pot last night, so I went to the café around the corner and bought pastries and coffee." I beckon them into my apartment, leading them to the tiny kitchen. I have to maneuver around all the boxes in order to reach the pastry box.

When I turn around, I run smack into Levi's chest, smashing the pastry box between us, almost dropping it. Levi grabs the box, his hands landing on mine as we both attempt to keep it from falling. The surprise of his hands on mine has me jerking them back. I'm glad he already had a hold of the box, otherwise, it would've fallen to the floor this time.

"I'm usually a lot smoother than this," Levi says, a sheepish smile on his face. All I can do is quirk an eyebrow at him. It's not hard to imagine how smooth he is with the ladies. He exudes a confidence that I'm sure makes any woman around him swoon. I refuse to acknowledge the effect it has on me. He clears his throat again, and I almost laugh at how unbalanced he seems.

"Right. Quinn, I have creamer and sugar if you need it."

"I'll take both, please," she says from across the room. "You've gotten a lot done. I thought we'd have more to pack up before loading the truck. We'll be finished in no time today."

"I don't have much, so it's made the process much faster." I walk into the living room, handing Quinn a coffee, then turn back to the box I was taping before Levi and Quinn got here.

"Cooper is on his way with the truck. I have to be at Paint and Paper when we're done, so I drove separately. We'll have the boys start loading the big things when he gets here. What else do we need to get into boxes?" Quinn manages the art gallery in town and is a very talented artist herself.

I point to what's left in the living room, and Quinn and I start putting the remaining items in boxes. Levi hangs out in the kitchen, eating a pastry, since there's not much for him to do until Cooper gets here. I can feel his eyes on me the entire time I'm packing. It's a little disconcerting. Why he would want to look at me right now is beyond my comprehension.

Between my ratty hair, leggings, and T-shirt, I'm not exactly stare-worthy. I didn't know my handsome stranger would be here, so I dressed for moving, not for impressing anyone.

My handsome stranger? He's not *my* anything. Even if I thought I'd want him to be. Which I don't. *Why am I thinking about this?*

It's not like it matters if he's impressed anyway. I still don't need a man in my life just because he might like me.

Luckily, Cooper's knock and subsequent entrance disrupts my thoughts. He crosses the room quickly with his long stride, holding out his hand to introduce himself.

"It's nice to meet you, Hope." His smile is warm, and I find myself blinking rapidly at his attractiveness. His light brown hair, golden hazel eyes, and strong jaw are intimidatingly beautiful. My eyes find Levi's, then bounce back and forth between the two men. They look so similar with the exception of their eyes. If Levi wasn't wearing a backward navy blue baseball hat, they'd look like twins.

Oddly enough, Levi's hat looks like the one that guy at the store was wearing. I wonder if they're the same person, and I never realized.

"Yeah, nice to meet you, too." I clear my throat, then look at Quinn, who's grinning at me.

She leans in and whispers, "My reaction was pretty much the same when I first met him."

Cooper winks at Quinn, and I think I may swoon. Jesus, this is too much to handle in one morning. "Let's start with the furniture, then we can pack the boxes around it," Cooper suggests.

I lead him and Levi into my bedroom, showing them what all needs to go. While they start loading furniture, Quinn and I finish packing the last boxes.

We get the truck and cars packed to the gills, but don't quite get everything in one trip, which means we'll have to come back. All things considered, I'm pretty happy. It's been a surprisingly good day despite having to move all my stuff. Levi and Quinn's relationship is hilarious. He treats her like a sister, constantly teasing her, which she returns in full. Then they'd team up to tease Cooper, which is equally hilarious.

There have been many times I've gotten distracted by Levi's laugh or the way his eyes light up when he smiles. His joy fills the room to the point you have no choice but to smile with him. Each time he caught me staring at him, his smile would grow wider. I'm not sure what that means, to be honest, or what him staring back at me means, either. I usually ended up making the interaction awkward and then quickly moved on.

Carrying a box into my new rental house, I'm blown away by the beautiful space. Quinn is definitely letting me pay far too little for the house. There are French doors to my left, and the hallway continues toward the back of the house. Stairs are directly in front of me, and to my right are the living room, dining room, and kitchen, each room opening to the next. The sunlight flowing through the windows makes the space bright and airy. It's perfect.

"Okay, Hope. How about you and Levi head back to your apartment to get the remaining boxes while Cooper and I get things organized here?" A little glimmer in Quinn's eyes makes me frown. Her suggestion doesn't make any sense to me. Shouldn't I be the one to organize the boxes in my own place? Before I can argue with her, she turns around and walks back to the kitchen.

A touch on my arm has me flinching away, and I cringe at my reaction. When I glance up, Levi is staring at me, a frown lining his face. "You surprised me. I didn't know you were standing right next to me," I offer as an explanation. It's not particularly true. I've known where he's been the entire day. I just wasn't prepared for him to touch me.

His touch feels different than anyone else's, though. When Claire accidentally brushes against me, it feels as if my skin is being peeled off my body. The couple of times Levi has touched me have been met with electricity that buzzes across my skin. It's alarming and a little addicting if I'm honest.

I'm tempted to keep touching him to fully understand what is happening to me. I want to explore the prickle on my skin that makes goose bumps raise on my arms. Except that would be crazy. To seek out touch voluntarily goes so far out of my comfort zone, it would be insane.

He nods his head and gestures for the door. "Let's head out."

I follow him out to the truck while taking a deep breath. This is going to be interesting, to say the least.

9

LEVI

"There are only a few boxes left in the living room and the ones in my bedroom," Hope says as we enter her apartment. She leads me to the living room and grabs a box from the floor. I avert my eyes to the other boxes to keep from staring at her ass. Her tight leggings highlight every curve she has. It's been practically torture having to watch her bend over a million times these past few hours.

"This is one of the easier moves I've helped out with. Thanks, by the way," I joke and am graced with one of Hope's rare smiles. She's been so serious most of the day. The few times I've managed to pull a smile from her made me feel like the king of the world.

When she opened her door this morning, I almost fell over in surprise. I hated the frightened look she had on her face when she saw it was me. I'm not sure why my showing up scared her, but it made me want to wrap her in my arms and protect her from that fear. Which would've been the exact opposite of the right thing to do. Luckily, Quinn showed up before Hope had a chance to truly freak out or I did something stupid.

Hope. Her name fits her perfectly. I'm glad I didn't have

to wait too long to gather that information. I wish I could get a better read on her, though. I've caught her staring at me several times over the course of the morning, and it gives me a little thrill each time I do. Granted, she's caught me staring as many times as I've caught her.

"This apartment didn't lend for collecting much stuff, so I can't take all of the credit." We both start grabbing boxes to finish loading the truck.

"It is pretty small, but it's a cozy kind of small."

"I thought so, too!" She smiles, and all I can do is stare at her. She's so beautiful when she's happy. It makes me want to do anything to keep her that way.

"My apartment is pretty small, as well, but it's not cozy like this."

"Typical bachelor pad?"

"Definitely." I grin at her, and she blushes. "I'm saving up to buy a house to renovate, so buying a bunch of furniture I'm not sure will fit in the house seems dumb."

"I get that." Hope puts the box she is carrying onto the tailgate of the truck, then pushes it against the others. "I've always wanted to decorate my own house. Most of the places I've lived in were already decorated when I got there." A small frown pulls at her mouth, then she shakes her head as if trying to remove whatever thought came into her head. I want to ask her what she was thinking about, but it feels too personal. I don't want her to close up on me again. She's finally feeling comfortable enough to have a conversation.

She starts back up the stairs with me trailing behind her. "As a contractor, I have to follow the wishes of the people I'm building the house for, so I'm looking forward to making all the decisions myself instead of going with what the client wants."

"I wish I knew how to do that kind of stuff. I'm pretty sure I'd hurt myself if I tried."

A laugh falls from my chest in surprise at her joke as we

walk into her bedroom to grab the rest of the boxes. Her flowery scent floats through the room, both leftover and from her standing next to me. Being in the very small space has my heart beating against my ribcage.

I do my best to move about the room without touching her. Her reaction earlier told me she doesn't like to be touched. She didn't say those specific words, but no one flinches the way she did because they're surprised. It was almost as if she were bracing for my touch to be harsh instead of gentle.

A slice of anger passes through me at the thought of someone hurting her to the point of causing her fear. How a person can physically or mentally harm someone else will never make sense to me.

"I've been doing it for years, and I still hurt myself," I respond, attempting to pull myself from the thought of Hope being harmed.

"Sounds dangerous."

"Eh, it's mostly just me working too quickly or not paying attention."

"I'm that way with roses. The thorns get me regularly, no matter how many times I work with them," she says, picking up a box. As soon as it's in the air, the bottom falls out, letting the contents spill everywhere. "Shit."

I crouch down to start piling up the clothes scattered on the floor. It's not until my hand wraps around something silky that I realize what I'm picking up.

Hope's underwear is scattered all over the floor, and I have to clear my throat at the sexy display of lace, silk, and cotton.

"Oh, my god," Hope gasps. She scrambles to pull the clothes toward her as a deep blush creeps up her neck. All I can do is smile. A chuckle sneaks through despite my attempts to hold it in. She glares at me, which only has me laughing harder.

Her hands slow down as she sits back on her heels with a deep sigh. Then to my utter surprise, she starts laughing, too. "I can't believe this would happen to me," she says, dropping her head into her hands, giggles still filtering through her words.

"Don't worry about it. It's not like I saw you naked," I tease as the image of her naked filters through my brain, her smooth, olive-toned skin glowing against my work-roughened hands. I have to clear my throat again in an attempt to remove the visual. I quickly stand, leaving the bedroom to run to the kitchen to get the tape dispenser.

Returning to the bedroom, Hope holds out her arm, and I place the tape into her hand. Once she gets the box back together, I move to help her put her clothes back into the box.

"Don't you dare!" she says, and I freeze where I am.

"I've already seen them."

"You don't need to touch them, too." She huffs, and I laugh.

"Fair enough." I grab the next box and start toward the truck, leaving her to clean up her clothes. It's probably best if I don't see what they look like in any detail. It's going to be hard enough to get the fantasy of a naked Hope out of my head. I don't need any additional information to add to the vision already forming.

On my way back up the stairs, Hope passes me with a box in hand. She keeps her eyes averted from mine, and I inwardly sigh. We're back to the distance again. I was enjoying getting to know her. The longer we talked, the more she opened up, giving me a small glimpse of the woman underneath the steely exterior.

There are only a few boxes left, and we get them loaded up quickly. When we're back in the truck, headed to the house, silence descends, the only sounds coming from the hum of the engine. I give her a few minutes of space before I do what I've been wanting to do from the moment I met her.

"Hey, Hope…" I start, waiting for her gaze to meet mine before I continue. "I want to put it out there that I am very attracted to you and would love to take you out to dinner sometime. I think we would have a blast if you'd be interested in going out with me." When she doesn't immediately answer, I glance over at her again.

Her eyes are wide, and her mouth is gaped open. I'm not sure if she's surprised or freaking the fuck out, so I quickly try to follow up my statement with an out. "You don't have to say anything right now. I just wanted you to know how I felt. I mean, I have horrible table manners, so you may not even want to be seen with me."

I look over at her to see how much damage has been done. Her lip is pulled up at the corner as she bites the side of her thumb. Almost like she's hiding a smile from me. She still hasn't replied, and I let her get away with keeping silent for now. I'll let her come to me when she's ready.

In any other circumstance, I'd probably take her silence as a no, but there's something about Hope. Something calling to me I'm not sure I can ignore. I want to get to know her on a deeper level. I don't just want to sleep with this woman; I want to learn everything I can about her. What she likes and dislikes, what she wants from life. All of it.

Every time she looked at me today, I saw a longing in her eyes as if she wanted something she could never have. Each of her reactions to me was so inconsistent. She couldn't stand for me to touch her or get close, but the attraction was shining in her eyes every time we made eye contact. She started to relax while we were by ourselves today, then immediately closed herself off after a minor incident.

She's an intriguing puzzle. One I'm willing to do whatever it takes to figure out because I'm pretty sure her pieces are going to fit my own.

I've never felt something like this with anyone before. The women I've dated were more like a distraction than something I wanted to pursue seriously. I know it's going to take patience to get Hope to open up to me again. I'll need to give her space to decide if I'm worth her time, even if it goes against what I normally would want to do.

In the past, it's taken all of a perfectly timed wink to get a woman to go out with me. Granted, the women I went out with before weren't anything like Hope. Which means, this matters a whole hell of a lot more.

It's all new territory for me, and I know if I mess it up, I'll lose any chance at finding out what Hope and I could truly become.

10

HOPE

The bright sunshine warms my skin through the window, creating a feeling of utter contentment I haven't felt since I was a child. I close my eyes to better soak in the moment as images of my grandmother and her flower garden come into my mind. A small smile pulls at the corners of my mouth at the memory. I can almost smell her roses.

God, I used to be so carefree. Running circles around my grandmother, keeping her constantly on her toes. She always hated how curious I was because she could never find me. I'd follow a butterfly across the backyard and end up under a bush, pretending a fairy family lived there.

Then one day, I woke up, and my entire life changed within hours.

I open my eyes again before I get too lost in my past, focusing back on my book. The library in Quinn's rental house is one of the best things I've ever gotten to experience. Since the house came mostly furnished, the space is perfectly decorated with comfy gray reading chairs, a couch, a yellow and gray patterned rug, and an entire wall of books.

The French doors are to my right and the chairs sit across from the couch in front of the wide window. It's the perfect place to read, and I'm taking full advantage of the house I now get to call mine.

As the week has progressed, I've slowly started to feel comfortable here instead of like a guest. I need to get some decorations to make the space a little more to my tastes. Not that Quinn's decorating is bad, it's actually gorgeous, but I think adding things I picked out myself will make it feel more like my house instead of someone else's.

My stomach rumbles, reminding me I haven't eaten anything all day because I haven't gone grocery shopping. I haven't decided what I want to make for the week, therefore, I have no motivation to go to the store.

Walking out of the library, I take in the space around me again and feel like pinching myself for the umpteenth time since I moved in. The large gray sectional and navy blue rug in the living room invite me to cozy up for a nap, the white six-person dining room table has me wishing I had friends I could invite over for a meal, and the white cabinets, granite countertops, and silver appliances in the kitchen have me itching to create an extravagant meal.

The parties you could host here would be phenomenal, and for the first time since I moved to Sonoma, I wish I could be more outgoing and create friendships with people I would want to invite over.

For so long, I was taught to not be seen or heard. It's hard to suddenly break out of that mold when you spent years being conditioned to expect a certain response if you slipped up.

Shaking my head at my pointless thoughts, I walk out to the garage. A sandwich from the café sounds delicious, and once I'm fueled, I'll head to the grocery store. If I can keep the reward of a delicious meal in mind, I might be able to get through it.

Once I'm in my car, I make my way to the café. I do miss being within walking distance, but the store is still close, so I can easily grab a coffee or breakfast there anytime. Most people go to the café for their amazing sandwiches, so I'm sure they'll be busy on a Sunday afternoon. It's worth the extra wait time, though.

The smell of toasted bread floats around the room as I step into the café. It's loud, too, which isn't a surprise for a Sunday afternoon. My stomach rumbles hard, and I'm glad I decided to have lunch here instead of finding something at home.

The restaurant has a counter with a window box displaying the pastries of the day. Unsurprisingly, there are only a few trays left since it's lunchtime. I jump in the long line to order, trying not to get overwhelmed with the number of people here. The line slowly moves forward, so I grab my book out of my tote bag to read while I wait.

Something catches my eye, making me look up from my book to find Levi's gaze on me. A gorgeous smile fills his face when I finally make eye contact. My stomach quivers when I realize he's here for lunch, too. How can I have lived in this town for over a year and never have run into him before, but now, when I can't seem to stop thinking about him, he's everywhere I am?

Why is this my life?

I swipe my sweaty hands across my pants and force my eyes to go somewhere other than to the handsome man who hasn't stopped being on my mind since he stepped foot in my store. I swore I would never allow a man to influence my decisions again, yet, here I am, wanting to flee this place because this dazzling guy makes me nervous.

"Can I help you?"

Startled, I look at the cashier. I didn't even notice it was my turn. *Damn you, Levi.*

"Hi, um…" I clear my throat in an attempt to get my thoughts to focus. "Can I have a BLT and a bowl of chicken noodle soup, please?"

The cashier rings me up and takes my cash, then hands me a number stand for my table. I turn to scan the room, hoping for an open table on the opposite side of the café, away from Levi. Every single table is taken despite how hard I'm wishing someone will move for me.

"You're welcome to sit with me."

I jump, my heart lurching in my chest. "How are you so sneaky?" The words fly out of my mouth before I can reel them back in.

Levi laughs, and I take a moment to appreciate the joy radiating off him. His smile lights up his entire face while his laugh bubbles up inside me, creating this oddly euphoric feeling. I don't think I've ever been around someone with so much happiness buzzing around him. It's unsettling. And unexpected. He's the first man I've ever felt comfortable around. Even though my nerves are through the roof, I'm not afraid. I'm curious.

"I apologize. I don't mean to keep sneaking up on you. I wanted to offer my table. It doesn't seem like there's any other option."

I sigh, looking around again. He's right, of course, so I resign myself to enduring his company. The problem isn't even Levi. It's having to deal with the constant barrage of thoughts that filter through my head when he's near me. On top of that, I seriously enjoy looking at him, even though I know I shouldn't. Sitting with him will allow me to get to know him better, and the more I get to know him, the more tempting he becomes.

All I can do is nod my head, but looking at Levi, you'd think he won the lottery. His happiness spreads to me, making my lips twitch up in a smile.

We sit down at the table, and both of our metal number stands sit to my left, leaving the middle of the table clear. I start drumming my fingers, not knowing what else to do. The quiet stretches between us, becoming awkward and uncomfortable. This is weird. *I'm* weird. Why am I sitting here?

"Maybe I should get my order to go," I suggest, standing from my chair.

"Wait. Don't go."

I freeze in an awkward crouch, my body reverting back to obeying commands on instinct. I look at Levi but am surprised by his expression. Instead of the hard lines and angry eyes I expect, they're soft and pleading. Almost apologetic in their deep, soulful gaze.

"Okay, I'll stay, then." My voice is barely above a whisper, the instinct to run flitting away as fast as it came. The tightness in my muscles releases, and I plop back down into my chair. Why does he never do what I expect him to do? Between constantly apologizing to me, making me laugh, and his overall happy demeanor, I don't know how to interact properly with him.

Anger and aggression have always been the leading emotions in my interactions with men. They never cared about how I felt, and they certainly never apologized to me. If anything, they expected me to be the one apologizing to them. Between their manipulations and the complete isolation I was kept in, I am utterly lacking in the right skills to handle this situation appropriately.

What would it be like to have a man like Levi in my life? My past has taught me there's more risk than reward in relationships with men. But right now, as I stare into Levi's warm gaze, I'm not so sure that applies to him. Being in his presence fills me with an ease I've never experienced when I've been around a man—*any* man—before.

The ever-present fear I'm used to feeling has morphed into more of a wariness, an uncertainty of doing the wrong things, not because I'm afraid of the consequences but because I don't want to push him away. I'm utterly perplexed by this odd turn of my emotions.

"Is the store closed today, or are you taking a break?" Levi's words pull me out of my head.

"We're usually closed on Sundays. Although, most of the time, I'm still at the store, working on something." I shrug my shoulders. I work a lot since I don't have much else to do.

"I'm almost always working, too. I have a hard time sitting still except to eat." Levi's smile is engaging, and mine follows quickly after his.

"I meant to ask you the other day how the flowers worked out for you."

Levi's eyes light up at the mention of his friend. Again, I feel like there could be more there than he led on. "She loved them, but I wasn't let off the hook until after a shopping trip for her zoo."

My brows furrow. "Zoo?"

"Yeah, Sara is a vet tech and has a soft spot for strays. She has what feels like a million animals who each need a good home. I took her on a shopping spree at the pet store to make up for my idiocy." Levi chuckles, shaking his head. "She came close to buying out the store but stopped just shy of it."

"I'm glad she made you work for it. Forgetting a birthday is a pretty big deal."

"I have definitely learned my lesson. Trust me." Levi winks, and my stomach swirls at the sight. It should make me feel better knowing he potentially has someone else in his life. Someone he obviously adores. It would mean he's not a threat to me or my carefully crafted life here. But instead, there's a little niggle of disappointment in my gut. A small part of me wants this outgoing, beautiful guy to see the real me. See the woman I'm finally becoming and want more from me than friendship.

Our food arrives, interrupting our conversation. I'm grateful for the reprieve from both the intense look Levi was giving me and my ridiculous thoughts. Sometimes, I hate how analytical I can be. For a good chunk of my life, it was necessary. I had to make sure I knew the potential outcomes of every step I made before I made them. Now, the constant barrage of analyzing thoughts can be overwhelming.

The delicious smell of my BLT wafts into my face, making my mouth water. I glance at Levi; a BLT and chicken noodle soup sit in front of him, as well.

"Copycat."

Levi's head whips up at my quip. A grin stretches across his face when he notices we've ordered the same thing. "I'm pretty sure I was here before you. Doesn't that make you the copycat?"

"Nope." I pick up my sandwich, dip it in the soup broth, and take a bite. Damn, so good.

Levi stares at me for a few seconds before shaking his head, a chuckle falling from his lips. "Sunrise or sunset?"

I swallow my bite before I answer. "Sunrise. It signals the beginning of a new day and a new opportunity to live the life you want." I reply, a little thrown off by the randomness of his question.

"But sunsets are when the fun begins."

"You can't have fun in the morning?" I lift my brow in objection, causing Levi's grin to widen.

"Touché. Salty or sweet?" he continues.

"Salty."

"No way! You'd choose chips over ice cream?"

"Every day." A laugh bursts from me at his look of indignation.

"Take out or dine in?"

"Depends on the situation. I don't mind eating out alone."

A look of teasing humor crosses Levi's face as he raises an eyebrow. I play back my words, realizing the unintentional innuendo I said. I groan, pushing my hands into my face. Levi's boisterous laugh has me giggling with him. Despite how heated my face is, I meet his smiling gaze.

"Your laugh brightens everything around you," he says, and my smile dims at his observation.

"I've never had much to laugh about."

"Why?"

"Life has very rarely been kind to me." My eyes widen at my unexpected honesty. There's something about Levi that makes me feel so incredibly comfortable. Almost safe.

"I'm sorry you've had that experience."

"Dogs or cats?"

Levi pauses at my quick change of subject but nods his head in understanding. "Dogs."

"We finally agree." I grin. Levi's phone starts ringing, interrupting our conversation. He answers as soon as he reads the caller ID, an apologetic look in his eyes.

"Hey, Mom." He pauses, listening for a minute. It's always a little weird to be on one side of a conversation, having no idea what the other person is saying.

"Sure, I can be there," Levi says, then hangs up after saying goodbye.

"Sorry, it's usually best to answer Mom when she's calling instead of putting her off."

"I can absolutely see that about her." Ignoring Alice Jackson seems like it would be a terrible idea. My phone starts ringing, and a laugh pops out of my mouth when I see who's calling.

I hold my phone to show Levi, and he laughs, as well. "Hello, Mrs. Jackson," I answer.

"Hi, sweet Hope. I am calling to invite you to dinner. Does Tuesday work for you?"

Surprised by both the invitation and the demand, I pause before answering. Glancing at Levi, his smirk tells me he knows exactly what I'm dealing with right now. "Um, sure. Tuesday is fine."

"Great! I will send you our address. Talk to you later, dear."

I realize she hung up before I could respond, which shouldn't be a surprise. Claire was right, she definitely used my phone number.

"So, I'll see you at dinner on Tuesday?"

"How did you—"

"She invited me to the same dinner. More than likely, Cooper and Quinn, as well."

"Right. That makes more sense than you being a mind reader."

Levi laughs. "Not a mind reader, but I wish I could be sometimes." His gaze is intense as if he's trying to do it now. Thank God, he truly can't.

"I should go," I say, standing from the table and gathering my trash. I need to step away from this insane pull I feel and attempt to organize the swirling thoughts running through my head. My brain is telling me to protect myself just in case I'm wrong about Levi. To stay far away from the potential danger, but my heart is longing for the deeper connections I've read about. The one where you can't get enough of the other person, no matter how much time you spend together. It's absurd and absolutely perilous to be feeling this way, but I can't help the need that's suddenly taken root.

It seems fate is going to make it harder to resist the temptation, as well. Between the random run-ins and Alice Jackson, I believe I'll be seeing Levi around a lot more frequently.

Whether I want to or not.

11

HOPE

"You can do this. You know everyone who will be there. There's no reason to be nervous." A deep sigh falls from my chest.

And now, I'm talking to myself. I hate how my fear of the unknown creates this unsettled feeling in my gut. Logically, I know there's no reason to still have a fear of uncertainty, but it's been something I've lived with for so long, it's hard to stop despite how much work I've put into doing just that.

Being nervous about going to dinner at the Jacksons' house feels silly. Cooper and Quinn have started to become friends, and Alice, while a force to be reckoned with, is a truly genuine person. They're great people who have never given me any reason to feel this way, but the voice in my head keeps whispering for me to be careful. *Don't be seen. Don't be heard.* The mantra I've repeated every day since my grandmother died plays over and over in my head. Even though I don't have to live my life afraid anymore, the instinct is still ingrained in me. It'll be a long time before I'm able to completely relax in my new life.

I sort through my closet, attempting to find something appropriate to wear. T-shirts are my comfort zone, and I wear them every single day. I rarely have a reason to wear anything else, so my wardrobe lacks anything nice for an event like this. Maybe a shopping trip to get some new clothes would be helpful. Especially now that I have the closet space.

Pushing through my nerves, I send pictures of the two shirts I'm debating on to Quinn. She's been texting me regularly since I moved into the house. Mostly checking on me, making sure I'm settling in okay. She's been so incredibly kind. If I could come out of my shell a little bit, she could become a good friend.

Me texting her first this time is a step in the right direction. I hope.

ME: I can't decide what to wear to dinner. Thoughts?

To MY SURPRISE, she responds right away.

QUINN: The green one. It'll look beautiful against your skin.

Me: Thank you. I'm nervous.

Quinn: You have nothing to worry about. I was nervous for my first dinner, too, but the Jacksons are incredibly welcoming and kind.

Me: Thanks for your help.

Quinn: Anytime! See you soon!

WITH ANOTHER DEEP BREATH, I take Quinn's advice and put on the green blouse. It's a little bohemian with flowy three-quarter sleeves and a V-neck with strings hanging down the front. I slip on a pair of skinny jeans to complete the look, knowing it's not much, but with Quinn's endorsement, I'm feeling much better about my choices.

I head downstairs to gather my things. This will be the first get-together I've been to since I moved to Sonoma. I'm sure I missed out on some connections I could've made when I first arrived, but I wasn't in any state to make them. I was unsettled, afraid, and constantly worried about my ability to hold myself together.

There were so many things I needed to be in control of before I attempted to make friends. Not only in my own head but also in my store. It took every ounce of determination I had to get the place ready for customers. Now that I feel slightly more in control—along with some serious pushing from my therapist—I'm finally feeling ready. Having lunch with Levi and hanging out with Quinn and Cooper while I moved also allowed me to realize how lonely I'd started to become. This dinner will be the perfect first step in putting myself out there.

Walking out to my car, I take another deep breath to settle my nerves. This could be a really great chance for me to get out of my comfort zone. I'll have a chance to talk with Quinn a little more, maybe even attempt to become better friends. I can socialize with people outside of my store in a safe place with people I trust. It's going to be good. I'll just have to watch out for Levi and the crazy pull I feel toward him.

I've never experienced something so intense before. Every time I'm next to him, a deep part of me feels safe, comfortable. It's a ludicrous feeling, as well as potentially dangerous.

No man has ever been safe for me. Plus, what are the odds he'd be interested in dating me when he most likely has several other options waiting in line? Taking a chance on Levi being different would be monumentally stupid. Deep down, I know it's the truth, even if I'm a little disappointed with my decision.

I use the time it takes to drive out to the Jacksons' house to shore up my wacky feelings for Levi. "Nothing can happen. Even if I want it to... which, I don't. *I don't.*"

I roll my eyes. I'm talking to myself again. *Can I get any crazier?*

I pull into the driveway of a beautiful two-story farmhouse with a welcoming red door. As dusk settles in, the lights shine through the windows, creating a warm, inviting look to the house. I grab the flowers I made earlier today and walk up to the front door, knocking swiftly against the wood.

My breath hitches when I see Levi standing on the other side, a wide smile planted on his face. His gray T-shirt pulls tight across his chest, highlighting his muscles, while his tight jeans make him look casual and comfortable. He looks yummy standing there.

So much for not being affected by him.

Why does he have to do this to me? Why can't I ignore him like I've ignored every other man who has attempted to talk to me? What is it that makes him so different? I wish I had the answers to those questions. All I have instead is a fading resistance to this larger-than-life man.

He beckons me inside the house with a jerk of his head. Stepping into the small entryway has us standing unusually close to each other. The buzz in my body at his nearness is alarming. Heat moves through me as his scent invades my senses. He smells like cinnamon spice and a warmth I want to curl up to.

I look into his golden-brown eyes, and the impact almost knocks me over. The intensity I see in them is spellbinding. I divert my gaze, stepping further into the hallway to break the contact. My resolve is deteriorating at a rapid pace. The chemistry between us is almost too strong to resist. *What if it's one-sided?* He did make it seem like he already has someone in his life. What if he doesn't feel the same things I'm feeling?

I hate my brain sometimes.

I turn to take in the house, forcing my thoughts to stop spiraling. There's a staircase to my right and a wide doorway to my left that leads into the living room and dining room. Alice comes around the corner from the dining room, walking directly toward me.

"I'm so glad you made it!" She pulls me in for a hug while I stiffly stand there, wishing I could handle these things better.

"Thanks for inviting me, Mrs. Jackson."

"Call me Alice, please," she says, pulling away from the hug but keeping her arm wrapped around me. As the shock wears off, the loving embrace feels kind of nice. I guess that's one way to start being okay with touch again. Constant exposure.

Alice guides me through the dining room into a beautifully decorated kitchen with gray countertops and white cabinets. Levi follows closely behind us, staying quiet as his mom tells me all about the dinner she's making.

"I thought a nice roast sounded good. With summer around the corner, it's going to start getting too warm to have the oven going for hours."

"I love the summertime. I'm starting to get some of my favorite flowers in at the shop. I actually made these for you." I hand Alice the bouquet.

"Oh, your summer bouquets are always so pretty. Thank you!" She takes the flowers around the large island in the middle of the kitchen and grabs a vase from under a cabinet. "Please, have a seat; chat with me while I finish up dinner."

I sit down in the chair at the island while Levi pulls out the chair next to mine. I feel as if we're on top of each other, but he's several inches away. His imposing presence radiates off him, surrounding me in his orbit.

"So, how are you settling into the house?" Alice asks, placing the flowers in a vase, then on the counter next to the sink.

"I've been settling in nicely. It took a bit to get used to the size, but I love it."

"Hope's old apartment was tiny. Made for easy moving, though," Levi adds.

"I'm glad you were able to help, Levi. This one works so much, I worried he wouldn't be able to make time." Alice jabs her thumb at Levi, making me laugh.

"Of course, I was going to make time." Levi rolls his eyes.

"Well, I never know with you." Alice huffs as only a mother could. Watching their dynamic makes me smile while also filling me with a small sense of sadness. I never got the chance to know my mother. She died giving birth to me, and my grandmother raised me instead. At least, for a while. Then I had to live with my father, who acted more like a prison guard than a parent.

"Anyway, Hope, do you have any weddings coming up?"

"Thankfully, no. They are a huge time commitment for a little shop like mine."

"I can only imagine. All those centerpieces to make by yourself."

"Is supper ready yet?" a booming voice asks, coming around the corner. It makes me jump a little in surprise. I'm assuming this is Rob, Levi's dad, because he looks exactly like Cooper, only with a few gray hairs and laugh lines around his eyes. Levi looks a lot like his dad but has enough of his mom not to be identical.

"Just about, dear," Alice responds, leaning in to kiss his cheek.

"You're not one of mine." Rob looks at me with a friendly smile.

"This is Hope. She owns Blooming Beautiful."

"So, you're the one who's been filling my house with beautiful flowers. It's nice to meet you." He grins.

"Guilty. It's nice to meet you, too."

"Hey, guys!" Cooper's voice matches his dad's boom as he and Quinn step into the kitchen. I'm glad they're finally here. Having a few extra people will help take the focus off me. Hugs are given out before Alice asks the boys to set the table. Quinn and I help get drinks together while Alice grabs up the serving dishes.

We all make our way to the dining room; Quinn and Cooper sit on one side of the table, Levi on the other, and Rob and Alice at each end, which leaves only one chair left for me.

Right next to Levi.

If I hadn't been through worse, this would probably rank up there with one of the most stressful nights I've been through.

The smell of him alone is enough to drive me crazy. Having to sit within touching distance is going to test every ounce of self-control I have.

12

———

LEVI

H ope's soft laugh spreads through the room, making everyone smile when she does. I don't think she has any idea of the effect she has on people. It's been fascinating to watch her slowly grow in confidence as the meal has progressed. It's as if I'm talking to a totally different person.

Having to sit next to her throughout dinner has been both amazing and agonizing. I've wanted to grab her hand or put mine on her thigh the entire evening. Anything to create a connection between us that's more than just the tension sparking in the air.

I know she felt the same thing I was feeling when she arrived. Standing so close to her in that tiny hallway was a test of my self-control. I was two seconds away from grabbing her and kissing the fuck out of her, so I'm glad she broke the connection when she did.

Ever since then, I've had to almost sit on my hands to keep from touching her. I wish I could understand her allure. I've never had such a strong need to be close to a woman before. They've always been either a distraction or an energy release. No one has ever created a buzz inside me I never want to expel.

"You should come out with us sometime! The girls are a riot," Quinn says to Hope, and I smile at the invitation. I can only imagine what will happen when Natalie gets her hands on Hope.

"I think I'd like that," Hope replies.

"I'll make sure the girls keep things low-key at first." Quinn winks.

"There's no way Natalie Carlisle can be low-key." I laugh.

"Facts." Cooper points at me in agreement. Our entire group has been friends since we were in kindergarten, and despite being a year younger, they included me in all their plans. I was lucky to have an older brother who actually wanted to hang out with me.

"Megan and I can help keep her reined in, Hope. Promise."

Hope grins, nodding her head.

"How is Natalie doing?" Mom asks. Natalie got trapped in a house fire set by a lunatic arsonist, and we weren't sure she was going to make it. It was a scary time for all of us.

"She's healing up really well. Home now from the hospital and already back to being her spitfire self." Quinn grins, shaking her head.

"Good. I hope you guys can get together soon," Mom says, looking at Hope with a great big smile on her face and a gleaming look in her eyes. I suddenly understand exactly why this little dinner was planned. The crazy, scheming lady. She knew Quinn would invite Hope out with the girls if given the opportunity, and her plan is falling into place exactly how she wanted.

"Hope, have you put up any decorations in the new house?" Mom asks.

"There's already some up from Quinn, but I was thinking about buying some others."

"Oh, what a great idea. Make sure you get Levi's help hanging them. You don't want them to break if they fall."

Hope's brown eyes flick up to mine, apprehension and desire swirling in them. Seizing on Mom's continued scheming, I say, "I'd be happy to help. Here," I lean over to grab a business card from my wallet, "this is my cell, so give me a call when you've picked out some things." I hand over the card, being careful to give her plenty of room to grab it without having to touch me.

"Thanks."

"We need to head out," Cooper says, looking as if he can't wait another second to get Quinn home. He stands, taking their plates to the kitchen. Since dinner has been over for a while, we all follow suit, standing with our dishes to put them by the sink.

"Shouldn't you be exhausted after the honeymoon, Coop? You just got back a few weeks ago. Maybe you're not doing it right. I'd be happy to give you some pointers," I tease. Cooper punches me in the arm as I laugh. I glance over at Hope, a blush blooming in her cheeks. When her eyes find mine, I can't help but wink at her. Her smile grows, and I've officially won a gold medal for the evening.

Dad, Cooper, and I quickly clean off the table together as the girls talk. Something about this scene feels incredibly right. Like all the pieces of the puzzle are finally where they should be.

Cooper gives Quinn another look that says he's dying to get her home, and a little niggle of jealousy worms its way through my stomach. What would it be like to have a person you want to spend all your time with? To have someone who, with just one look, knows exactly what you're thinking. I stopped believing I was ever going to have it until I met Hope. Now, it feels like my future is only standing a few feet away.

My eyes find her across the room, laughing at something my mom is saying. I could watch her laugh all day and not tire of it.

"You should ask her out," Cooper says from my left.

"I did; the ball's in her court now."

"When have you ever waited for someone else to tell you what to do?"

His words make me pause. He's right. I've always been the one to jump in headfirst instead of waiting around.

"She's different, man. Treat her that way," Cooper continues, then slaps me on the shoulder.

"See you later, Levi." Quinn gives me a quick hug, then walks over to Hope to say goodbye.

Cooper's advice unlocks something in my brain. Hope is different from any other woman I've ever encountered, which means my actions need to be different than they normally would be. I've never had to work hard for a date, which only solidifies the point. My dating history has been flighty at best and playboy at worst. If I want Hope to know how special she is to me, I need to woo the shit out of her until she has no choice but to say yes.

"Hope, would you and Levi mind doing the dishes for me?"

"I don't mind doing them by myself," I offer, giving Hope an out.

"No, I should help since I got to enjoy the meal without making it."

"Thank you so much, dear," Mom says, leaving us in the kitchen alone. Her matchmaking tactics hit me the minute she leaves. She's devious.

Hope and I work together to gather all the dishes, then make a game plan for how we want to tackle the massive pile. It looks like we're going to be here awhile. Thank God.

"Popcorn or candy?"

"We're starting this again?" She raises her eyebrow, one of my favorite expressions of hers.

"Of course. How else am I supposed to learn everything about you?"

Hope looks at me for a bit, almost as if she's trying to get a read on me. "Popcorn for movies. Candy for road trips."

"Interesting distinction. But I'd have to agree with both. Beach or mountains?"

"I don't know. I've never seen either."

"What? Seriously?"

Hope shrugs her shoulders, keeping her face blank. I make a plan right then to take her to a beach as soon as possible.

"Which one would you pick?" she asks.

"Beach all the way. Although, I do enjoy the mountains, as well."

"Books or movies?"

I grin, happy she's joining the game with her own questions. "Movies."

"No way! The books are always better."

"I wish I had the attention span to read."

"You should try an audiobook. You could do it while you work," Hope suggests. It's an incredibly insightful idea. I shouldn't be surprised. Hope seems to be the kind of person who would notice every detail about you, cataloging it to use later, if needed.

"What do you like to read?"

Hope's cheeks grow pink, and I raise my eyebrow back at her in anticipation of the answer. "I like a lot of different things, but my favorite is romance."

"Well, I never would've guessed." I grin at her. An image of Hope reading sexy books pops into my head. I wonder if she ever gets turned on by them. I clear my throat. I do not need to be thinking about her like that while she's standing right next to me. It's hard enough to keep my hands to myself without any dirty thoughts in my head.

"You should try them. I bet you'd like some of the military ones. They've usually got quite a bit of action in them."

"If you send me an audiobook, I promise I will try it out."

Hope looks at me for a moment, trying to gauge my sincerity. I genuinely meant what I said. If she sent me the book, I really would try to listen to it.

We keep the game going back and forth while we finish up the dishes. I'm learning so much about Hope that I would've never gotten to know if it weren't for Mom. I'll have to thank her for it sometime.

We have a lot more in common than I thought we did. Each topic we bring up seems to provide more interests we share, but our answers vary slightly. We both love coffee entirely too much, but I drink mine black while she likes it sweet. Neither one of us enjoys playing sports, but she likes watching baseball, and I like watching football. Italian food is both of our favorites, but she's a red sauce fan whereas I prefer white sauce.

This connection growing between us is something I've never experienced before. The more I learn about her, the more I want to keep digging to get at the heart of who she is as a person. I want to be the only one she shares her deepest desires with.

Disappointment flows through me as we finish up the dishes. With our task done, we're both going to have to leave soon. I'm not ready for the night to end, but there's no way Hope would be ready to go somewhere alone with me. Plus, I don't want to push her too far too quickly. I want to do this right. Prove to her that I can be someone she can trust to take care of her.

We both gather our things and walk toward the front door. I holler up the stairs to say goodbye to Mom and Dad, who shout a goodbye in return. Opening the door for Hope, she steps through, and I follow closely behind her. As I walk her to her car, the cool evening air feels refreshing after being inside for so long.

Hope stands next to her car, keys in hand, looking up at me through her dark lashes. For the first time since I met her, I feel like I can get a read on her, and I don't think she wants to leave any more than I do. I step closer, mere inches between us now.

"When you get your decorations picked out, give me a call. I can help you put them up."

"I will. Thank you for offering."

"Just don't want you to smash a finger or something." I grin down at her.

Hope's eyes hold mine for a minute, the whole world reflecting back at me. Without much thought, I gently wrap my hand around her arm, tugging her toward me. I want to kiss her with everything I have, but instead, I slowly wrap my arms around her shoulders, embracing her in a hug that feels more intimate than any sexual encounter I've experienced.

Hope's body is stiff for a second before she melts into my arms, wrapping hers around my waist. We fit so perfectly together as if we were always supposed to find each other.

I place my nose to the top of her head, inhaling her flowery scent, then gently press my lips against her head. Hope drops her arms and steps away from me, my body chilling from the sudden loss of her body heat. I shake my head, trying to get my raging body under control. How one moment can send me into a tailspin will never be clear to me. Nothing even happened.

"Good night, Levi," Hope whispers, then quickly gets into her car.

"Night," I say as her door closes on my words.

Stepping back, I watch her pull out of the driveway. In all my dating history, a hug has never affected me the way Hope's body against mine did. There's something inside her calling to the heart of me. Something wild and free that she's holding close, too afraid to let it out.

I'm determined to be the safe place for her to soar. To prove I have what it takes to set her free.

13

"ROSEMARY"

SIX YEARS AGO

"Can you make sure you're careful around the roses, please?" I ask the gardener. His tanned skin shows signs of being outdoors for long periods of time. I think he's my age, but it's hard to tell between his sunglasses and wide hat.

"Of course, ma'am. I'm sorry if we've messed anything up."

"Oh, you haven't yet. The last guy to mow got too close, so I wanted you guys to pay a little more attention."

"I'll let them know," he says with a nod of his head and a smile. I return his smile, then walk back toward the house. I love walking through the gardens. They have been a place of solace to me over the past few months. I'm not sure how well I would be coping without them.

The house is quite large. Even after living here for the past three months, I'm still struggling to adjust to the size. With five bedrooms and four bathrooms, it's a lot to take care of every day, but I'm finally finding my groove. As well as what is expected of me.

That's been the hardest adjustment. I thought living with

all my father's rules was difficult, but Antony is something else entirely.

Stepping through the foyer, the grand staircase is the first thing you see. To the right is a formal sitting room and to the left is Antony's office. The door is always closed, no matter if he's inside or not. Everything feels almost like a museum, like if you touch anything, it'll be detrimental to the piece of furniture.

Past the staircase is the kitchen and one of the bedrooms. I spend most of my time in the kitchen. It has the best view of the flower garden in the backyard. All the windows give the chef-worthy kitchen a bright and cheery look.

"Marta, did you get everything we need for the party this week, or will you need to make a run to the store?"

"Rosemary, I need you in my office," Antony says from behind me, startling me with how quietly he moves. I clench my fists to keep my words in check, then slowly turn to face him, attempting to keep my face blank. A little smirk pulls at his lips, knowing he got the drop on me. He enjoys playing his cat and mouse games.

I nod my head, following Antony back to his office. I have no idea what I could've done to require this meeting. I probably didn't do anything, and he decided to change the rules just to have a reason to punish me. Keeping me on my toes is one of his favorite things to do. Right behind inflicting pain.

"Is everything running as it should? I heard you asking Marta about dinner this week." Antony motions for me to sit in one of his brown leather visitor's chairs sitting in front of his desk. His whole office is decorated with dark brown tones. Each piece of furniture chosen to show off his wealth, I'm sure.

He leans against his desk directly in front of me instead of sitting in his chair. His position gives him a height advantage to make me feel even smaller.

"Yes, since we added the dinner party to the schedule this week, I wanted to ensure Marta had what she needed."

"Good. I'm glad to see you thinking of those details."

You've ensured I won't make those mistakes again. The words stick in my throat. I so badly want to say them out loud but know what will follow immediately if I do.

"Did you talk to the gardener today?"

"Yes, I wanted them to watch out for the roses," I reply.

"Was it necessary to flirt with him?"

My eyes shoot up to Antony's, his blue eyes steely and hard. What was he talking about?

"I wasn't flirting."

Antony's fist clenches. "Don't lie to me," he growls.

Keeping my eyes locked with his so he knows I'm not lying, I defend myself again. "I wasn't. I asked him to tell his guys to watch out for my roses, nothing more."

Antony's arm lashes out so fast, I barely have time to register it's coming. The backhand throws my body into the side of the chair. If it hadn't had arms, I would've been thrown to the floor from the impact. My right cheek throbs as tears spring to my eyes. I manage to hold my cry inside. I'm so used to the pain at this point, crying out does nothing but make me look weaker.

"I saw you, so don't bother lying again. You are not to speak to any male again. If you need something done, you tell either me or Marta, and we will relay the message."

I look up at Antony, his eyes gleaming with satisfaction. He catalogs the redness of my face and the tears filling my eyes. After a few painful minutes, he finally dismisses me.

I stand on shaky legs to walk out of the office, closing the door behind me as I go. When I'm back in the kitchen, Marta hands me a cold compress, knowing exactly what happened. Sometimes, I'm grateful for her help, and other times, I want to scream at her to do something. Ask her how she can watch this happen every day, and never say a word about it.

"I have everything I need for the party, Mrs. Malatelli."

I nod my head, then leave the kitchen, needing a moment alone in my room.

I thought I'd have found an opportunity to get out of this long before now, but I haven't.

I'm not sure I ever will.

14

HOPE

The smell of rubber and tools greets me as I step into the hardware store. Aisles of every home improvement item you could possibly need span the large space. It's overwhelming, to say the least.

There are entirely too many options here. Where do I even start?

I step down an aisle with wood glue, paintbrushes, and paint. Nope. Not what I need. Down the next one I go, one after the other, still having no clue what I'm even looking for, at this point.

Finally, one aisle seems promising as I start browsing the nails collected in clear plastic bins. Now, which one do I need? Where are the employees when you need them?

"Hope?"

The sound of my name startles me, and the nails I had in my hand go flying into the air.

"Jesus." My hand flies to my chest as my heart attempts to thump out of my body. Turning, I find Levi smirking at me from the end of the aisle. I shoot him a glare. "I'm going to buy you bells to wear so you won't do that anymore."

He laughs, and I can't help the smile growing on my face.

I don't think I've ever smiled so much around another person. How can he have such infectious joy surrounding him? I lean over to pick up the nails I dropped, placing them back into their respective bins.

"Are you doing some remodeling?" Levi asks, a teasing lilt to his question.

"No, just trying to get the stuff to hang the paintings I bought at Paint and Paper." Quinn helped me pick out some great stuff to match the decorations already at the house.

"I thought you were going to call me when you picked out some decorations."

I cringe. I did say I was going to do that, but I wasn't sure if he genuinely meant he'd be happy to help or if he was only being nice. "I didn't want to bother you. I figured it couldn't be too hard to hang a few pictures myself."

"Well, those are drywall nails."

"Hmm…" My brows furrow as I look at the selection. "I guess those won't work, then?"

"Definitely not." Levi laughs. "Here," he reaches up, grabbing a clear box hanging on a peg, "these are what you need."

The box says *picture hanging kit*. These make way more sense than loose nails. I turn to walk back out of the aisle, then start toward the cash register. Levi walks next to me with a few supplies in his hands.

"Um, not to question you or anything, but do you have a hammer?" His words are hesitant as if he doesn't want to straight-up ask if I know what I'm doing since it would be rude.

"Yes, of course, I do!" I say indignantly.

I don't actually have one; I just don't want him to think I'm a total idiot. Which, I am. How could I have forgotten that I would need a hammer? I casually look up at the lists of items at the end of each aisle, trying to find where the hammers would be located.

"Okay… I'm sure you'd do fine on your own, but I can

still come help you. I've got some time right now," he offers a little sheepishly. He knows I'd probably put a million holes in the wall if I did this on my own.

"It's driving you crazy thinking about me doing it myself, isn't it?"

"No! I'm just trying to be helpful."

I raise my brow at him, and he crumbles like a dried flower.

"Okay, yes! I keep picturing the hammer going straight into the wall, and it's killing me!"

"All right, fine. You can help." I walk up to the cash register, setting my kit on the counter. "Um, you have a hammer, right?"

"Oh, sweet Jesus," Levi groans, which makes me laugh.

If I'm being honest with myself, I didn't call Levi because I'm afraid of my feelings for him. Ever since dinner a few nights ago, I haven't been able to stop thinking about how amazing it felt to have his arms wrapped around me. Being surrounded by Levi's strong embrace made me feel safe for the first time in a very long time. Naturally, I freaked the frick out as soon as I got home. Despite having given myself a few days to calm down, I still couldn't gather enough courage to call him to help me with the paintings.

I should probably thank fate for letting us cross paths again.

After I finish checking out, I grab my small paper bag and step out of the store with Levi following close behind me. "I'll meet you at your house?" he asks, his own bag hanging from his fingers.

"Sure. See you in a minute." Once I'm in my car, I pull out of the parking lot to head home. Driving down Main Street always makes me smile. The sidewalks have wooden awnings covering them, and timeless black lamp posts are stationed between beautiful flower boxes. One of my favorite things is how the city changes the flowers for each season. Each box is always well maintained, which makes my flower-loving heart happy.

I pull into my driveway, opening the garage door as Levi pulls in behind me. Once I'm out of my car, my stomach starts to quiver at the thought of being in my house alone with him. It's not like I haven't been alone with him before, but something feels different this time. *I feel different.* The resolve I'd been holding on to so strongly seems to have evaporated with the bubbles of dishwater.

I wait for Levi to get out of his truck, his muscles flexing under his T-shirt as he lifts his toolbox out of the back. His tight jeans highlight his butt so well that I find myself wanting to give it a firm squeeze. The paper bag in my hand crinkles when my body tightens at the sight.

There have always been men I found attractive, but no one has ever made my body heat with only a flex of muscles like Levi does. I wish I had the gumption to make the first move. I don't possess that amount of courage, though. Plus, I have no idea if he still has any desire to date me. Why would he when I'm an absolute disaster? I mean, he could have his pick of women; picking me would be a bad bet.

Levi turns around, catching me staring, and a cocky, little smirk grows on his face. I quickly turn to walk inside so he won't see me blush. The garage door leads into the kitchen, and I set the hardware bag on the counter as Levi comes in behind me.

The three paintings I picked out lean against the wall in the kitchen where I want to hang them. Each painting is a part of a whole picture, and when they're hung, you'll see a full sunrise coming up over the lake here in Sonoma.

"These are great," Levi says, walking over to the paintings. He sets his toolbox down on the floor, the tools rattling against the metal.

"Quinn painted them. I thought they were pretty fitting."

"Definitely." Levi smiles at me, and I have to turn away

before I get pulled into his magnetism again. Grabbing the kit from the bag, I hand it over so Levi can hang the paintings.

His large hand slides across mine as he takes it from me, his eyes gauging my reaction. Instead of feeling the need to pull away, a tingle races up my arm. I grit my teeth to keep from gasping at the sensation. I wish I understood this connection between us. It's unlike anything I've ever experienced before. My body and mind are in turmoil, pulling in two different directions.

I want to know how it would feel to touch him completely uninhibited. To kiss him with the passion I've only dreamed of experiencing. At the same time, I am terrified of the consequences of getting too close, of allowing a man into my life when they've only ever led to pain. There's something about Levi that's pulling me in so hard, I'm having a hard time fighting it. What would happen if I gave in?

Levi's eyes shine with an emotion I can't read before he turns to the paintings, turning them around, then grabbing what he needs from the kit.

"Can you hold these for a second?" he asks, holding out the gold hooks. I take them from him and watch as he measures out where each painting will go. He double-checks the placement with me, then hammers the nails into the wall.

After hanging the paintings on the hooks, he steps back. They look perfect. I take a photo to send to Quinn, and she sends me the heart-eye emoji in return.

"Thank you for helping me. I would have made a mess of that."

"I know." Levi winks. My hand snaps out, whacking him in the arm. My eyes go wide at the move, and I freeze. Fear races through me so fast, I'm almost dizzy.

Levi chuckles as he rubs his arm. He turns to look at me, the smile dropping from his face. "Hey, what happened? Are you okay?" Concern is laced through his voice as he steps closer to me. My brain is moving in hyperdrive, trying to predict the outcome of the moment. I don't know how he'll react to my brazen move. I'm frozen in place as self-preservation takes over my body.

"Hope," Levi whispers, desperation lacing his words. His hands come up to my face, and I cringe into myself, keeping my eyes closed in preparation. The moment his soft touch runs across my cheeks, my eyes fly open in surprise. "You're safe with me."

His hazel eyes are full of concern as they implore me to hear his words. His thumbs rub across my cheeks, making my body relax. The adrenaline pumping through my system begins to dissipate, and I have to close my eyes as embarrassment floods me. When tears burn behind my eyelids, I grit my teeth to keep from letting them fall. I can't believe how quickly I was triggered. He didn't even do anything wrong. It was my own body reverting back so fast, there was no stopping it.

Levi's lips press against my forehead, his words whispering against my skin, "I will never hurt you. Ever." His arms wrap around my shoulders, pulling me into him. My head lands on his chest, his comforting scent surrounding me. All I can do is lean into the embrace.

It's been so long since I've been held like this. So long since I've felt the gentle touch of someone who cares about me. It's overwhelming. I sink further into Levi, deepening our connection. As his hands soothingly run up and down my back, a few of the shattered pieces of my soul begin to mend themselves. Even though the cracks will always remain, they'll serve to remind me of how strong I am.

15

LEVI

My headlights illuminate the front of Max and Lucy's little cottage as I pull into their driveway. I turn my truck off, grab the six-pack of beer I bought, and walk into the house. After so many years of friendship, knocking is sort of pointless.

The smell of food permeates the open living space, making my mouth water. I slip off my boots, then make my way into the kitchen, where Max and Lucy are moving around each other with an ease I've always found fascinating. It's as if they know each other's moves before they make them, creating this intimate interaction I will never be a part of.

"Hey, guys!"

Max turns his head at my voice, a smile breaking across his face. His brown hair and dark chocolate eyes have always been warm. Between Lucy's constant kindness and Max's generosity, they are two of the nicest people I know. Which is saying something because the rest of my friend group is amazing, as well.

"How are you, man?" Max asks, pulling me into a bro hug,

our hands clasped at our chests and a quick slap to the shoulder.

"Doing pretty good. How are you guys?"

"Just great." Lucy smiles. I give her a quick kiss on the cheek. Her stick-straight, blonde hair is pulled back into a ponytail while her brown eyes shine with happiness.

"Can I help with anything?" I set the six-pack I brought in the fridge, grabbing two out before closing the door.

"Nope, it's just about ready," Lucy says, moving around the kitchen, taking out bowls and silverware. She gives the chili on the stove another stir, then lets us know it's ready to dish up.

Once we all have our bowls prepped, we sit down at the table to chat about everything going on in our lives. Despite co-owning the company, Max and I don't spend every day together. Most of his day is spent at our small office in town, drawing designs and running the day-to-day stuff while I'm on-site at each build. We have regular dinners so we can catch up on our lives.

"What's on your project list right now?" I ask Max.

"I've got a couple of things, but no major time sucks. Why?"

"Well, I may have a project for you soon."

"Did you find a house?" Lucy asks excitedly. They've been a part of this search since I started looking months ago, knowing it's my dream to fix up a place of my own.

"I think I might have." I pull out my phone to pull up the pictures. "I'm going to put an offer in tomorrow but wanted to make sure you had some time to help me design the renovation."

"It's going to take a lot of work. You've got a mess on your hands there," Max says, looking at the pictures with Lucy.

"I know, but it's got the right bones to make it exactly what I want."

"I think it's perfect." Lucy grins at me.

"I agree. I couldn't have picked out a better house for you." Max smacks me on the shoulder.

"You'll help me with the design?"

"Of course. We'll charge you a nominal fee. Give you the family discount." He winks. "We've got a baby to think about now."

I freeze. "What?"

"Oops." Max sheepishly grins at Lucy, who laughs at him.

"You're having a baby?"

"Yeah, we found out a couple of days ago." Lucy blushes.

"Holy shit, guys!" I stand from my chair and walk around the table to give them both a hug. "Congrats. Does anyone else know?"

"Nope, you're the first one we've told. We were going to wait a while before we shared, but it sort of slipped out there," Max says. Lucy grabs his hand with a smile as I sit back down in my chair.

"This is great!" The look Max and Lucy share has something in my chest constricting. I've never felt the kind of love they have for each other. The kind of love that consumes you so fully, you don't know what you'd do without the other person. It's not something I ever thought much about, but now, I feel like I'm missing out.

As they usually do, my thoughts drift to Hope and the connection between us. She's the first woman I've ever considered wanting more with. No one else has ever captured my attention like she has. I want to be with her all the time. It took every ounce of strength I had to leave her the other day after I hung her paintings. I knew we both needed a little space after the heaviness of what happened. I'm still not sure why we took such a hard left turn.

She was being so playful, then something happened to make her utterly terrified. It was like a switch was flipped, and she became a different person. She folded in on herself, even flinched away from me when I tried to figure out what was going on. All I wanted to do was protect her from the bad things in life, and based on her reaction, some pretty bad things had to have happened to her.

I had to keep complete control over my emotions because rage was coursing through me so strongly, I knew she'd see it if I let it slip. I can only guess at the horrors Hope has endured, but her fear speaks loud and clear. If someone hurt her, they deserve to rot in hell after being made to endure the same pain they inflicted on her.

I hate that she felt the need to cower away from me. I would die before I ever did anything to hurt her. I was surprised she let me comfort her afterward but was really glad she did. It eased some of my worries about her being afraid of me.

"You okay over there?" Lucy asks, her brows furrowed in concern. I must've had a look on my face to make Lucy notice I wasn't paying attention anymore.

"Yeah, sorry. Thinking about something."

"Do you need help working it out?"

"Actually... I met someone." I tell them all about meeting Hope and how much I've come to like her. I don't want to share too much of what happened the other day, but I think having someone else's perspective could be helpful. Over the past week, I've done my best to establish myself in her life. I've brought her lunch from the café, coffee in the mornings before work, anything I can think of to see her.

I'm ready to push us to the next level, but I'm worried Hope isn't. If I move too fast, I'll be guaranteeing my future as a sad, lonely schlub, reliving my glory days in a bathrobe that covers nothing.

"It sounds like she's feeling things for you, too. What would you normally do in this situation?" Lucy asks.

"I'd ask her out. I wouldn't leave it up to chance or give her time to decide she doesn't like me anymore."

"Then, there's your answer. You need to be able to be

yourself, Levi. If she can't handle it, then maybe she's not ready to be with you yet."

I nod my head in response as my brain speeds twenty steps ahead, trying to figure out the best way to move forward. I've done all I can to show her how much I want her. It's time to see if she wants me in return.

I hope I don't screw things up too badly. Being in a relationship isn't something I'm used to, but I can't risk losing out on the potential of finding the person I am meant to be with. After spending a little bit of time with Hope, there's no doubt in my mind she's special.

There's always going to be the chance of getting hurt. That's life. Sitting on the sidelines and watching it pass me by seems monumentally stupid. Letting Hope go because I'm too scared to jump in would be even worse.

I've never been one to shy away from something out of fear. Usually, I do it *because* I'm afraid, and there's never been one time I've regretted my decision. This feels like something I would regret not doing.

Now, I just have to plan the best way to ask her out and hope like hell she doesn't say no.

16

HOPE

"Can you grab me the rest of the peonies from the back?" I ask Claire as I place some more greenery into the centerpiece I'm making. I've got about ten more to go for the city council banquet tomorrow afternoon.

Smaller events are much easier to handle than weddings. They are a lot less stressful for a multitude of reasons, the main one being I don't have to worry about a bride freaking out because the flowers she wanted didn't come in on time. It hasn't happened to me since I opened my shop, but it happened at the store I worked at in high school. I was so glad it wasn't my job to deal with the bridezillas.

Claire comes back, placing the bucket of peonies next to me on the counter. "Thank you. You can head home if you want. I can handle any last-minute walk-ins." The store is only open for another hour, and we're usually slow at the end of the day.

"Okay! I'll see you tomorrow." Claire beams at me. Her infectious joy has made my day even better. Without her around, I would've wallowed in the embarrassment of my behavior in front of Levi. It's been four days, and I still haven't been able to get over it.

The way he held me, comforting me after my panic attack, was a totally new experience. I thought he'd want to talk about what happened, but instead, he hugged me. He hasn't brought it up during any of the times he's come to see me since, which I'm glad about. I'm not sure how to describe what was going through my head or why I reacted the way I did. I don't fully understand it myself.

All I know is one minute, we were teasing each other, then the next, my brain went into survival mode after I hit him. I would have never gotten away with something like that in my old life, and my body reacted before I could rationalize what I was doing. He was sweet about it, though, which made my feelings for him grow exponentially.

Since then, each coffee or food delivery has been met with both nerves and excitement. I've loved every minute he comes to see me, even though my brain keeps screaming, *"Danger, Will Robinson."* But for once, it's not my body I'm worried about. It's my heart.

I don't know what to do with all the feelings he's stirred up inside of me. They're all foreign, making it very difficult to dissect each one over the past few days. The surprising thing is how safe I feel every time he's around. It's as if something deep inside me is calling out to him, telling him exactly what I need at any given moment. I've never had an experience quite like it before.

The door chimes, and I look up to find Levi striding into my store, a goofy grin on his face I can't help but return. He's still in his work clothes, his shirt splattered with paint.

"Hi." A blush creeps into my cheeks as he steps closer to the counter.

"Hi. I have a question for you."

My brows furrow and worry flits through me, hoping he doesn't want to talk about *the incident* as I've come to think of it. "Okaaaay."

"What kind of flowers would you suggest for asking someone out?"

Disappointment flows through me swiftly and furiously. I do everything I can to keep it from showing on my face. "Um… roses would probably be good."

"Sure, that makes sense. What would be your favorite flower to receive?"

"*My* favorite?" I ask, not quite sure I understand what he's asking.

"Yeah, what's your favorite flower?"

"Well… I love tulips and white orchids."

"Okay, can I have an arrangement with those two, please?"

I press my fingers between my eyebrows, studying Levi. "Are you sure?"

"Yep." He smiles at me as if he's in on a joke I don't understand. I sigh, shrugging my shoulders before I turn to the coolers behind me. Grabbing out the flowers I need, I put together a beautiful arrangement—one I would love to receive from Levi, then wrap it with a pretty, white ribbon and bring it over to the register.

"Can I have a card, please?"

"Um, sure," I say, handing over a white and silver card to match the flowers.

Levi quickly writes something down, tucking it away before I can see what it says. He hands his credit card over to pay, then picks up the flowers when he's done.

"When are you done working?"

"Not for another hour."

"Okay. See you later." He grins, then walks out of the shop, leaving me standing there in utter confusion.

What the hell just happened?

It takes me a bit to focus back on the centerpieces, but I manage to finish them, leaving myself time to work on some lingering paperwork I haven't gotten to. I was glad no one else came in, so I had plenty of time to do both.

A knock at my front door pulls me out of the dull task of balancing my inventory list. I stand from my tiny desk and walk out to the front. We've been closed for the last half hour, so I'm not sure why someone would be trying to get in.

When I come around the corner, I find Levi standing on the other side of the door with the flower arrangement I made him earlier in hand. I unlock the door, inviting him inside with a frown.

"Everything okay with the flowers?"

"I hope so." He hands them to me, and I automatically start examining them to see if something weird is going on. Levi's laugh has me looking up at him.

"Here, open it," he prompts, holding out the card.

I take it, pulling the card out of the envelope.

*Hope, **will you go on a date with me?***

I BLINK AT THE CARD, momentarily stunned. "You want to go out with me?"

"Why do you think I asked about your favorite flowers?"

I look down at the arrangement. "These are for me?"

"This is not going how I planned." He huffs out a laugh. "Hope, I want to take you out on a date."

"Okay." The word slips out before I can think about the consequences. Between his bumbling idea of giving me flowers that I made myself, and him looking so cute while trying to help me figure out what's happening, there is no way I can say no.

"I want to spend more time with you—okay?"

"Yeah." I shrug, smiling at his confusion. "I'd like to spend more time with you, too."

"What are you doing tomorrow night?"

"Going on a date, apparently." I grin at my own words. I don't know how he does it, but every time I'm with Levi, I become the person I've always wanted to be. The girl who says what she's thinking, who can crack a joke with the best of them. When I was young, there wasn't much that held me back, but the more life pushed me down, the more I retreated into myself. With Levi, I feel like I'm finally able to be that carefree girl again.

"Okay, then. I'll pick you up at seven?" I don't think the smile on Levi's face could get any brighter.

I nod my head, grinning from ear to ear as Levi walks out of my store. I walk back to my office when I freeze in place.

Holy shit, I'm going on a date.

I don't know how to date. What the heck am I supposed to do now? I'm going to need help, and I know just who I should call for it.

* * *

"OKAY, show me what we've got to work with," Quinn says, rubbing her hands together.

"Not much." I grimace, pulling out the only three dresses I own from my closet. Quinn is sitting on my bed, helping me get ready for my date. I called her right after Levi left yesterday, knowing I was not going to be able to do this by myself. She squealed at the news, then immediately agreed to help me out.

"These are great choices. This yellow one is adorable."

"It's my favorite, but is it too much?"

"No, it's fun and flirty."

I grab the dress and step into my bathroom to change. The dress is sleeveless with a high neckline; the top is tight, then flares out at the waist, and the skirt has billowy layers that end a little bit above my knees.

I step out of the bathroom to face a grinning Quinn. "It's perfect!"

"Are you sure?"

"Absolutely." She hands me my wedge sandals, then checks the time on her phone. "Okay, he's going to be here in about twenty minutes. Do you need me for anything else? I don't want to be here when he shows up."

"I think I'm okay. Should I do something with my hair?" I finger my curls that are hanging loosely around my shoulders. There's nothing I can do with it, but I figure I should double-check.

"No, your curls look great." Quinn walks over to hug me, squeezing me tight. These embraces are getting easier to handle. The frequency must be helping me desensitize. "I am so happy for you. Levi is a great guy; you're going to have a blast."

"Thank you so much for your help."

"Anytime!"

I follow Quinn out to the living room, shutting the front door behind her when she leaves. I still have ten minutes before Levi's supposed to get here.

I pace around the living room, picking up random items and putting them in other places to keep myself occupied. I think I've been on a total of three dates in my entire life. I have no idea what I'm supposed to do. I'm hoping Levi will take the lead for most of the evening. Then, I won't have to worry about looking like a complete idiot.

Headlights shine through my living room windows, making butterflies set up camp in my stomach. He's finally here.

When he knocks on my door, I grab my purse from the couch and open the door to take in the beautiful specimen before me. A green button-down shirt is stretched tight across his chest and tucked into khaki pants that are tight around his thighs. He's styled his light brown hair into a messy, just-woke-up look while his hazel eyes shine bright green against the color of his shirt. He looks amazing and a little intimidating. Why anyone as good-looking as Levi would want to go out with me is anyone's guess.

"Wow. You look beautiful!" Levi says as his eyes scan my body, causing goose bumps to race down my arms.

"So do you. I mean… Well, you know what I mean."

Levi's guffaw has a little of the tension seeping out of my shoulders. He holds his hand out for me. "Are you ready?"

"I think so." I take his proffered hand, and he leads me out to his truck, opening the passenger door for me. "Thank you," I say as I climb into the cab. I close the door, keeping my gaze on Levi as he walks around the front of the vehicle to get in on the other side.

The inside of his truck is clean and smells like one of those car fresheners.

"I thought we could go get dinner first, then I have an idea for later that's a little out of the norm."

"Dinner sounds great. What do you have planned?"

"I kind of want it to be a surprise."

"Well, then, you'll have to risk it being a bad idea."

Levi laughs. "Fair enough."

We drive for a little longer until he pulls into the parking lot of one of my favorite restaurants in town, Cantina Laredo.

"I hope Mexican food is okay. I was going to take you to La Mensa, but they didn't have any reservations available on such short notice."

"It's perfect. Mexican food ranks right up there with Italian for me."

"Totally agree. Chips and queso will always be one of my favorite snacks."

As we walk toward the restaurant, Levi stands close but doesn't touch me. For the first time ever, I'm wishing he would. When we get inside, the smell of Mexican spice hits my senses, making my mouth water. All the cliché Mexican restaurant decorations are scattered around the room with the exception of one completely random thing. The trunk of a turquoise Oldsmobile sits off to the side, and a full nacho bar is set up inside of it. I have no idea where the idea came from, but everyone loves it. It's become a huge draw for the town.

We sit down at the table the hostess leads us to and start digging into the chips and salsa.

"How did your week go?" Levi asks before crunching on his chip.

"Fine. I've been getting busier with different events, which is great for recognition, but exhausting. How was your week?"

"That's great, although, being overwhelmed with business can be hard. I heard back from my realtor yesterday. I'm officially closing on my fixer-upper."

"Congratulations!" The passion in Levi's voice when he told me about buying his own fixer-upper while he helped me move was inspiring. I could tell it was something he'd wanted for a long time by how animated he got talking about it.

"It's going to take a lot of work, but I'm looking forward to it."

"Are you doing it by yourself, or will some of your crew help you?'

"My crew will definitely be helping. It would take me forever to finish it by myself."

We keep talking about his house while we wait for our food to arrive. The longer we talk, the more I settle into the moment. Despite the butterflies still flapping around, I'm finally finding my groove. I just hope I can hold on to it for the rest of the evening.

LEVI

Excitement buzzes through my system with every glance I steal at Hope. Dinner was amazing, and I've learned so much more about her than I ever thought I'd get the chance to learn. Things like how she wants to go on adventures but has never had the opportunity or how witty she is when she's finally comfortable in a situation.

We're back in my truck now, headed to our next stop. This is either going to go fantastically or disastrously. I didn't want to take her on the cliché dinner and a movie date, but now that we're on the way, I feel like this could potentially backfire. If it doesn't, I know we'll have a blast.

"So, where are we going?" Hope asks, her melodic voice filling the quiet cab.

"A place in Westlake."

"You're still not going to tell me?"

"Nope."

"Okay, then. But I reserve the right to say no," she says quietly.

Kind of an odd thing to say.

"Of course. That was always a given."

"Not always," she mumbles.

"Hey." I glance over at her to make sure she's looking at me. Her features are shadowed in the dark truck, but I can see the hesitation in her eyes. "I would never ask you to do something you didn't want to do. I promise. You always have a choice."

She sighs, a small smile pulling at her lips. "Thanks."

"Has that happened before?" I ask slowly, worried about wading into territory I probably shouldn't.

She pauses, almost as if she is debating whether to answer my question or not. Finally, she says, "Yeah it has. My dad wasn't the nicest person to me. He didn't care much for what I had to say and made a lot of plans without consulting me or giving me a choice."

My hands tighten around the steering wheel. While her words are gentle, the meaning behind them is not. Her dad was an asshole. "I can't imagine how hard that was for you. Was your mom around?"

"No, she died when I was born. I lived with my grandmother until she died when I was fifteen. Then I had to live with my dad. My grandmother is the one who inspired my love of flowers. She used to call me Rosebud because I loved her roses so much." Her quick change of subject to her grandma tells me she doesn't want to keep talking about her dad. I don't mind since I don't think I have the strength to keep my anger out of my voice. Going through all of that before you're an adult would be incredibly difficult. Not only did she have to deal with the death of a loved one, but she then had to live with someone who didn't give a shit about her.

"What was your grandma like?"

"Beautiful," she breathes. "My mom had me when she was young, which made my grandmother incredibly young, as well. She had this silky, dark hair that curled like mine."

"And it was just the two of you?"

"Yeah, my grandfather passed away before I was born. It

was hard on my grandmother, losing both her husband and daughter, one quickly after the other. She always told me I was the greatest gift to come from the suffering."

"She sounds like a wonderful woman." I pull into the parking lot of the bar, then turn off the truck. "Ready?" I ask, glancing over at Hope in the dark cab.

She nods her head in response and opens her door. I hold my hand out for Hope when I meet her at the back of the truck. The fact that she grabs it without hesitation gives me so many feelings, I can hardly name them all. Elation, hope, desire. They're all coursing through me as we walk into the bar.

It's noisy as we step inside. People are standing at the bar or sitting at the tables surrounding the dance floor. No one is dancing despite the music playing. Right now, it's a pop song, but it'll change to something different in a little bit.

"Do you want a drink?" I know I'm going to need one.

"Tell me what we're doing first."

"Two-stepping."

"Sorry?" Confusion lines Hope's face, and all I can do is laugh.

"Tonight, we are learning how to two-step. I know a little bit already, but I thought getting some lessons would be fun."

"We're dancing?"

"Yep." I watch Hope's face as she starts to understand what's happening. Her smile grows so big I think it might split her face in half.

"I've never two-stepped before, but I've always loved to dance. I haven't in many, many years." A line furrows her brows as an emotion I can't catch flits across her face. "I'm going to need a drink first, though."

"You got it." Keeping her hand in mine, I lead us up to the bar, catching an empty bar stool. I gesture for Hope to have a seat while I flag down the bartender.

"I'll take a jack and coke and a—" I pause, looking at Hope.

"Vodka cranberry, please," she supplies. The bartender nods, grabbing bottles to make our drinks while I turn to take in Hope. The lights in the bar are dim, making her olive skin look exotic. Her dark eyes hold so many emotions, I wish I could read what they were. Her tongue peeks out, wetting her lips. She's fucking beautiful.

"I was worried dancing would be too much," I say, leaning in close to be heard above the noise of the bar.

"Why?"

I debate about being honest or altering the truth. With the little bit I know about Hope, honesty is probably best. "Well, I've noticed you don't like being touched, so I was worried dancing with me would be a bad idea."

Hope looks down at her lap in what I'm guessing is embarrassment. "Physical touch hasn't always been soft for me."

"Someone hurt you," I say quietly, attempting to keep the steel out of my voice. My teeth clench in anger at the confirmation of my assumptions. I've wondered since the first time I touched her and was afraid my suspicions were true.

Her eyes find mine, an ocean full of vulnerability swirling in them. It takes everything I have not to scoop her into my arms and promise to protect her forever. I wish I could've protected her from the beginning.

The bartender sets our drinks down, interrupting the moment. It's probably for the best. Being in a bar isn't the right place to discuss such a heavy topic anyway. At the same time, though, she was finally opening up to me. Hopefully, she'll still feel like talking after we leave.

"So, you've two-stepped before?" she asks, changing the subject.

"Yeah, I have. Megan and Quinn wanted to try it out one day, so we all decided to go for it. Nat and Tucker never even attempted the moves. Todd and Megan tried, but Todd was horrible, though Cooper and Quinn and Max and Lucy were amazing at it."

"Who did you dance with?" A little line between her eyebrows has me wondering if she's jealous. The thought makes me want to puff out my chest.

"Sara. She's like the sister I never had. I feel that way about all the girls because we've been friends since we were little. Sara was awful, but I didn't do too bad."

Hope smiles at me, her shoulders relaxing a bit, which only confirms my theory about her being jealous. "I think I'll be the judge of that."

"Oh, really?"

Hope nods, her smile growing wider. I love how she's excited about this. I was worried she would want to go home the minute she found out what I had planned.

We finish our drinks at the same time the instructor tells us to gather on the floor. There are about ten other couples surrounding us while others are sitting around the bar, watching the lesson.

Hope and I watch the instructors explain how to do the first steps while a popular country song plays. When it's time for us to try on our own, I turn to Hope with my hand held out to her. The minute she grabs it, I pull her in close to me, wrapping my other arm around her waist.

"This okay?"

"Yeah," she breathes, biting her lip as she stares up at me with desire sparking in her dark brown eyes. I squeeze her hip, then start leading her in the moves, trying to distract myself from the lust coursing through my body. It backfires, of course, because Hope is an amazing dancer. The way her body moves against mine only has my hormones racing faster. I have to keep my hips angled away from her so she doesn't feel the effect she has on me.

We start attempting more advanced moves, the instructor

helping us to move on faster than the rest of the group. I spin her around, causing her yellow dress to flare out. Each spin makes Hope's smile grow. Our eyes never stray from each other as our bodies find the perfect rhythm together.

In all the time I've known her, which admittedly isn't long, I've never seen happiness radiate off her like this. She's glowing, and being the one to bring her this joy has created this bubbly feeling in my chest I never want to go away.

We start to wind down on the lessons, and people start walking off the dance floor to get drinks. I keep Hope in my arms for a few more minutes because I'm not quite ready to let go.

"I have to say, I'm impressed." Hope grins up at me.

"I'm glad I didn't disappoint you."

"Do you want to grab another drink?"

"In a minute. Let's finish this song first."

Hope graces me with a happy smile, nodding her head in agreement. I can't take my eyes off her. For the first time in my dating history, I don't want this night to end. I'm not looking for an out or a way to move things along quicker. I would be content to stand here, holding Hope in my arms for the rest of the night.

Seeing Hope slowly lower her walls has made me feel like I've won the best prize. Being the one she's chosen to open up to is the best gift I could ever receive. Especially knowing it's not easy for her to lower her guard around others.

I'm nervous I'm going to screw this up somehow. She deserves the world, and I want to be the one to give it to her. If that means it takes every ounce of effort I have to prove I'm worthy of her, then I'll do it. I have a feeling she's every-thing I've been looking for in a partner because, right now, with her body against mine, I've never been happier.

It always felt like the women I dated didn't think I was good enough for a long-term relationship—like I didn't have the right qualities. But having Hope in my arms proves I just hadn't found the right person to settle down with.

As the song ends, I realize we're going to have to leave soon. Neither one of us are huge drinkers, and since the lesson is over, the bar is getting louder, which will make talking difficult.

We step off the dance floor, my hand on Hope's lower back as I lead her back to the bar. "Do you want another drink?"

"No, I think I'm okay." Hope's eyes are on me, cataloging every expression I make. I can see the tension in her shoulders; I'm just not sure where it's coming from.

"Are you ready to go home?"

"Um, I guess." Her hesitant answer has me wondering if she's not ready for the night to end yet, either.

I take her hand to lead her out of the bar, her fingers twisting around mine so delicately, I want to squeeze them tight so she can't get away. We make our way back out to my truck, and I help her up into the cab.

How can I ask her to keep the night going without it sounding like I want to sleep with her? I mean, I do want to sleep with her, but not tonight. Tonight, I want to keep learning more about her. Keep getting closer to her so we can both be comfortable with the idea of dating each other.

My thoughts keep swirling as I drive us home. Hope must be in her head, as well, because she doesn't say much, either. The rumbling engine seems loud with the radio off.

My nerves return as I pull into her driveway, my headlights shining on her house, highlighting the small front porch, wooden porch swing, and black front door. I turn the truck off, then step out onto the driveway. Hope beats me to opening her door, and I meet her at the front of the truck. We walk side-by-side up the sidewalk, the front porch light guiding our way to the door. The air is perfectly tepid, making me want to spend a little more time in the fresh air, looking at the stars.

Standing outside her front door, I watch her fiddle with her keys. I can't stand the unknowns anymore. "I'm not ready for the night to end yet."

Hope's eyes fly to mine, uncertainty and hope glowing in her gaze.

"I don't have any expectations, I just want to spend more time with you. I'm not ready to go home to an empty apartment and sit on the couch, watching TV alone, when I could do the exact same thing with you."

Hope grins at me. "You want to come in for a cup of coffee?"

I grab her hand, an elated smile on my face. "I'd love to."

18

"ROSEMARY"

FIVE YEARS AGO

The sound of boisterous laughter follows the scent of cigar smoke all the way upstairs. My anxiety runs through me with such strength, I can't focus on the words of my book. I stand, pacing around my small bedroom to try to dispel some of the tension. My bed sits directly in the middle of the room, leaving enough space for a chair and dresser on opposite sides.

I hate when he has his friends over. They drink entirely too much, and Antony is always unpredictable when he's drunk. I've grown accustomed to his mood swings, predicting when I need to make myself scarce, but when he drinks, his behavior is never the same. I end up saying the wrong thing or not saying anything at all, which also pisses him off. Luckily, he doesn't host gatherings here very often. Otherwise, my life would be much worse.

I got lucky tonight when he requested I stay upstairs instead of joining them. Normally, I have to wear uncomfortable clothes and stand silently next to Antony the entire evening. He enjoys showing me off to his friends like I'm the winning trophy. What's worse is it usually ends in some form of punishment for me. I was either too silent, my facial expression too severe, or some other completely made-up reason for Antony to hit me.

I pick up my phone to open one of the three apps I'm allowed, a silly game based on the *Harry Potter* series, where you get to pretend to be a wizard. It helps take my mind off what will happen when the men leave. Before too long, I hear the sounds of goodbyes, indicating they're finally finished with their get-together.

My hands start to shake while my heart races with the sounds of footsteps on the stairs. I stand stock-still in the middle of my room as the door to my bedroom opens. Antony steps inside, his blue eyes glassy from the alcohol.

"Rosemary. You've been quiet as a mouse tonight," he slurs, scanning my entire body as he moves further into the room. He's been more and more affectionate towards me these last few months, caressing my body and giving me lascivious looks that make my skin crawl. I wish I had the freedom to tell him to stop. Instead, I'm trapped in this prison of pain, where my needs don't matter.

All I can do is stand there and attempt to read his next move. He seems to be in a good mood, albeit under the influence. Unfortunately, with the alcohol in his system, his good mood can change on a dime. Even without alcohol, his brutality is a hair-trigger away.

He steps closer to me, towering above my small frame. When he raises his hand, I flinch unconsciously, hating myself for the reaction.

His smile grows vicious, knowing he got to me, as he runs the back of a finger down my cheek. "I knew I wanted you the minute I met you. I let your father rack up his debt, knowing full well he'd never be able to pay it off, which would lead to my very generous request of taking you off his hands. He was only too happy to oblige."

Stay quiet. Don't give him anything. But, God, do I hate my father even more now.

"I've given you time to settle in; now, it's time for you to show your gratitude." His gaze turns salacious as he stares down at the small amount of cleavage showing from my V-neck T-shirt.

The blood drains from my face. I should've known this would happen. It was only a matter of time before he was going to want me for more than my house-running abilities. With the way he's been acting these last few months, I'm surprised it hasn't happened sooner.

His hand runs from my neck into my hair, gripping it so tightly I wince. He shoves me toward the bed, and I stupidly try to fight against his demands.

"Please, Antony. Don't." Fear makes my voice break at the end. It doesn't seem to matter how strong I've built up my walls. Deep down, I'm still the weak fifteen-year-old girl, hoping someone will keep me safe while my life implodes.

His answering chuckle tells me my pleas will only fall on deaf ears.

I don't want to do this. I don't want any of this. Why did my life have to turn out so horribly?

A quick fist to my side forces out a gasp, the pain making me wilt. Antony's hand in my hair is the only thing holding me up.

"I would suggest you get with the program, Rosemary, or this will be worse," Antony growls.

He shoves me onto the bed, and all I can do is lay there, tears streaming down my face, resignation setting in that this will be my life forever.

19

HOPE

Hands. All I can feel are hands. Everywhere. I fight against them as hard as I can. I thought I was safe. I got away. I got out.

"Hope. Baby, wake up."

The words echo through my head, but I can't make sense of them. Fear pulses through me while I continue pushing against the hands holding me.

"Sweetheart, please open your eyes. You're safe."

The soft tone has my eyes shooting open. I move my head around, trying to get my bearings. The soft gray couch underneath me, the sunlight shining through the windows, and the gentle hazel eyes staring at me allow my brain to catch up. I'm in Sonoma. I'm safe. I got away.

"Baby, you were having a nightmare." Levi's soft voice caresses me, helping my body calm down from the adrenaline of the too-real nightmare. I turn my body on the couch so I am chest to chest with Levi, my back facing the living room.

"Are you okay?" he asks, concern filling his eyes. He lifts his hand, and I flinch. A residual reaction from the dream. He freezes where he is, a hint of anger radiating off him.

"Sorry."

"Don't you dare apologize," he says vehemently. He slowly lowers his hand, his eyes asking for permission, and I nod my head. He pushes my hair off my forehead, then gently strokes his thumb across my cheek. "I wish I could fix it for you," he whispers. His words create an emotion I've never felt before. An ache sets up shop in my chest, forcing me to take deep breaths so I don't lose it in front of him.

"You're helping," I whisper back. Between his gentle nature and constant zest for life, he's helped bring me out of my shell. I just wish I could move on from my awful past.

"How did we end up here?" I ask, finally realizing we're laying on the couch together. "The last thing I remember is starting *Remember the Titans*."

Levi's chest rumbles against me as he chuckles. "Well, I was sitting there enjoying the movie when, all of a sudden, you fell over on me. Hand still in the popcorn bowl."

"I fell asleep?"

"Like a rock."

"Oh, my god. That's embarrassing." I shove my face into Levi's chest, trying to hide my mortification. Levi's hand runs through my hair, and I want to purr at the sensation.

"You were so cute, asleep on my lap, I couldn't stomach moving you. I guess I ended up falling asleep, too."

"That's all any girl wants to be. Cute."

"Hey, you could've snored. Although, I'm pretty sure you drooled on me."

"No, I didn't!" I start to get off the couch, but Levi grabs me around the waist, pulling me in closer to him.

"I'm teasing. You didn't drool." He smirks at me, humor glowing in his eyes. His sandy brown hair is all messed up from sleep, making him absolutely adorable this morning.

"That wasn't very nice," I say sullenly. Levi presses his soft lips against my forehead in apology. I've never felt this comfortable in a man's arms, this safe. I don't want to ever get up.

"Do you want to talk about the dream?"

I look into Levi's eyes, finding only patience there. I don't even want to think about the dream, let alone talk about it. My past is just that, the past. There's no reason to rehash it.

Allowing someone in could help you push past some of your insecurities. Joy's voice echoes in my head, but I push it away. No one needs their lives darkened by my history. Especially someone whom I want to see me as more than the battered girl who barely made it out alive.

I shake my head no, willing Levi to take my mind off the fear still simmering under my skin. Maybe I can do it on my own. Be strong enough to take what I want for a change. I glance down at Levi's plump lips, only inches from my own.

I've only kissed a handful of men my entire life. Each one was less thrilling than the last. But I know kissing Levi would be my undoing. He already consumes all my thoughts. Kissing is the next logical step.

And dammit, I just want to. I want to feel the unbridled joy in his soul spread into my own. I want to know what it's like to be swept up so deep into a kiss it makes all other thoughts leave your head.

Without another thought, I press my lips against his.

For a second, Levi freezes in surprise at my boldness. But he quickly recovers, taking over the kiss. He explores my mouth, teasing my lips with his tongue and teeth. Little nips are soothed away by a swipe of his tongue. The erotic glide stirs something in my body I never knew I possessed. There's a fire exploding in my core I didn't know I was capable of experiencing.

My tongue sneaks out to meet Levi's, and his chest rumbles with a groan. Power courses through me, knowing I made him make that noise. I slow the kiss down, needing a minute to pull myself together.

Our breathing is ragged, chests heaving into each other. I relax my fingers, having unknowingly curled them into Levi's button-down shirt.

"Wow," he whispers against my mouth.

"Yeah."

He leans in to kiss me again, but my stomach lets out a growl to rival Levi's earlier. Embarrassment floods me as he drops his forehead to mine, a quiet chuckle shaking his chest.

"Shall we get some breakfast?" he asks.

"Only if you'll kiss me again afterward."

"I can guarantee I will be kissing you again."

My grin stretches across my face so wide it's threatening to split my face in half. I'd be embarrassed, but Levi's smile matches the width of mine, making me feel less alone.

We both get up from the couch, slowly making our way into the kitchen. I start on some coffee while Levi grabs bacon and eggs. Elbow to elbow, we make breakfast together, speaking only a few words while sharing heavy glances that hold an abundance of meaning.

"Are you going to do something with the fork in your hand?" I ask, realizing Levi has mainly just stood next to me the entire time I've been cooking breakfast.

"I'm helping."

"With what?"

"Something important." He pokes at the bacon with his fork. "See?"

An unexpected laugh bursts from my chest.

"Fine, so I have no idea how to cook. I'm enjoying being next to you while you cook, though." He grins at me, and for a short moment, I'm swept up in his playful teasing. I'm not thinking about how awkward I am or how he could find someone with fewer broken pieces.

"Me, too." My lips tip up as Levi leans in to kiss me before I turn back to the stove to finish breakfast.

This feeling of comfort is foreign but so welcome. I both

want to stay with him all day and have him leave to give me room to analyze the whole night. He's been so unfailingly patient with me. Despite all my triggers, he's still here this morning. And God knows why. I'm a mess. Getting involved with me is destined to be a disaster.

I mean, I'm a pretty bad bet in the first place, so why the hell would he even want to date me?

"Why did you want to go on a date with me? Out of all the women falling at your feet, why me?" I ask, my thoughts spilling out of my mouth as we sit down at the breakfast bar with our full plates.

Levi pauses, surprised by my out-of-the-blue question, I'm sure. "Because you captivated me from the moment I met you. You're the only woman who's been able to make me stop and sit down." He levels me with a stare so filled with emotion, I can't pick everything out. Admiration, desire, strength.

All the things I've dreamed of seeing in my partner's eyes are finally reflecting back at me. "I'm a lot of work. I'm still gluing my broken pieces back together and am bound to do things wrong."

"So am I, sweetheart. We'll just have to go into this with an abundance of grace, knowing we're both going to mess up."

"Okay," I whisper, overcome with emotions I never believed I'd have a chance at feeling.

Levi grins, then returns to his breakfast. I have too many feelings swirling inside me to eat now, but I'm perfectly content to sit here and enjoy his company.

"I'm starting work on the house next week. I'm hoping I can make it habitable relatively soon so I can sleep there."

"I can't wait to see it."

"It's a mess right now, but I can't wait to show you my plans."

Our conversation flows naturally from one topic to the

next. Our childhood memories, embarrassing stories, every-thing. It's amazing to have this connection with another person. I don't hold back on anything except for my one deep, dark secret.

Maybe one day I'll tell Levi what happened to me, but not today.

2 0

LEVI

"I think this is worse than the Korneski house we did two years ago," Max says as we walk through the disaster of a house I bought. Giving it a quick glance, the initial impression would be, *yikes.* Between the peeling wallpaper, unusable stairwell, and an ugly kitchen from the fifties, it's a mess. But when you look a little closer, you'll find original crown molding, beautiful stone fireplaces, and a bone structure waiting for the right person to make it gleam.

"I know, I know. It's in rough shape, but look at all of the original woodwork in the corners here." I point to the carved pieces of molding in the corners of the room. "All they need is a bit of sanding, a new stain, and they'll be back to their original glory."

"Oh, I have no doubt we'll get her into top shape. I'm just glad you're the one doing the work." Max laughs.

"Let's start on my reno plans. The demo alone is going to take a while, so I'd like to get your opinion on what we can get started on now."

Max walks over to the sawhorse table I set up in the middle of what will be the living room. He lays out his preliminary drawings to discuss everything that will and

116

won't work now that he's seen the space in person. It's a little surreal to have this dream finally become a reality. I've wanted to do this since I started the construction company, and to be taking the first steps is unbelievable.

I've always had a love of restoring houses. There's something special about taking an unwanted place and making it beautiful again. Now, I'm finally getting a chance to create my own vision instead of someone else's.

Looking around this house, I see what it could be one day. A place for my family to be safe, happy. To create memories that will last forever. It's a dream I've harbored since I picked up my hammer on my very first job site. Having met Hope, I can see my potential future a little clearer than I've ever seen it before.

A little niggle of doubt sneaks into my stomach at the idea of a future with Hope. Am I really going to be able to give Hope what she needs? She deserves the world, and I'm not entirely sure I'm the best choice to give it to her. I've made a lot of stupid choices when it comes to dating. How the hell am I supposed to navigate this minefield of unknowns without a map?

"Levi?"

"Huh?" I snap out of my distraction, realizing Max asked me a question.

"You okay, man? You're not normally this distracted when we're on-site."

A sigh falls from my chest, knowing he's right. I hate when my brain goes into overdrive like it's doing right now. "I'm fine."

"Thinking about the woman you were talking about at dinner? Have you asked her out?"

"Yeah, I did. We went out a few nights ago, and it was… I don't even know how to describe it."

"Based on your grin, I'd say it went pretty well." Max chuckles, waggling his eyebrows. I realize he thinks we had sex. In any other circumstance, that would probably be true. Now, for the first time, I feel guilty about my dating history. Hope is so much more than a quick fuck. She's brilliant, stunning, and more than I ever expected her to be.

"It was phenomenal, but we didn't sleep together."

Max's eyes bug out. "Holy shit. She really is different, isn't she?"

I nod my head because there's nothing more to say. He's right. Hope is so different from anything I've experienced before. I also want her more than I've ever wanted anyone else. For both her mind and body.

"I thought she might be when you brought her up, but seeing you now, I know for sure. I'm happy for you, man." Max's smile is knowing and full of something I'm not sure I can interpret.

"But I've never been in a relationship. I'm a glorified play-boy, Max. How do I do this without fucking up?"

"We all have pasts, Levi. Ugly parts of us we don't want others to see, but the key is knowing when you've found the person you can trust with those ugly parts. None of the women you went out with had the qualities you needed for a relationship. I'm sure they were great people, but you needed someone specific, someone special. It sounds like Hope could be that person, and if so, you'll know what to do because she's the right one for you."

Something in Max's words resonates deep inside my chest. None of the women I went out with were the right fit for me. I always thought I didn't have the right qualities for a long-term relationship, that something was wrong with me. Looking back, I know it's because the women I went for weren't the ones who were capable of taking me seriously. If I'm being honest with myself, I think I sought them out specifically for that reason. They didn't fit into the puzzle I'd been building, which kept my heart safe.

But Hope does.

I knew she was different the minute she didn't fall for my typical lines. I was so caught up in her magnetism, I fell back on my typical ways of getting a woman, thinking it was the easiest route. When she didn't fall under my charms as most women do, I knew I'd found someone who finally deserved more from me.

I may not do everything the right way, but I'm going to put everything I have into making this the best thing for both of us. "Thanks, Max."

"Can we get back to work now and stop gabbing like teenage girls?" He winks at me, and a guffaw flies out of my mouth.

"Asshole." I punch him in the shoulder, then turn back to the plans. I'm not used to having to ask for dating advice. I've never needed it before, but knowing my friends have my back, no matter how much they tease me, eases a little of the pressure in my chest.

With so many unknowns still in my future with Hope, it's reassuring to have my best friends standing behind me to give advice whenever I need it. We've always been there for each other, no matter the circumstances, supporting each other through all of life's challenges.

It makes me want to bring Hope into the group so she can experience the same comfort. To know that, no matter what, she has friends who will be there for her. Even if we don't work out in the end.

The thought of us ending makes my stomach turn. I don't even want to think about never getting to see Hope again.

I need to text Quinn to make sure they make plans to go out sometime soon. I'd venture to guess Hope doesn't have many friends here, based on how she first interacted with me. Plus, I remember Mom talking about how no one could get the full story on the new flower shop owner when Hope first moved here.

Knowing she's shared more with me than any other

person makes me feel incredibly special. Despite how much we shared on our date, she's still pretty closed off, which is understandable. It'll take time for her to feel completely comfortable with me, to trust I'm not going to hurt her. Every ounce of effort will be worth it when she's able to be fully open.

Max and I make a game plan to finalize the designs for the house. He invited me over for dinner, but I declined so I can start demolishing some walls. Until I finish the Silvey project, I'll only be able to renovate at night. It'll make for some long days, but it will be worth it in the end.

Since this is an old Victorian-style home, there are a million walls sectioning off the main floor. I'm going to start with tearing down the walls in the kitchen, dining, and living rooms so they will all be open to each other. Then, once I get the stairs repaired, I'll make the master bedroom bigger. With five bedrooms upstairs, we've got plenty of room to spare.

I've been thinking about getting Hope in on some of the plans. When she mentioned always wanting to decorate her own house, I thought she might enjoy helping make decisions. Plus, I'm hoping she'll be spending a lot of time here when it's done, so she might as well have a say in what goes into it.

My vision for the house fills my head as I start removing the wall between the kitchen and dining room. I can see busy weekday mornings, rushing around the kitchen, slow Sunday mornings with coffee on the porch, and constant love filling the whole place.

It's everything I've ever wanted.

21

HOPE

My muscles strain as I drag a huge fern from the front corner window to the other side of the room. As the end of May brings warmer temperatures, I have to rearrange my floor displays so the right plants get all of the sun they need while others don't get too much.

Despite the effort, it's one of my favorite things to do. Caring for plants, knowing they wouldn't survive without me, fills me with an enormous amount of satisfaction. It's amazing how happy I can be when I'm finally starting to feel like myself again.

Even Claire asked me what was going on, so I finally told her about Levi. She squealed throughout the entire retelling of my date, then asked a million questions I only had half the answers to: Are we going out again? Did I want to go out again? How could I resist having sex with the flaming hotness of Levi Jackson?

I blushed from head to toe when she asked that last one.

It felt so good to share my life with someone for once, even though participating in girl talk with Claire was an interesting experience. I struggled to share all my thoughts with her, but I do feel a certain sense of camaraderie between us now. Sometimes, a small sliver of regret will hit me because I didn't take advantage of the friendships I could've made when I first moved here. I have to keep reminding myself that I wasn't in a place to be open with those people like you should be with friends.

I needed to do things on my own first before I attempted to bring others into my life. For too long, I was under the thumb of someone else's decisions with no say in the matter. I was constantly shoved into this tiny box of limited choices, unable to do anything other than survive. Once I had the freedom to make my own choices, I needed to know I could do it on my own without anyone else's influence.

If I'd attempted to make friends when I moved to Sonoma, I wouldn't have been able to discern if it was my choice or someone else's. But now, as I rearrange my store's display to my own specifications, I know I'm ready to start letting people into my life again.

I'm tired of being stuck living my life day to day, too afraid to believe something better is out there. I want to start making plans beyond what I'll do tomorrow, even if I'm terrified those plans will be taken away from me. My past will always be a part of me, but I think I'm finally ready to see what my future could look like. If Levi is a part of it, I wouldn't mind one bit. If he's not, I'd still be okay.

Although, thinking about never seeing Levi again has my heart lurching in my chest. I had so much fun on our date. The dancing and conversation were so much more than I ever thought possible with a man. On top of everything, the way he took care of me after my nightmare was heart melting. And the kiss! I've replayed our kiss a million times in my head, going so far as to imagine things that could come after another kiss like that.

He made sure to get my number before he left my house, then proceeded to text me the rest of the day. We've both been so busy with work this past week we haven't been able to find a time to get together again. I think that's a good thing, though. It's given us time to talk, to get to know each other on a deeper level. Sometimes, we chat about silly things, other times, we'll discuss our hopes and dreams.

In the evenings, he video calls me while he's working on his house. I never knew a tool belt could be a turn-on. It's not just the wardrobe I'm enjoying, either. It's everything about Levi. His humor, his mind, his hazel eyes. Everything about him calls to me, and despite all our chats, I've started to miss him. Being on video doesn't quite match the feeling of actually being in his presence. I've been dying to see him in person again, and I wish I was brave enough to tell him.

I want to feel his arms around me, holding me close. I want to experience all the sensations of his body next to mine while his lips devour me whole. I just want… him.

The door chimes, bringing with it the sound of heavy chatter between friends. A smile forms as I right myself from dragging the fern around the room. With hands on my hips, I take in the group of women who walked into my store.

Quinn, Lucy, Sara, and Megan—the girls Levi is best friends with—spend a few minutes checking out my new displays. It still has a secret garden vibe, but it's a little more summery with all of the seasonal flowers available now.

"This looks amazing, Hope!" Quinn says, walking toward me.

"Thanks. I finished updating it today." I walk back to the counter, cleaning up some of the scraps of greenery littering the surface to keep my hands busy. "Can I help you guys find anything?"

"We actually came in to talk to you!" Lucy grins at me from Quinn's side.

"Are you doing anything next weekend?" Quinn asks.

"I don't think so." I hesitate, confused about where this is going.

"Want to have dinner with us? We're getting together at

Nat's house and wanted to invite you to come, too. We figured this would be more low-key than a night out at Donna's."

"Oh, wow. Um… yeah, that would be great." Surprise floods me at the invitation. When we had dinner at the Jacksons', Quinn invited me out with them, but I figured she was only being kind. I never imagined she'd follow through. They're such a close group of friends, it's hard to believe they'd want to add another person into the mix.

"Yay! Does Sunday evening work for you?" Megan asks. Her blonde hair and blue eyes give off a barbie vibe, but paired with her genuine smile and kind demeanor, she comes off more friendly than stuck up.

"I think so."

"Fantastic! We'll see you next Sunday, then." Quinn grins at me, then ushers the group out of the store.

The exchange happened so quickly that I didn't even ask about details. What am I supposed to do at a dinner party? I've never been to one before. Do I bring food? Or drinks? I have no idea where Natalie lives, so that's a whole other detail I'll need to get sorted. My anxiety is going to go crazy over the next week. Claire's footsteps jingle as she comes out of the back room, carrying a potted hibiscus plant.

"Did I hear you getting invited somewhere?" she asks, setting the plant down in the perfect place. I didn't even need to tell her where I wanted it.

"Yes, you did. Quinn Jackson and her group of friends invited me over for dinner."

"Well, look at you, miss social butterfly!" Claire winks. Her teasing makes the tension in my shoulders loosen.

"This is crazy. Making my own friends was always frowned upon in my old life. What the hell have I gotten myself into?"

Claire's stricken expression has me replaying my words. It was probably the most I've ever said about my past to her.

Despite being willing to put myself out there, sharing what happened before I moved to Sonoma is difficult. I'm sure my statement is both shocking and confusing for her. Out of context, it doesn't make much sense.

"You've made a new life with the freedom to do what you please. Making friends seems to be on the agenda now," she says softly. I wonder if she understands my past more than I give her credit for. After all this time, it's probably obvious what I went through without needing to share the details.

"I have friends. Well, *one* friend."

"Who?"

"You, silly girl." I laugh.

Claire beams at me as she walks closer. "I'm glad you think of me as a friend. I think the same of you, but you need more. Ones who are closer to your own age and don't work for you."

Knowing she's right, I heave out a sigh. I was never very good at making friends. I didn't have much opportunity when it truly mattered. I had friends in school growing up, but I lost them after my grandmother died.

When I moved in with Dad, I was stuck in survival mode. I never had the time to make new ones. Then, after he died, I wasn't allowed to talk to anyone save for a couple of people. Looking back, I realize how lonely I was. I didn't have the headspace to acknowledge that loneliness until now. I had more important things to worry about.

"This is a good thing," she continues, and I nod. It is a good thing. It's time to start making those friendships I've always wanted.

It's probably going to end horribly, but at least I can say I tried.

22

LEVI

The bell over the door chimes as I step through the threshold of Blooming Beautiful. The entire store has been rearranged, taking me by surprise. It looks phenomenal. Every plant is perfectly placed, showing off how talented Hope is at her job. A burst of pride flows through me as I take in all the changes. She's incredible.

"Hope?" I call out into the seemingly empty store. She comes around the corner from the back, her brows furrowed in confusion. Her tight T-shirt and high-waisted shorts show off her curves, making her legs look a mile long. Damn, she's pretty. Our video calls do not do her justice.

As soon as her eyes land on mine, her frown melts into a beaming smile. Talk about making you feel like a million bucks. Her smile is only for me. She walks toward me, and I open my arms, allowing her to make the connection if she wants. To my utter amazement, she wraps her arms around me, squeezing tight. With my arms around her shoulders, I hold her close, soaking in the moment of having her back in my arms.

My nose finds the top of her head as I breathe her in, the scent of fresh flowers filling my senses. God, I missed her. I don't even know how that's possible since we've only spent a little bit of time together.

She pulls back, pink tinting her cheeks. "Hi."

Her dark eyes shine up at me, making me grin as I run my thumbs across her smooth cheeks. "Hi there." My eyes drop to her mouth. I've been dreaming about our kiss since the moment I left her house. Unable to wait any longer, I press my lips against hers.

She tastes incredible. Addicting. Her soft and pliant lips mold to mine as I deepen the kiss. Our tongues twine together, teasing each other. Her moan pushes my body into overdrive as I explore her mouth.

I pull back before I get too swept up in the moment. Being in the middle of her store with windows on three sides of us is like putting a spotlight on our activities. The gossip train would have a field day if they saw us. Not that they aren't already talking. I took her to dinner at one of the more popular restaurants in town and have been fielding calls from my mom for the past week, trying to get the scoop on what's happening between us.

She's not super happy with me because I refuse to share anything with her. I think she was hoping I'd have the inside track on all things Hope. Instead, she's received only vague confirmation about us dating. Hope's and my relationship is no one else's business but ours. No one else needs to be a part of it unless we decide it's okay.

"Are you ready to go?" I ask before I get too carried away with our kisses.

"Yep, I just need to shut everything down." Hope turns to start closing up her shop. I invited her to come see the progress I've made on the house this week. I've shown her parts of it these past few days over the phone, but it doesn't quite do it justice. I've gotten a good chunk of the walls torn out, and with the stairs finally fixed, the master suite is just about finished.

When everything is shut down, we walk out the front door toward our cars.

"You want to ride with me? I'll have to come back this way when we're done anyway."

Hope nods her head. "Sure."

I lead her over to my truck and open the door to help her inside. When she's settled, I walk around the front to get in on my side. It's only been a minute, and my truck already smells like her. It's fantastic.

I start toward my house, excitement buzzing through me at knowing Hope is finally going to see all the work I've done. I've been dying to get her into the house since I first bought it. I want her to be a part of the whole process, get her opinion on my plans. Every time I'm there, I imagine her in each room and wonder if she'd like what I've done with it. That's why I kept video calling her at night. I'd subtly ask what she thought of whatever I was working on, adjusting my plans based on her suggestions.

As I drive, I reach across the console to grab her hand. Her fingers slide through mine like they were always meant to be there. A small smile pulls at the corner of her lips when I squeeze her hand. Utter contentment flows through me. For once, I don't feel like there are a million things I should be getting done or feel like I could crawl out of my skin with how restless I am.

I never knew being with another person could feel like this. As if my whole world is only right when she's next to me. I don't think I can ever let her go.

"Quinn and the girls came to the store this afternoon to invite me out with them."

"Really? That's great. Are you guys going to Donna's?" I never got a chance to text Quinn about inviting Hope out, so I'm glad to hear she did it already.

"No, thank goodness." Hope laughs. "They invited me to dinner next weekend at Natalie's."

"Good. You'll have a great time with them," I say as I pull into my driveway. I kiss Hope's knuckles before letting go of her hand to get out. She follows my lead, jumping from the truck and standing in the driveway, looking up at the house.

"Levi…" she breathes. "This is beautiful."

The Victorian-style house gleams in the sunset, highlighting the blue siding and white decorative molding. "You like it?"

"It has a turret, Levi! How could I not like it?" Her exasperated tone makes me laugh as I wrap my arm around her to pull her closer. She fits perfectly under my shoulder like she was always meant to be there.

"Ready to see the inside? It's a mess since we're still in the middle of demo, but I've gotten a lot done."

"Absolutely."

I guide her across the porch and through the front door. The wide foyer greets us with plastic tarps hiding the gorgeous cherry wood floors. Those were an amazing surprise hiding under the ghastly carpet from the seventies. A sitting room is open to the foyer on the left, and a study with French doors is to the right in the turret. I've been debating about closing off the sitting room to make a second office, but I haven't quite decided yet.

Despite my progress, walls still block most of the downstairs since I've been focusing on getting the master ready this week. Hope makes comments on all the rooms, giving opinions that match my own for what to do with each space. It's crazy how in sync we are with our thoughts, each of us building on the other's ideas.

I lead Hope into the room I want to be all hers one day. The top of the turret has dark wood, built-in shelves lining the two straight walls, and the rounded side has three large windows brightening the room.

A gasp flows from Hope as she steps into the room.

"There used to be a ladder running around the room, but

it was in pieces when I bought the place. I'm planning on getting a new one when we're done refinishing everything."

"Levi, this is amazing. I could spend every minute of my day here. Can you imagine how many books could fit on these shelves?"

"I know. It was definitely one of the perks of this house. Do you think we should brighten up the shelves? They're a little dark."

Hope looks at me with wide eyes, a multitude of emotions passing over her face. "We?"

"Yeah, I figured with us dating, you'll be spending a lot of time here, so you should get a say with what it looks like," I clarify. In all actuality, I meant when she moves in here one day, but I know the idea would push her too far, so I keep the thoughts to myself.

"You'd really want me to make decisions for your house? I mean, giving my opinion is one thing, but to actually make choices is something else entirely."

"Of course, I do. I want you to have a say in everything we do."

Hope's body practically melts at my words, and I can't stop myself from pulling her closer to me. I gently lay my lips against hers, trying to express all my feelings for her with my actions. I want to prove to her how different I am from those of her past. I can tell her she can trust me until I'm blue in the face, but until my actions back up my words, she'll never believe them.

"Come on, you," I say as I pull back from the kiss. "It's time to get to work."

Hope's dazed expression makes me grin as she tries to come out of the haze of lust our kisses always seem to bring.

"What do you mean, it's time to get work?" she asks as I pull her down the hallway toward the master suite. The space is huge now, having combined it with another bedroom. All I have left to do is paint, then I can bring in some furniture. The bathroom is still disgustingly outdated, but it's functional.

"Yeah, I didn't bring you here to sit and look pretty. We've got things to do." I grab my tool belt off the floor, snapping it around my hips. After so many years of wearing it, I barely notice the weight anymore. Once it's settled, I grab the small belt I bought for Hope. It has a hammer, tape measure, and a couple of screwdrivers on it. Even though she'll never need the tools I put on it, I still wanted to see her wear it, knowing how hot she'll look with it around her flared hips.

I turn to give it to her and catch her eyeing my chest and hips where my belt is slung low. I suppress the groan bubbling up my throat when she clamps her teeth on her bottom lip. "So, the tool belt does it for ya, huh?" I tease.

Hope's eyes jump to mine, a full blush blooming across her cheeks. An embarrassed smile creeps across her face as I walk toward her. "It's nice to know you approve of the uniform," I tell her, leaning down to kiss her cheek. "Now, a proper handywoman needs a tool belt, and I happen to have one right here." I hold up the belt to show her.

"I would have no clue how to use any of those tools," she says.

"Don't worry. I'll teach you everything you need to know, but for now, you won't need to use them. I just want to see you in a belt." I wink at her.

Her sparkling laugh filters through the room. "So, the tool belt does it for ya, huh?" she echoes, her eyebrow raised. God, she's something else.

"You're damn right, it does. You do it for me, belt or not, though, so…" I shrug. "Ready?"

She nods her head, and I reach around her to put the belt on her hips. It looks just as good as I imagined it would.

"Perfect. Now, we need to pick out a paint color. I've got three options I haven't been able to decide between. Will you help?"

"Sure," she says as we walk over to the painted squares on the wall. I have one I like the best, but I'd like to see if Hope likes it, too. Hopefully, she does because I already bought the paint.

"I like this light gray the best." When she points to the one I bought, I have to clench my fists to keep from wrapping her up in my arms and spinning her around.

"I agree. I think it's my favorite, too." I grab out the paint can, then pour it into two trays. After handing Hope a paint roller, I look at her seriously. "Now, this is a paint roller. This soft bit is where the paint goes. Don't—"

Hope punches me in the arm while I bust out laughing. "You're such an asshole. I know how to paint." She pouts as she fights a grin from forming.

I lean in to kiss her temple. "I'm sorry. I couldn't help myself."

She rolls her eyes, but the grin she was fighting breaks through, making her dark eyes sparkle. The change I've seen in her since I helped her move is like night and day. She's way more comfortable in her own skin, not afraid to be a little more outgoing with me.

We both turn toward the wall and start painting, keeping up a steady stream of chatter the whole time.

"You never sent me that audiobook you were talking about," I remind her.

"Oh, I completely forgot. I'll go through my books tonight. There's one I think you'd enjoy. It's got everything: action, adventure, as well as romance."

"Sounds great. I'll listen to it while I work on the house since it'll be a little quieter here than on our normal job sites."

"Good idea. Action or horror movies?"

I love that Hope has taken to my game. I don't even know where it came from. It was just a way to get to know her without having to ask any personal questions.

"They both have their merits, but action is more fun."

"I hate horror. My life used to resemble a horror movie, so I'll pass on those any day." Hope stills, the paint roller frozen mid-roll against the wall. I don't think she meant to share that information with me. Her doing so tells me she's starting to feel comfortable enough to share her past, which is a pretty big deal.

"I hate how hard your life was before you came here," I say into the quiet room. "I want you to know you're safe to share whatever you want to with me. I will be here to listen. Always."

As Hope begins painting the wall again, her whispered words pack a punch. "I haven't felt safe in a very long time, but with you, I finally do."

"You will always be safe with me, no matter what."

Hope's eyes find mine, almost as if she needs to ensure I mean what I say. I stand there, keeping eye contact with her so she can see I truly mean it until she nods her head and goes back to painting.

The room feels heavy with her confession. Hope's life should've been carefree, beautiful. I want to do that for her. I want to show her how much fun life can be if you're open to it.

An idea pops into my head of how to liven things up again. It's probably going to end up in a mess, but it'll be so worth it. I have to suppress my grin so she doesn't see my intentions coming.

I run my finger down my roller, then turn to Hope. "Hey, you have something right here," I say, running my paint-covered finger across her cheek. Hope's eyes grow wide, her mouth gaping open.

"You didn't."

"Didn't what?" I ask with fake innocence. "I thought you'd want to know you had paint on your face."

"That you put there!" Hope lunges, wiping her hand down my stomach, streaking gray paint down my blue T-shirt.

I breathe in a dramatic gasp as I look down at my shirt. "I can't believe you'd do something so mean when I did nothing to you."

Hope giggles at my theatrics. The sound slams into my chest like a punch. If I can keep a laugh on her lips forever, I'll die a happy man.

"Payback's a bitch." She winks. *She fucking winked at me.* God, I am falling so hard for her. I reach down and wrap my hand around my roller again. Paint covers my wide palm, and I look back at Hope with my hand turned toward her so she can see it.

Her eyes grow big, and she shakes her head, her smile as wide as her eyes. She backs away from me as I step closer. "Levi! Don't you dare."

"Payback's a bitch, babe."

She takes off running across the room, her laughter flowing behind her. I race after her as she makes it to the hallway, running toward the staircase. She runs into the library, turning around when she realizes she has nowhere else to go. Her chest is heaving, cheeks pink from exertion, while her eyes shine with happiness. She's fucking stunning.

I hold my hand out, showing her the paint covering it, and she shakes her head, her grin growing wider.

I lunge, her squeal echoing in the empty room. She turns to get away, but my arms wrap around her from behind, my paint-covered hand sliding down the front of her black T-shirt. She squirms in my arms, making me lose my footing, and we fall to the floor in a tangle of limbs and paint. I turn at the last second so she falls on me instead of me crushing her.

Our breath comes out in pants from our fake fighting. Hope gazes down at me, her eyes full of emotion. Fear, lust, and affection are all fighting for top billing.

I slowly lift my paint-free hand so she can see it before I slide it across her forehead, pushing her hair out of her face. "You've beguiled me, Hope. You're everything I've ever wanted in a partner. I'm so glad I met you."

She stares at me for a moment. "You overwhelm me in the best ways. For so long, I thought I'd never feel this way about anyone. You've made me feel safe for the first time in a very long time, and I'm terrified. I'm putting a lot of trust in you, Levi. So much more than you know." Vulnerability flashes in Hope's eyes, covered by the strength I've come to recognize as her armor. I am beyond floored at her admission.

"I swear, I will do everything I can to make you happy, to keep making you feel safe."

Hope gazes at me for a second longer before leaning down to press her lips against mine. The kiss is tentative, explorative as she starts to learn my mouth. It takes most of my strength to not take over, allowing her to learn at her own pace.

As she deepens the kiss, I wrap my arms tight around her body, pulling her as close to me as I can get her. It never feels like enough. The soft slide of her tongue against mine has my control slipping entirely, and I take over. Flexing my muscles, I pull us into a seated position, her straddling me. Hope naturally drops her knees on either side of my hips as my hand slides up her spine into the silky curls of her hair.

Before I'm ready, I have to pull away from the kiss in order to breathe. I lean my forehead on Hope's as we both pant. Her eyes stay closed as I take in every soft feature. She's stunning. Every inch of her calls to me, making me want her more every time I look at her.

"Come away with me," I blurt out.

Hope's eyes fly open at my words. "What?"

"Have Claire take over the shop tomorrow, and come away with me. I want to take you somewhere for the weekend."

She stares at me for a minute, debating about agreeing to my request. I can see she wants to but is still nervous about being alone with me.

"You can say no, and I'll take you to dinner tomorrow instead, but I want to go on an adventure with you." I run my hand down Hope's spine, and a little shiver moves through her. The lust in her eyes tells me it was a good shiver instead of one of nerves.

"Okay. I'll go on an adventure with you." Hope's smile is slow in coming, but when it finally hits its full wattage, I feel it all the way through me.

She's got me falling so hard for her that I can barely tell what's up or down. She has no idea the effect she has on me.

But I plan to tell her very soon.

23

UNKNOWN

T he jingle of keys echoes down the white-washed hallway. The small cell doesn't allow me to see who's coming, but it wouldn't matter anyway. I've solidified my strength in this hell hole well enough that trivial things, such as who's coming to my cell, are no longer a concern. It's amazing how quickly you can establish your leadership over a group of thugs needing the validation of someone higher than their station.

"You've got a phone call, boss," the guard says, stepping up to the bars to open the door. It was just as easy to get the guards on my payroll. A few well-placed threats and a greased palm or two got me any luxury I could need. I've always been good at getting exactly what I want, no matter the situation. It's what has made me so successful.

I stand from my cot, waiting for the door to open. When it does, I step into the hallway while the guard cuffs my hands. My teeth clench in annoyance at being treated like every other criminal. Someday soon, I'll be free of this fucking charade. I'm far too important to continue being degraded by people inferior to me.

The guard escorts me into the room with a bank of phones. "Last one on the left." The guard motions to the end of the row of *phones, then steps out of the room. At least I'll get a small amount of privacy.*

I step to the booth, picking up the phone from its cradle. "Yes."

"Boss, we found her," my associate says through the line. His words send a bolt of triumph through my system. I knew we'd find her; it was only a matter of time.

"Good. Where is she?"

"Some hick town in North Carolina."

"Hmm. Interesting. I'll want a full report."

"Yes, sir."

"What about the other matter?"

"In the works. Should only be another week or two."

"Fine. If this goes sideways, it's on you."

"It won't, sir."

"We'll see." I hang up the phone, not waiting for a sign-off. If he needed coddling from me, he wouldn't be in my employ.

As I'm escorted back to my cell, my plans play over in my mind. I'm so close to having all the pieces in place to have everything back the way it was. I'll have her exactly where she's supposed to be.

With me.

24

HOPE

It's the butt crack of dawn, and I've never been more excited to be awake this early. Levi will be picking me up for our adventure in ten minutes. I am terrified... and ecstatic. I have no idea where we're going. Levi refused to tell me, saying it would ruin the surprise. You'd think after what happened in my past, I would be freaking out over the unknown, but after our conversation last night, I fully trust Levi to keep me safe.

The one thing I'm most concerned about is spending the whole night together. Since the first time was an accident, I'm nervous about navigating this situation without looking like a total idiot. The man is seriously sexy, and I am... not. I don't even know how to be sexy. Am I supposed to be?

This is going to be a nightmare.

Levi has completely turned my world upside down. He's reached down into the darkest parts of my soul and pulled out all my secret desires. Things I never dared to dream about have suddenly been laid in front of me. They're so close, within reach, all I have to do is say yes. And, God, do I want to say yes. I've never wanted anything more.

If I do go through with taking our relationship to the

physical level, I'm going to need the courage to share my history with Levi. At least in the sex department. He deserves to know that part of my story. He deserves my whole story, but I'm not sure I'm ready to give it to him yet.

Levi's headlights shine through the window as he pulls into my driveway. I grab my small overnight bag and walk out the front door, excitement buzzing through me. My smile is wide as Levi jumps out of his truck. He looks comfortable in loose-fitting jeans and a T-shirt, but it doesn't give me any indication of where we're going.

When I'm close, Levi takes my bag from my hands, placing it in the back seat next to his duffle. As soon as he turns back around, he scoops me into his arms for a hug, wrapping his arms around my waist. My arms naturally go around his neck, his spicy, cinnamon scent filling my senses.

"Good morning." He grins down at me, and after a quick peck on the lips, he leads me around to the passenger side door, opening it for me to get in. He's moving so quickly, I can barely keep up with him.

"Good morning," I say when he's in the truck behind the steering wheel. His excitement is almost palpable in the small space.

"Are you ready to get on the road?"

"I think so. Are you going to tell me where we're going yet?"

"Nope." He twists around to back out of the driveway, sending me a wink as he does. All I can do is shake my head at him. I have no idea how he knew I would enjoy an adventure like this. We haven't even gotten to our destination yet, and I'm already having more fun than I've had in a long time. It further proves how different Levi is from every other experience I've had before.

"What I can tell you is we'll be on the road for a while, so I thought we could cue up the audiobook you sent me last night."

"Yes! Let me get it going." I take Levi's phone from his outstretched hand, clicking on the app to open the right book. I sent him a couple of great military romances with tons of action. The narrator is phenomenal, which is a bonus. A good narrator can make all the difference in the world.

The man's voice blares over the speakers, starting right in on the action. The story follows a group of Navy SEALs as they fight bad guys across the ocean. It's thrilling to listen to their adventures as they try to fight against the evil of the world.

As the story progresses, Levi grabs my hand, interlacing our fingers, and setting them on his lap. I went so long without being touched like this, I forgot how amazing it can feel. And I love that Levi doesn't hesitate to touch me now. It makes me feel like he sees me as more than the broken girl he first met.

I also love how much he likes holding my hand. It's almost as if he can't stand not touching me, so he holds my hand to make up for it. I feel the same way about touching him. I want to be close to him always. His scent comforts me while his strong arms make me feel safe from the world.

The feeling has become addicting.

The narrator begins to read the first sexual encounter between the two main characters, and I realize how bad of an idea this was. I didn't even think about how explicit these scenes are. I'm not sure I'm brave enough to listen to this while sitting next to the man I've started to have some seriously heady sexual fantasies about.

'I CAN'T WAIT ANYMORE, Heather. I need you now.' Tom's hands slide down Heather's body in a sensual glide. He starts to take her clothes off, slowly revealing her silky skin. When she's bare, Tom kisses down Heather's body, pulling her taut nipple into his mouth.

• • •

LEVI CLEARS his throat as the narrator describes every aspect of Tom and Heather's passionate encounter. My face is flaming as my body reacts to the erotic images the story paints. Normally when I read these scenes, I tend to be unaffected. They always feel so far removed from me.

But sitting next to Levi, every word from the story has my imagination picturing him doing the same moves, creating a fire in me so hot, I'm not sure how to tamp it down.

Apparently, it's getting to Levi, as well, because he moves our joined hands from his lap to his lips. He presses his mouth against my knuckles, then gently bites them, nipping at the back of my hand with his teeth. I gasp, the sensation going straight to my core. I can't take my eyes off the sight as the narrator ends the scene, picking up the next chapter.

"So, these are the books you enjoy. Very spicy." Levi smirks at me with an eyebrow raised.

I pause the book, working to push past the embarrassment flowing through me. "Yes, but if I'm honest, those scenes have never affected me quite like that before."

"Oh, really?" The wolfish grin on Levi's face makes me laugh. "Care to elaborate?"

"No."

"Come on! I need to know what was different about this one compared to the others. It was me, right?" He waggles his eyebrows, which makes him look ridiculous.

I shake my head, but he keeps pushing, pleading for me to tell him. Eventually, I give in, unable to handle how cute he looks when he's pouting. "Fine! Yes, it was you. Happy?"

"Ecstatic." He laughs. "Now that we're being honest with each other, tell me, were you imagining me doing those things to you?" His voice goes deeper, lust punctuating every word. "Because I was definitely imagining doing them to you."

I bite my lip as my heart rate increases. "Yes, I was

thinking about you." My boldness surprises me, but I've come to realize that's the effect Levi has on me. He pulls out the characteristics I haven't felt free enough to show.

"Good."

I wait for him to ask what my thoughts were, fully expecting him to want to know everything. When he doesn't say anything else, I look over at him. My eyebrows furrow as I take in his relaxed position. His hand is still holding mine, his thumb running across the back while it rests in his lap.

"That's it?" I finally ask.

"What do you mean?"

"You don't want to know what I was thinking?"

"I have a guess, but no. I figured you'd tell me if you wanted to."

My shoulders deflate a little. I'm even more confused now than I was a minute ago.

"Are you disappointed I didn't ask?" Levi asks, amusement lining his face.

"Apparently, I am." I huff out a laugh. I can't keep up with myself. I would've been incredibly embarrassed to share what I was thinking with Levi. It also would've been an incredibly arousing experience that I'm a little sad I didn't get to have.

"Well, maybe you can tell me later." Levi gives me a gentle smile followed by a wink. I grin. His winks get me every time.

I press play on the audiobook again, and we both fall quiet, listening to the narrator continue the story. It still amazes me how Levi never does what I expect him to do. It's like he knows exactly what will keep me at ease while pushing me out of my comfort zone at the same time. He also gives me the space to make my own choices despite his efforts to coax me out of my shell.

I know I'm likely to fall for this man quickly. If I haven't already.

We drive for a couple more hours, our conversations bouncing between free-flowing and contented silence, reinforcing how comfortable I am with Levi. I've not once felt uneasy or worried about what we're doing or where we're going. I'm still not sure I can trust these feelings for certain, but I do know I can trust Levi to keep me safe, wherever we end up.

He finally pulls into the driveway of an adorably tiny cottage. The sun has risen fully, making the morning bright and cheerful. The air is cool, and the hint of salt in the breeze sends a buzz of excitement through me. I have a feeling I know exactly where Levi has brought me.

"The key should be in the lockbox on the door. Can you get it for me while I get our bags?"

"Sure." I race up the tiny porch to unlock the box with the code Levi gave me. I get the door open right as Levi steps onto the porch. I'm brimming with anticipation, hoping he really did bring me to the beach like I've always wanted.

We walk through the door, the interior of the cottage confirming the beach vibe with its blue walls and seashell decorations. The living room is cozy with a small loveseat and chair facing a television. A half wall separates the kitchen and breakfast nook that's only slightly bigger than my old apartment's, and at the back of the house is a wall of windows looking out at the beautiful blue ocean.

Levi drops the bags at the bottom of the stairs at the back of the cottage. "You ready to go see the ocean for the first time?" He grins at me.

I squeal, unable to contain my excitement any longer. I race toward Levi, launching myself at him as he laughs, catching me around the waist. My arms wrap around his neck in a tight hold. "Thank you for bringing me here," I whisper against his lips before kissing him like I've wanted to since he picked me up.

He takes over, sliding his tongue against mine, sending

me into a whole other dimension. Without conscious thought, my legs wrap around his waist as his hands slide down my spine to grab my butt. Our kiss turns passionate, frenzied, our lust for each other skyrocketing.

Levi pins me against the wall, his body pressing tightly to mine. I can feel every muscle, ridge, and stone plane of his body, not to mention the steel rod in his pants pressing against my center. The fire coursing through me right now feels untamable. Like it's going to incinerate me if I don't get some relief.

I pull at the strands of his hair in my fingers, trying to direct Levi to do something more.

I have no idea what.

I just need more.

25

LEVI

I'm going to explode. My entire body is on fire with the press of Hope's body against mine. Every kiss before has been slow, exploratory. This one is ravenous, erotic. Fucking fantastic.

I run my tongue down Hope's throat, allowing us both a chance to breathe. God, she tastes good, like the most decadent dessert I've ever eaten. I sink my teeth into the space where her neck meets her shoulder and smile when a shiver moves through her.

I want to strip her bare and take this moment to a whole other level, but when I catch Hope's eyes, I see lust swirling around so much apprehension. I know it would ruin the entire moment if I pushed her too far right now, so instead, I gently kiss her lips in an effort to tamp down the inferno in our bodies.

"You're one of a kind, Hope. I'm so grateful you've given me a chance to prove myself to you."

Hope sighs against my lips, the corner of her mouth tipping up. "Thank you for being patient with me."

I lean in to kiss her once more before setting her back on the floor. The loss of her body against mine feels as if I'm missing an integral part of who I am. Like I'm no longer whole if she's not next to me.

It's still a little baffling how this woman became so important to me after only a few weeks of being in my life. I guess I've spent enough time with all the wrong women that when the right one came along, it was a no-brainer. Now, I'm determined to keep her by my side for as long as she'll let me.

"Let's go check out the beach. Then we can head into town to get some groceries."

"Perfect."

I open the back door of the cottage and follow Hope outside. The crashing of the waves greets us as we walk along the path leading to the beach. Since it's still early in the season, I was able to get this little rental on short notice. The ocean views alone are worth the price, but having our own path directly to the beach was the reason I picked this one specifically.

Since we're only here for a short time, I wanted her to spend as much time at the beach as possible. With direct access, we'll be able to come out here anytime we want without it being a big deal.

The minute we're on the edge of the sand, Hope kicks her shoes off and runs towards the waves. She looks so light-hearted, my chest aches at the sight. She bends over to roll her pant legs up to her knees, then immediately runs into the ocean waves.

A squeal echoes across the beach, making me laugh. When I finally catch up to where she's splashing, she looks up at me with the widest grin. Her eyes dance with mischief before she kicks her foot up, sending an arcing wave of freezing cold water at me.

"You didn't."

"Oh, I so did." She giggles. I run full speed at her, crashing through the water. Hope squeals as she tries to get away, but I catch her around the waist, pulling her up into my arms. I pretend to throw her into the ocean as she screams out *no* while laughing so hard, I'm afraid she can't breathe.

I carry her out of the water and set her down in the sand, taking in the sight that is happy Hope. I've always thought she was beautiful, but right now, she's radiant. She looks up at me, her eyes shining brighter than I've ever seen. I can't stop myself from kissing her. Those plump lips are calling out to me to take them in a deep, drugging kiss. If we weren't in public, I'd be tempted to take this kiss even further, but I pull away before we get too swept up in each other.

"Thank you so much for bringing me here, Levi. This is the best weekend I've ever had."

I wrap her up in my arms as we stand there looking out at the ocean. "And it's only just begun."

* * *

I SLIDE my hands through my hair for the millionth time this evening, unsure of the best move to make. I have very few options, and not a single one is good.

"You have to make a move at some point," Hope taunts. I glare at her, but it only makes her smile grow wider. I pick up my little, plastic warrior pieces, moving them around the board.

Hope is beating me handily at *Risk*. At this point, I'm just trying to save my pride since I have no chance of making a comeback. "How are you so good at this game?"

"Mostly luck since I've had good rolls. I'm also very analytical. I examine the entire situation before making a decision."

"I've always been impulsive. I make decisions entirely too quickly."

"No wonder I'm beating you so badly." Hope laughs, and I grin at her, happy she's happy despite getting my ass kicked.

After we left the beach, we cleaned up from our water

escapades and drove into town. We had lunch at a small café with the best potato soup I've ever eaten. Then Hope insisted we go grocery shopping so she could make dinner. I offered to take her out on a date, but she said she wanted to cook for me instead. Who am I to turn down a home-cooked meal?

When we got back, she wanted to go back to the beach, so we grabbed some chairs and lay out in the sun, listening to the waves. After eating Hope's phenomenal enchiladas, we found a closet under the stairs with stacks of board games. I've since learned that Hope is super competitive, and stone-cold when it comes to defeating me. If she hadn't kept the little sheepish smile on her face while destroying me, I'd be wondering if she was playing up the innocent act.

"You know, we should just call it. You've already clearly won, and my pride is heavily dented. I don't know if I can take much more."

"You have plenty of pride to spare, so I'm not too worried about you."

I dramatically slap my hand over my chest. "Drive the knife in deeper, why don't you?"

Hope throws a potato chip at me, making me laugh. "Fine, we can be done." She sighs. The smile she's hiding tells me she's not put out in the slightest.

"How about you pick out a movie while I clean up?"

"Perfect." As Hope heads into the living room, I gather all the game pieces, sorting them back into the box. When the game is put away, I turn to find Hope snuggled up in the middle of the couch. Her feet are tucked under her with a blanket lying across her legs. I love that she chose a spot where I would have to sit right next to her, no matter what.

"What did you pick out?" I ask, sitting down next to her.

"A superhero movie. This one has the two hot guys who start off as best friends and then become enemies."

"First of all, I'm sitting right here. I'd rather not have my girlfriend lusting over a hot guy who isn't me. Fictional or not. And second of all, fantastic choice."

Hope's head whips around so fast, I'm worried she might hurt herself. I knew my nonchalant statement would get a rise out of her; I'm just not sure which part caught her attention. The girlfriend bit or the preference that she doesn't fantasize about other guys.

"First of all," she echoes, a little heat behind her words. I have to fight my grin at seeing her get fired up. "I've never lusted after anyone else but you, however, there will be people I find attractive. I mean, I'm not dead, so you'll have to get over it. Second of all, when did I become your girlfriend?"

So, it was the entire statement. Good to know. "Your point on the attraction thing is fair, so I'll concede that one. As for being my girlfriend... You became mine the minute I woke up on your couch with you in my arms, never wanting to wake up alone again. Just as I became yours the minute you woke up terrified and allowed me to hold you."

Hope's eyes bore into mine as if the harder she stares, the better she'll be able to read my mind. I hold her eye contact, needing her to see me, see what we could be together. "I'm yours..." she says slowly like she's deciding how the words feel out loud.

"Just as I'm yours," I repeat.

Hope continues to stare at me, vulnerability radiating off her in waves. I'm worried I pushed her too far too soon, but it was time she knew exactly what was going on here. I don't want to pussyfoot around, waiting on her to decide if we're doing this. I know she wants me as much as I want her. We can figure out the rest later.

She nods her head decisively, then suddenly straddles my lap, knees on either side of my hips. She holds my face in her hands, her gaze serious. "Don't let me down."

I slide my hands up her back and into her hair. "Don't run away from me when you get scared."

We lean in at the same time, our mouths meeting in the middle. Her lips are soft and pliant against mine as I take control of the kiss. Everything I've dreamed of is in my arms right now. She's the one I never truly believed was out there. The future I always hoped I'd have.

My hands start roaming all over Hope. Down her back, around her hips, up her rib cage. Her curves feel phenomenal in my hands like I always knew they would.

As mine continue to explore, Hope's do the same. Around my arms, across my chest, down my sides. Her hands feel like electricity is buzzing across my body, sending blood straight to my cock.

Hope rocks her hips, grinding her center against me, making a groan rumble through me at the sensation. She boldly starts kissing my jaw, nibbling her way to my ear, then down my neck. I wrap my hands around her hips, my long fingers stretching around her ass. Gripping her hard, I pull down while thrusting my hips up to grind against her center. Hope's moan has my body feeling like it's going to explode.

I stand with Hope still in my arms, carrying her through the kitchen and up the stairs. The bedroom has a comfortable queen bed and a nice, attached bathroom despite its size. There was a small part of me that worried about getting a one-bedroom cottage, but I also knew Hope wouldn't have agreed to come away with me if she was uncomfortable with the idea of sleeping in the same bed.

I lay her down on the mattress, our kisses continuing to wreak havoc on me. As my body comes down over Hope's, my hips fitting snugly in the V of her legs, I feel her body tighten with tension. And not the good kind of tension, either.

I pull back, scanning Hope's face to figure out what's going on. Lust is still the forerunner in her eyes, but nerves are settling in quickly. "Tell me," I whisper against her mouth, sliding my lips across the soft skin of her cheeks and up to her temples. Her body relaxes a fraction, which tells me it's not me she's worried about.

"I've never done this with someone who cared about me. With someone I wanted to do it with."

My head flinches back to look into Hope's eyes. Her words slowly sink in, realization dawning on me. "Oh, sweetheart," I exhale. My fists clench by her head, my body taut with anger and sadness that Hope's life was a living hell for her. My forehead drops onto hers as I try to get my feelings under control. She doesn't need to see my anger when what she needs is gentleness.

"We're going to need to talk about this, but not tonight." Her tense body relaxes even more underneath me. "Look at me," I say softly, then wait until she opens her eyes again, giving me her full attention. "Tonight, the only people allowed in this room are you and me. You tell me when you like something and when you don't. You tell me when you need more or when it's too much. I may lead, but you have control. Okay?"

Hope's dark eyes melt, the vulnerability changing to something I'm not sure I'm ready to acknowledge yet. I know mine are reflecting the same things in return, but neither one of us is ready to say those particular words out loud.

"I need your words, Hope."

"Okay," she whispers. My lips find hers again in a slow, passionate kiss that spurs the fire in my belly into an inferno. Our tongues glide, exploring all these new feelings and desires. I slide my hand from her shoulder to the hem of her T-shirt. Her skin feels like silk under my work-roughened hand as I move up her stomach. I reach the underside of her breasts, slipping my thumb under the cup of her bra while my mouth explores the line of her neck.

The pad of my thumb rubs the underside of her breasts;

the soft flesh tears at every ounce of control I have. Hope pushes her chest further into my hand, giving me every indication she wants me to keep going. I oblige, pulling her T-shirt over her head and quickly removing her bra.

My first look at Hope is more than anything I ever imagined. Her olive skin glows under the lamplight; her full tits are fucking magnificent. "You're everything I ever dreamed about and more," I whisper against her skin as my lips and hands continue to explore her body. My tongue glides across the slope of her breast until I hit the peak, pulling her nipple into my mouth.

"Levi," she moans, her hands starting to get into the action. They move into my hair, wrapping around the strands at the back of my head.

I play with her nipples using my mouth, hands, and teeth. Learning what makes her crazy. Every sound she makes has my cock pressing harder against my zipper. I'm worried I'm going to come before I even get inside her.

I move down her body, stopping at the top of her jeans. I pop the button, slowly lowering the zipper to give her plenty of time to stop me if she wants. Hope looks at me with heavy-lidded eyes, her hands resting on her stomach, looking serene and fucking beautiful.

I take her jeans and underwear off simultaneously, baring her completely. Her trust in me is overwhelming.

I vow right then to never break that trust.

HOPE

Being completely bare to Levi should make me feel incredibly vulnerable, but with the way he's looking at me, I couldn't feel sexier. The lust in his eyes makes me squirm on the bed, needing him to touch me, be with me. "You're a little overdressed for this party." I grin at him.

He shakes his head as if he's coming out of a stupor and grins back at me. "Sorry, I got distracted."

I laugh, happy the intensity from a moment ago has lightened again. It feels like we're back to our normal selves instead of trying to navigate the bomb of my confession. I didn't want to tell him about my awful experiences with sex, but I knew it wouldn't be fair to him if I wasn't honest. There's a chance I could end up having a panic attack, so I wanted him to know why in case it happens.

I sit up to help him get rid of his clothes, grabbing the hem of his black T-shirt. He grabs it from the back of his neck and slides it over his head.

When he settles his arms back down at his sides, all I can do is blink at him. He has muscles on top of muscles. I didn't even know guys could look like this in real life.

With a mind of its own, my hand reaches out to touch his

abs. He flinches at my touch but stays still, letting me explore. He's as hard as a statue and just as sculpted as one. "Seriously? This is what you look like?" My question comes out almost incredulously.

Levi laughs, then starts to undo his pants.

I bite my lip as he slides his jeans down, revealing gray briefs that are molded to his thick thighs, highlighting his impressively hard package. "Jesus," I whisper, swallowing hard.

"Lay back, I'm not done exploring you yet."

I comply with his demand, needing his body against mine with every fiber of my being. He follows me back, pressing his bare chest against mine. His hard muscles against my soft body are almost my undoing. He kisses me, starting his explorations over again while his hands slide over my skin. The rough calluses on his palm bring goose bumps to the surface.

The slow, sensual movements of our bodies together have my senses going into a frenzy. I've only ever experienced fast and aggressive. To have someone who genuinely cares about me taking the time to explore every facet of my body, learning what makes me burn… It's indescribable.

"Levi, I need more," I finally squeak out. He's setting every nerve ending on fire with his hands and mouth. They're everywhere on my body except the one place I'm desperate for. I think I might explode if he doesn't move to the spot he hasn't touched yet.

"I'm still learning your body, but I'm willing to move a little quicker." He slides further down my body, using his shoulders to widen my legs. His lips press against my inner thigh, right above my knee, then slowly glide their way to my center.

The closer he gets, the more I moan in both pleasure and frustration. My hips undulate, trying to relieve the ache spreading into my stomach. Levi's tongue slides up my sex, and I levitate off the bed. He has to grab my hips so I stay still enough for him to continue. Never in my life have I ever felt something as decadent as Levi's tongue.

My hands fist into his hair to help keep me anchored. I feel like I'm floating off the bed in ecstasy while something major is building in my core. Something I'm afraid to let go of because I'm pretty sure the fall is going to kill me in the end.

Two of Levi's fingers slide inside me, sending me into a desperate frenzy. I call out to him, not quite sure what I need. It's all too much and not enough.

"Let go, sweetheart. I'll always be here to catch you."

With those whispered words of safety, I detonate.

My entire body tenses at the onslaught of feelings taking me so far from here, I don't know how I'll find my way back.

When I finally begin to come down, I realize it's with the help of Levi, gently bringing me back to him with slow licks and smooth slides of his fingers like he promised. He wipes his mouth on my inner thigh, a beaming smile shining at me.

"That was fucking amazing to watch."

If I wasn't already flushed with arousal, my entire body would be blushing at his words. He leans up on his knees, sliding his boxers down his thighs to reveal his gigantic shaft.

"Holy shit." I continue staring at him as he wraps his fist around his impressive and overwhelming girth. "You're not real. No one is supposed to look like you."

Levi guffaws at my words. "I am real and so fucking in awe of you, Hope." He grabs a condom from his pants on the floor, slides it on, then settles himself back between my legs. Kissing from my neck up to my jaw, he nips at my ear. My hips lift at the sensation, connecting my center with his hard length. We both groan at the feeling of him sliding through my wetness.

I didn't think I could be aroused so quickly after the first orgasm, but with one move, Levi has me on edge again. He leans onto one elbow while his other hand starts to play with my breast. Pinching, pulling, sending bolts of pleasure straight to my clit. It's sensory overload with his lips and teeth nipping at the skin on my neck and collarbone.

"Levi, please," I moan out. I can feel his smile against my skin.

"Just making sure you're ready for me."

"I'm past ready for you." My words are desperate, wanton, so far from how I normally sound it's hard to remember the small, timid girl I used to be. He takes pity on me, adjusting his hips so he's lined up with my entrance. I can feel the pressure there already, and I tense up, nerves shooting through me faster than lightning.

"Sweetheart, look at me," Levi whispers. I didn't even realize my eyes had closed until he said something. When I meet his gaze, the look on his face makes my eyes well. The genuine affection there is almost too much to handle. "It's just you and me in this room," he says, running his thumb down my face. "God, I'm falling so hard for you."

"I'm falling just as hard, Levi."

Gently, he leans down to kiss me while simultaneously pushing through my tight muscles. The pressure is still there, but with his lips on mine, it feels like a decadent slide. He starts to pull back out, only to push back in, moving farther into me than before.

The sensation has me gasping, which allows him to push all the way to the hilt. We both moan at the tight fit. It's like nothing I've ever felt before. I never knew sex could feel like this.

"I need you to move, Levi. *Please.*"

He gives in to my plea, pulling out, then gently pressing back in, hitting a spot so deep inside me, I'll feel it tomorrow. My fingers dig into his back, desperate for him to get as close as possible. His hips start to move faster, building us both up higher than we went before.

He straightens, continuing to pulse in and out as he grabs the back of my thighs, pushing them towards my chest. This is the most vulnerable position I've ever been in, but he's hitting so deep inside me, I don't have the capacity to notice. With his muscles straining, he looks so powerful over me, heightening the entire experience.

Before I'm even aware it's happening, my orgasm hits me like a freight train. It barrels through my entire body, from my toes to my head. I clamp down hard around Levi, every muscle tightening as my body explodes. His hips start moving fast, slamming into me, prolonging my orgasm, while his dick jerks and spasms as he comes. It's a heady sight to watch this man succumb to his needs.

Levi drops my legs, falling down on top of me as our chests heave, trying to get more air into our lungs. His weight feels incredible as if he's holding me to the ground after I was soaring too high from him.

"I know I should be a gentleman and stop crushing you, but you feel so good under me."

I breathe out a laugh, running my fingers through his sweaty hair. "I like the way you feel on top of me. I'm not ready for you to move yet."

Levi nuzzles my neck, pressing his lips against my skin. He lifts his head to look me in the eyes. "That was incredible. Fucking fantastic."

I beam at him, returning his happy smile. "Yeah, it was. Nothing has ever felt as good as that." Levi's smile grows cockier, which makes me laugh. "Okay, muscle man, get off me before I run out of air."

He jumps off the bed and saunters into the bathroom, comfortable in his nakedness. He's magnificent in so many ways, but tonight, he's shown me how a man is supposed to treat a woman. He's proven there are truly good men in the world. No matter what happens in the end, I'll be forever grateful to him for giving me that.

HOPE

"What do you mean, you've never been to a football game?" Levi asks incredulously.

"I don't know how else to say it. I've never been to a game." I glance over at him; he's got one hand on the steering wheel, the other gently holding mine on his lap.

"Not even at your high school?"

"Nope."

"Absolutely crazy. Football is intense here. We'll go to a game when the season starts in the fall so you can see what I mean."

A warm, fuzzy feeling flows through me at the thought of still being with Levi in the fall. There's something comforting about him planning things out so far in advance when we've spent very little time together. I think it's the idea of Levi wanting to still be with me in the future, even after finding out how big of a mess I can be.

We left for home an hour ago, which turned out to be a lot more difficult than I expected. I wasn't ready to leave the beach yet, wanting to enjoy the little bubble we'd created in our cottage for a bit longer. We spent most of last night lying in bed, going from talking about anything under the sun to feeling each other up to distraction.

It was absolute bliss to feel so comfortable spending an entire night naked and getting thoroughly ravished.

This morning, we slowly made our way downstairs, had a small breakfast, then packed up our things to go home. Levi promised he'd bring me back again, which helped make leaving a little easier. I'm not sure what awaits us back home or what our relationship will look like when we get there, but knowing he'll be by my side gives me the confidence to handle whatever comes at me.

"I'm sure I'll enjoy it, as long as you're there with me, but I still think baseball is better. There was a field around the corner from the apartment I lived in when I was in high school. I'd go to the games in the evenings if I wasn't working."

"I played baseball in school. I wasn't good at it, but I enjoyed it."

"I bet you looked hot in those pants."

Levi throws his head back and laughs while shaking his head. "Did you play a sport?"

"No. For a lot of different reasons." I say a little more seriously.

"I don't want to push you, but I'm ready to listen if you're ready to talk."

I sigh, hating how dark my life was before I moved to Sonoma. Having opened myself up to making new connections with people, I don't want to bring the dark into the sunshine despite knowing it's time. "My life has never been happy, Levi. Are you sure you want to ruin the view you have of me?"

"Hope, nothing is going to ruin my view of you. No matter what happened in your past, it's still a part of you. It's turned you into the woman I'm falling hard for, and I want to know everything about you. Even if it's not all sunshine and rainbows."

Emotions swallow me up, closing off my windpipe. Levi lifts my hand and kisses my knuckles in the way I love. "Okay… you asked for it," I say as I try to figure out where to start.

"You know my mom died giving birth to me," I start as Levi nods his head in response. "I was given to my grandmother because my dad wasn't in the picture at the time. She was always loving towards me, but there was very little in the way of parenting from her. She suffered from severe depression, which was compounded by the deaths of my mom and grandfather, so I learned to be self-reliant very early on. I didn't mind because, like I said, I knew she loved me. We spent a lot of time in her garden, tending to her roses, which, of course, I loved. We had a good life.

"Then, when I was fifteen, she died. I woke up one morning, got ready for school, and when she didn't come to say goodbye to me, I found her in bed. I'm still not sure how she died; I was too young for anyone to feel the need to tell me. A social worker came, did some digging, and managed to find my father. From that point on, my life was a living nightmare."

Levi clears his throat, then squeezes my hand. "He was the one who hurt you? Made it difficult for you to handle physical touch?"

"He was my first experience with abuse, yes. He took a lot of his anger out on me. He didn't want me. I was a burden to him, which he reminded me of regularly. Mostly with his fists. Never with… anything else.

"In high school, I worked at a flower shop because we didn't have any other income. Dad was a gambler, and even when he won, the money would go straight into the next bet. If I had to guess, that was the reason he kept me instead of letting me go into foster care."

"Did you go to college after you graduated school?"

"No, I didn't have the money. I also couldn't get a scholarship because my grades were horrendous. I worked so many hours to make ends meet, my schoolwork ended up coming last."

"Jesus, Hope. You're Wonder Woman." He shakes his head, and I look at him like he's crazy.

"I'm not even close to Wonder Woman. I barely kept a roof over our heads. I think the flower shop owner paid me more than was typical for a high schooler because he knew a little about my home life."

"Hope, you were a teenager. Do you realize how strong you had to be to both graduate from high school and keep a roof over your head at the same time?"

I shrug my shoulders because he's making it sound like I did something wonderful. All I did was keep us from becoming homeless. "After I graduated, I worked full time at the flower shop. I would've moved out right away, but I didn't have the money for a deposit on my own apartment. I started squirreling my paychecks away in the hopes that one day I could move out. It was a slow process since Dad forced me to give him more money, but I still managed to save a little at a time, which gave me the strength to keep going.

"Then my dad got diagnosed with progressive lung cancer. He died a few months after he was diagnosed."

I pause in my story, unsure of how best to move forward. If I tell Levi everything, he could both see me differently and potentially be in danger. I can't allow either of those scenarios to happen. Especially putting him in danger. He doesn't deserve to have this hanging over his head. He's done everything to make me feel safe. If I can do the same, I will.

"Right before he died, I was told he had racked up a huge gambling debt, and everything we owned would go towards paying it off. I was then informed that I was a part of the deal, that my dad had basically sold me to his friend to repay his debt. I was to live with this man, doing whatever he asked of me because my father was a piece of shit." Bitterness creeps into my voice. Saying the words out loud makes my stomach burn with anger. I've only had to tell my story to one other person, and she's been instrumental to my healing.

I glance over at Levi before I finish the story. His jaw is clenched, his hand squeezing the steering wheel tight enough to make his knuckles turn white. With anyone else, I'd be nervous at his obvious anger, but he's gently sliding his thumb across the back of my hand. It's soothing my jagged nerves and helps me start the next part of the story.

"At first, it was okay. He lived in a nice house with a beautiful flower garden. Honestly, it was a lot better than anything I'd ever lived in before. Then, as time moved forward, things began to spiral from there. His aggression toward me slowly increased until it became… more."

Without any explanation, Levi swerves toward an off-ramp to exit the highway. We've still got another hour before we're home, and we don't need gas or anything. I don't say a word until he parks at the back of a large gas station.

"Levi?"

He leans over, unbuckles my seatbelt, then lifts me out of the seat and over the console to his lap. I open my mouth to say something, but Levi gently shushes me.

"I need a minute to hold you," he murmurs. My muscles immediately relax into his lap, taking advantage of the opportunity to be close to him. I stick my nose into his neck, breathing in his intoxicating smell. It's amazing at how quickly it's become calming for me.

"Will you finish the rest of it while we sit here? I don't think I can hear the rest without being able to touch you."

Nodding my head, I continue where I left off, keeping my head on his shoulder. "The first time he hit me was because

I'd left my coffee cup on the table. I'd gotten distracted by something and had forgotten to take it to the sink. From there, I was punished for any reason he deemed worthy. I was constantly kept on edge, trying to navigate the cat and mouse game he enjoyed playing.

"The first time he touched me sexually was after a night of drinking. He was always the most unpredictable when he was drunk. I tried to fight back in the beginning, but it only made him more vicious, so after a while, I just took it. It was a self-preservation tactic because the more I struggled, the worse it would be. Which, for a long time, made me feel guilty.

"Joy, my therapist, has helped me navigate the trauma I experienced. I've struggled with knowing I didn't fight back. That I just let it happen. I understand now that it was my way of coping with the abuse, and it doesn't mean I was okay with what he did."

Levi squeezes me tight, pressing his lips to my temple. Being wrapped in his arms, knowing he's not disgusted with me, is indescribable. I worried he wouldn't see me in the same light after I told him what happened, but the strength I feel with his body surrounding me makes me feel cherished.

"I was forced to stay for almost six years until I was finally able to make my way here. Sonoma was my grand-mother's hometown. From the stories she told about it, I knew it would be the perfect place for me to start over. It's taken quite a bit of therapy and time alone to heal. I'm not quite where I want to be, but I'll get there."

My stomach twinges a bit, knowing I haven't given my whole truth to Levi about how I got away or my relationship with Antony. He was more than my father's friend. He was my husband. A criminal.

I can't bring any of that into Levi's world, though. He doesn't deserve to have any more of my darkness covering him. He's been more patient with me than I probably deserve, so I'll do whatever it takes to protect him.

"The moment I met you, I knew you were strong. What I didn't realize was there was so much more to your strength than your ability to ignore my charms." Levi gives me a squeeze, and a small laugh huffs out of me at his teasing. "You're incredible, Hope. You went through a kind of hell I will never understand, coming out on the other side with your head held high. You deserve every happiness in your life, and I would love to be a part of it if you'll let me."

"I never knew there were men like you, Levi. In my experience, they were either aggressive or indifferent. You've changed the way I see the world, and I'll be forever grateful. Just… remember I'm still skittish. I'm going to react strongly to things that probably don't matter. Please have patience with me."

"My relationship experience is pretty limited, so as long as you're patient with me when I screw up, we'll be fine."

I look up into Levi's hazel eyes. There's a depth in them I want to fall into forever. It's gentle, protective, and another emotion I'm not yet ready to address. I know if I stare any longer, words I won't be able to take back are going to start pouring out of me.

He leans down, gently pressing his lips against mine. So many emotions pass between us as this kiss sweeps us into a moment I won't ever forget.

"Shall we get back on the road?" Levi asks, barely pulling away from me.

I nod my head. With one more peck on my lips, Levi helps me back over the center console to the passenger seat.

Once I'm buckled, we get back on the highway, my hand wrapped around Levi's. It seems to be his preferred driving position. We're quiet, enjoying the soft music playing over the radio, completely comfortable just being together after our weekend.

I don't know what awaits us back at home, but I can't wait to find out.

For the first time in years, I'm looking forward to my future instead of barely being able to see the next day.

28

LEVI

"How's your house coming along?" Quinn asks as she stirs something on the stove. She relegated me to the sidelines of their kitchen when I tried to stir something that wasn't supposed to be stirred yet.

Quinn invited Hope and me over for dinner tonight. When I stopped by Blooming Beautiful to pick her up after work, she was surrounded by a pile of greenery and was a little frazzled. There was a last-minute order for twenty centerpieces needing to be completed in only a couple of days. On top of that, she mentioned she was behind on her administrative tasks, so it was going to be a long night for her. She insisted I still come for dinner with the caveat that I must bring her leftovers when we're done eating. It was an easy deal to agree to, even though I'd rather have her with me instead.

Since our conversation on the way home from the beach last week, Hope has been much more forthcoming with me than ever before. It's as if once her story was out there, she felt free enough to fully be herself. There are no more secrets between us, which has allowed us to focus solely on each other instead of our pasts.

We spend most of our free time together now. When I'm done working, I pick Hope up at her shop, then we spend our evening at my house. Most of the time, she sits in the room and watches me work, but with some things, she's able to help or give me an extra hand when I need it.

When I'm done working on renovations for the night, we go back to her house to sleep. Even though I could sleep at my house now, I don't want Hope to have to rough it through the renovation mess. And there's no way I want to sleep by myself. I've gotten so used to waking up next to her that sleeping alone sounds dreadful.

"The house is coming along nicely. A little slower than I originally planned, but I don't mind."

"I'm guessing because of a certain florist?" Quinn eyes me with a raised brow; her passive attempt at digging makes me grin at her. "You know your mother has been relentless at trying to get details out of me."

A laugh bursts from me while I roll my eyes. I'm not surprised Mom has moved to bugging Quinn about my relationship. Since she wasn't getting anything from me, she had to go to the next likely source.

"I'm sorry she's been pestering you. I need time to establish our relationship before I let Mom get in the middle of it. Even when we are on more solid ground, I still probably won't give her any details."

"She just wants to know you're happy, Levi, while also learning Hope's entire background at the same time," Quinn teases.

Cooper comes in from the backyard with Piper on his heels. She's the sweetest mutt I've ever met. I'd love to have my own dog but have never had the time or the space to properly care for an animal.

Maybe when the house is done, Hope and I can look into getting a dog. I know she loves them as much as I do.

I mentally shake my head at my own thoughts. I swear I

barely recognize myself now. The minute I met Hope, something inside me changed. For a long time, I've lived a carefree lifestyle. Settling down never felt within reach, so I leaned into the idea of playing up my bachelorhood. And it was fun. I loved it.

At the same time, I felt like something was wrong with me since it never seemed like women wanted to spend more than one night with me. What was it about me that made them think I was only good enough for a night of fun? Not for anything more substantial. Maybe I'd done it to myself. I'd played up this persona of a bachelor, living it up with no attachments, so maybe women stopped believing they could be the one to settle me down.

Then I walked into Hope's shop and got completely turned onto my head. For the first time, I'd met a woman I couldn't get out of my mind. Weeks had gone by, and my obsession had grown each time I saw her. After our lunch at the café, I knew she was different from any other woman I'd ever been with. From then on, I knew my life would never be the same again.

"Are we talking about Mom?" Cooper asks after filling up Piper's water bowl.

"And her meddling ways," I respond.

"It's finally your turn!" Cooper laughs, rubbing his hands together with a look of straight glee on his face.

I flip him off when Quinn's back is turned to the stove, but it only seems to make Cooper laugh harder. He grabs my outstretched finger, squeezing it tight enough to hurt. I jab him in the stomach with my free hand to make him let go. My hand hurts like a bitch, even though I don't show it.

"Stop, you two. Just because my back is turned doesn't mean I can't hear you wrestling," Quinn says with disappointment in her voice. Cooper and I freeze, dropping our hands.

"Sorry, *Mom*," I say teasingly.

"Brown noser," Copper coughs. I punch him in the shoulder.

We both straighten up when Quinn turns around with a raised eyebrow. The small smirk she tries to keep under control gives her away as she instructs us to set the table. Cooper and I grin at each other while following through on the directions given. I love spending time with these two. I just wish Hope could've been here, too, but we're all getting together this weekend.

The girls originally planned to hang out by themselves at Nat and Tucker's house, but the guys didn't want to be left out, so it turned into a whole group hangout. I told Hope to expect it to happen every time the girls get together. The guys can never seem to stay away for too long, even when we're having a guys' night.

Before Hope, I never understood why that was the case. It didn't bother me when we crashed the girls' nights, but their need to end the evening with them never made sense to me. Now, I understand their feelings a lot better. Even being away from her for a few hours tonight has me wanting to leave early to get back to her.

"How much longer do you have to go on the renovations?" Cooper asks as we sit down around the table. Quinn made chicken alfredo with homemade sauce.

"Probably a couple more months at a minimum. I was telling Quinn they're going a little slower than I expected, but not too bad."

"That's how we got off on the topic of your mom prying into our lives," Quinn adds.

"Ah. Makes sense." Cooper pauses, glancing at me as if he wants to say something but isn't sure how I'm going to take it. "How much do you know about Hope?" Both the look on Cooper's face and his question have me on edge.

"Quite a bit. Why?"

After a quick glance at Quinn, Cooper looks back at me.

"I pulled her background like I do every time someone rents Quinn's house."

He pauses long enough to make my gut tighten. "And?"

"Well, there's basically nothing in her background until she moved to Sonoma. She's twenty-eight and has no history until a year ago? It's a little weird, Levi."

I grit my teeth to keep from yelling at my brother. I know he means well. He was looking out for his family. In fact, if I had dealt with a murdering lunatic who kidnapped my wife as Cooper did, I'd have done the same thing. It's just that this is Hope. Her history is her own. People don't need to know what she's been through unless she deems it okay.

"She's been through hell and back, Cooper. I'm not going to tell you anything else because it's not my story to tell, but know there's a good reason."

Cooper stares at me for a minute. I can tell he doesn't want to let it go. I keep eye contact with him, making sure he knows he won't get anything else out of me.

Finally, after a long beat of silence, he nods his head. "I trust you, Levi. If you say things are fine, I believe you. I just wanted to make sure everyone was safe."

"I know, but this isn't something to dig further into. If she wants you to know the story, she'll tell you."

I get another nod, and Quinn moves the conversation on to something else. The best thing about my family is knowing they aren't going to push Hope into telling them about her past. They respect that everyone has a story— backgrounds they don't want to share with the world.

It took Tucker months before he told us about his horrible childhood. Having gone to school with him, we could hardly believe he lived in such an awful situation. It showed us that no matter what it may look like on the outside, you never know what someone has been through.

We finish dinner pretty quickly, and I make my excuses about having to pick Hope up at her shop. I'm ready to see my girl. Especially after what Cooper told me tonight. I know her history made it so having an online presence wasn't likely, but if I'm being honest with myself... it doesn't make sense that she wouldn't show up at all.

She should've come up both from being in the system when her grandmother died and having worked full time for a florist. I don't want to question what she went through, though, because I've seen the effect it's had on her.

There are still times she flinches if I move too fast or sneak up on her accidentally. I know the abuse was real, so I have to trust that she doesn't show up in the system for a good reason.

I just thought all our secrets were out in the open already.

29

"ROSEMARY"

THREE YEARS AGO

"Hey, Jerry, I left my sneakers at home," I say to the one man I'm allowed to interact with, my driver. "I'll miss the first spin class, but there's another one right after if you don't mind turning around so I can get them."

"Sure, Mrs. Malatelli."

I sit back in the car, mad at myself for forgetting the one thing that's majorly important when you work out. I've been going to these classes for about a year; you'd think I'd have mastered packing a gym bag by now.

I'm glad this doesn't affect anyone but myself.

Jerry pulls up to the back of the house so I can sneak in and grab my shoes without disrupting anyone. I'm not supposed to be here right now, which is why I was allowed to start going to classes at the gym. Antony put it so nicely when he offered them to me. *I need you away from me for a couple of hours. Plus, you need to get rid of the weight you've gained sitting around on your ass. Spin classes will achieve both of those goals.*

I head inside through the back door, keeping my steps light so as not to alert anyone when I hear voices at the end of the hall. Antony must be having a meeting in his office. Since he has no idea I'm home, I take advantage of the moment to listen to their conversation.

With the door cracked, I can hear every word they're saying.

"What do you mean the whole shipment is gone?" Antony growls.

"It was seized right after it crossed the border, sir. We're still looking into the details, but there's an obvious leak in our operation." The voice of one of Antony's trusted advisors, Dominic, floats through the doorway. I've met him several times over the years. He's one of those men who, at first glance, seems like a decent human, but when you look deeper, evil swirls in his eyes.

"I want all the information as soon as you have it. This is the second shipment in the last year to be seized. I won't have this happening again. Find the mole." Antony's voice is hard, unrelenting. I would not want to be Dominic right now.

"The guns arrived at their destination as scheduled. We're outfitting the cars now to ship them out. Should be done this week."

Guns? I always knew Antony's business dealings weren't exactly legal. Me being the biggest example, but he trades in guns? And what shipment got seized? Something other than guns? This is monumental. I've never gotten an opportunity like this before to gather information. Now, I have to figure out how best to use it.

I'll also need proof.

A noise startles me, and I whip around to find one of Antony's men standing behind me. My blood freezes in my veins as nausea swirls through my stomach.

This is it.

I won't survive after this.

The small glimmer of hope I had vanished into thin air.

I escape the house, grabbing my shoes before Tomas can tell Antony I was spying. I know there will be hell to pay when I get home, but my life is already a living hell.

It can't get much worse.

30

HOPE

"Are you sure this is okay to wear?" I turn, inspecting my shorts and yellow tank in the bathroom mirror.

"You look beautiful as always, babe." Levi kisses me on the temple, then steps into my bedroom to get dressed.

We're getting ready to go to Natalie and Tucker's house tonight. I thought it was just going to be the girls there, but Levi said the guys were feeling left out, so they're going to be there, too. I started to laugh when he first told me, thinking he was joking. He then explained how these guys genuinely liked hanging out with their women, and I should be prepared for a bunch of alpha men to become marshmallows around their women.

Then, I actually did laugh.

After it set in that there were going to be several more people at this gathering, I started to get nervous. Even though I've met almost everyone, I'm still worried about how I'll interact with all of them. I know my old habits of staying out of the way aren't going to work in this situation.

I've been going over all of the couples in my head so I don't forget who they are. There's obviously Quinn and Cooper, who I plan on sticking close to until I get comfortable. Max and Lucy will be there. I met them one night at Levi's new house. Natalie and Tucker have a five-year-old boy, Noah, who they are trying to adopt. He doesn't live with them yet but spends the weekends with them and will be there tonight since it's not just a girls' night anymore.

Then there's Megan and Todd. I've interacted with Megan on several occasions since I moved here. She's one of the nicest people I've ever met. I've yet to meet her husband, Todd, though. I also have only met Sara a couple of times. She came in with the girls to invite me to dinner, but they were only there for a few minutes.

For some reason, I'm most nervous to connect with her. I think I've made her out to be some kind of competition, even though I know that's not the case. If Levi and Sara were supposed to be together, they already would be.

"You ready to go?" Levi peeks his head through the doorway. He's got on a green fitted T-shirt that makes his eyes pop and khaki cargo shorts. The funny thing is he actually uses all of his pockets. I don't know how his pants don't fall down with the things he puts in them. Usually, it's random nails or scrap pieces of wood, but he came home with a couple of screwdrivers once.

"Yes, let me grab my bag, then we can go."

We leave the bedroom and head out to Levi's truck. It's a short drive from my house since Natalie and Tucker don't live too far from me. When we pull up, there are cars parked all over the place, both in the driveway and on the sidewalk.

Jitters slide down my arms as I open the door to get out. It seems everyone is already here. The noise of the party is loud enough to filter outside.

Levi comes around the front of the truck and wraps his arms around my shoulders. "I parked on the street so we can leave anytime you want. We can be out of here in no time if you get overwhelmed."

I press up onto my toes, placing my lips gently against his.

I'm so grateful for how well he knows me. I don't know how he learned my body language so quickly. Over the course of the last couple of weeks, he's been so attuned to my every need. Never have I felt so seen or understood.

Levi quickly takes over the kiss as he usually does, twining his tongue with mine. His hand wraps around the side of my face, making the world fade around me so I only feel him. There are days I feel incredibly sad not to have known this could be my life. I've spent so much time alone, constantly on edge, afraid that if I allowed myself to slow down for even a minute, I'd suffer the painful consequences.

In this moment, as Levi's lips slow our kiss down, happiness envelops me so strongly, it brings tears to my eyes. There, deep in the hazel-green eyes I've come to rely on, I see the future I've longed for. It scares the hell out of me while simultaneously filling me with such joy. I'm going to fall in love with this amazing man—if I haven't already. I hope he doesn't take advantage of that.

Levi takes my hand, leading me up the sidewalk toward the front steps of the house. Instead of knocking, he opens the door, walking right into the loud chatter of his friends, bellowing out a *hello* to rival his brother's booming voice, and everyone responds in kind.

The small entryway leads directly into the living room. A staircase is to our left and a hallway goes toward the back of the house. It seems the party goers have already split off into guys and girls. The girls have taken over the side of the living room with the couches while the guys stand around the other side by the food.

Quinn jumps up from the couch with her wine glass in hand to give me a hug. I expect this will be how most of the introductions will go. With Levi's help, my sensitivity to touch has lessened drastically. It only feels mildly uncomfortable now when it used to feel like you were taking a cheese grater to my skin.

"Oh, I'm so glad you're here! Come on, let's get a drink in your hand before we force the madhouse on you," Quinn teases, easing some of my nerves. Levi squeezes my hand but lets Quinn pull me down the hall. The U-shaped kitchen is gorgeous with its granite countertops and dark cabinets. The dining room is open to the kitchen, and there are trays of food sitting out on the table. I'm pretty sure you could feed an army with the number of appetizers there are.

"What do you feel like drinking tonight? We've got a ton of wine, beer, and potentially even a cocktail or two." Quinn steps up to the counter where several bottles of alcohol sit.

"Wine would be great. Whatever is open."

Quinn starts pouring while I awkwardly stand there, waiting for her to finish. It's annoying how out of place I feel, all because I lack the courage to put myself out there. These people have been nothing but welcoming to me, but my insecurities keep telling me I'll never be good enough to fit in. Even though I know it's irrational, it's hard to get your brain to stop thinking the worst about yourself.

"I've already told the girls not to pry too much. We'd love for you to keep hanging out with us, so sit back, get to know the group, and you tell us what you want, when you want," Quinn says quietly.

I'm overcome with gratitude for her friendship, and, completely out of character, I reach out to pull her into a hug. "Thank you so much for including me, Quinn."

She gives me a squeeze in response, then pulls away to hand me my glass. We make our way back to the living room, and Levi catches my eye, silently asking if I'm okay with an eyebrow raise. I smile at him, happy to be included. He winks at me, making my grin widen. I love that wink.

I squeeze onto the couch next to Natalie and Megan, who both have glasses of wine in hand.

"I'm so glad you're here! Did you get food? I sort of went crazy with the appetizers." Natalie grins at me. Her beautiful red hair is swept back into a messy bun, and she's got on yoga pants and a long-sleeve T-shirt. It makes me feel so much better about the casual clothes I'm wearing. I know she's still healing from the house fire she was trapped in a couple of months ago, so I'm not surprised she has on long sleeves despite the summer heat.

"Not yet, but it looks great," I respond.

"We have news!" Megan says as if she's about to burst if she doesn't tell everyone right away.

"Spill!" Lucy grins. I swear she's one of the kindest people I've ever met. Her husband, Max, too, which was a surprise when I first met him. He came off as super intimidating before I got to know him.

"We're getting our first kiddo!" Megan beams.

A chorus of *yays* echoes across the group as they all ask questions simultaneously.

"Is it a boy or girl?"

"Do you know their name?"

"Can you adopt him?"

Megan laughs, gesturing with her hands for the girls to stop talking. "It's a boy, he's seven, his name is Nathaniel. We don't know a whole lot other than he'll be arriving tomorrow."

"This is amazing! I'll see if Noah would be interested in meeting him once he gets settled at your house."

"That would be great, Nat."

I look over at Noah right as Tucker throws the little blond boy over his shoulder, making him squeal. I have a lot of respect for these people who are so willing to open their homes to kids who would never know love without them. It gives me a little sense of peace knowing Nathaniel and Noah will grow up surrounded by so much love.

"Hope, how was the beach? I'm so jealous you got to go," Sara asks me after the group exhausted all their questions about Nathaniel.

"It was amazing but way too short. I'd never been before, so I wasn't ready to come home yet."

"You'd never been to the beach before? Where are you from?"

"West Virginia." My tendency to clam up about my life has me holding my tongue from saying anything else. Oddly enough, there's a large part of me that wants to share my life with them. I think having told Levi part of my story, I feel more accepting of my past than I ever have before.

I'm too used to holding things close to the vest, though, so I won't be sharing my past tonight. It's better this way. There are too many people here for a story as dark as mine.

"How'd you end up here?"

"My grandmother told me about this place. She used to live here when she was a girl and would tell me all these stories about how beautiful it was here. When I got my chance to move, I knew this was where I wanted to make my home." The stories my grandmother used to tell me made it seem so idyllic. When I actually got here, the stories didn't do it justice. It's everything I dreamed it would be.

"How long did she live here? I wonder if our parents might know her," Megan asks.

"She lived here until she graduated from high school. Then she moved to West Virginia with her husband's family while she was in college. Her last name was Langley—like mine—so you could ask, but I doubt it."

"Well, we're glad she told you about this place—for more reasons than one." Quinn nods her head over to Levi.

"Seriously, who knew Levi would be the one to settle down so quickly?" Natalie grins at me.

It's easy to forget that Levi used to get around before we started dating. He's still just as charming as he was the first day I met him, but after our trip to the beach, something about him feels almost… settled. Relaxed. Sometimes I wonder if he'll get tired of my broken pieces. If he'll decide it would be easier to go back to that easy, playboy life. It wouldn't surprise me if he did. I'm not the easiest choice.

"And I know I've never seen him this happy. It's a good look on him," Sara says, surprising me. Before Levi and I started dating, the two of them hung out frequently. I was worried she'd hate me for taking up all his time.

"Alice is over the moon despite being pissy about not getting any details," Quinn says with a sly smile.

"What do you mean?" I haven't heard anything from Alice about our relationship, so I'm surprised to hear Quinn say there's something going on.

"Oh, Alice was on a warpath when everyone found out you and Levi started dating. She wanted all the details and was royally pissed at Levi for not telling her about you two. Since he hasn't told her a single thing, she's been pestering the hell out of me and Cooper." If Quinn wasn't grinning at me, I'd feel awful she was being hounded by Alice.

I'm not surprised in the least that Levi kept this from me. He's always doing things to protect me. Keeping his mother at bay so I don't have to share the details of our relationship is yet another way he's proving how much he knows me. It would be incredibly difficult for me to say no to his mom, so him doing it for me makes me want to kiss him.

"I'm sorry you're taking the brunt of her questions, but also, thank you for taking the heat for me." I laugh, knowing we'll have to give in to Alice's request for information soon. Maybe I can invite her over for dinner one of these nights, and let her ask us whatever she wants. Levi is going to hate that idea.

I realize my glass is empty, so I stand to go back to the kitchen for a refill. When I walk in, Noah's little hand reaches up to grab a cookie from a platter on the table. He peeks around the corner of the dining room, keeping a watchful eye on the adults. He turns to escape when he spots me and freezes.

I lift my hand to my lips and slide my finger and thumb across them like I'm zipping them. He grins so big there's a chance it'll split his face in two. He comes into the kitchen, munching on his cookie.

"What's your name?" he asks.

"I'm Hope. You're Noah, right?"

"Yep. Natalie and Tucker are going to be my mom and dad one day. I can't wait. It's taking forever."

"I bet they're excited, too."

"Yeah. I like their friends. I used to be scared of new people 'cause my first mom wasn't a good one, but now, I'm going to have a great mom." Noah keeps munching on his cookie as if he didn't just drop a bomb. At only five, this little boy has had a hard life. Something I can relate to on a certain level. I may not have been as young as him, but I know what it's like to suffer at the hands of a parent.

"Yes, you are," I say in almost a whisper, overcome with emotion for a kiddo I barely know. I hope with all I have that this works out for him. He slips out of the kitchen and into the living room, most likely to find Natalie.

After taking a deep breath to clear my emotions, I grab a bottle of wine to refill my glass. My phone starts ringing in my pocket, surprising me. All the people who would call are in the other room. When I pull it out, *Unknown* is flashing on the screen.

"Hello?"

"Rosemary…"

My body freezes instantly.

No.

I wasn't supposed to hear from him ever again.

"That's not my name," I croak, barely able to get the words out.

"I know. Sorry, Hope. You know I wouldn't call if it wasn't important. I have news."

I don't say anything. I wouldn't know what to say, even if I could get the words past the lump in my throat.

"He's out. On a fucking technicality. His lawyers found an issue with some of the evidence, and they won the appeal."

My breath freezes in my lungs.

Even though the kitchen is empty, I still glance around the room, afraid he'll be standing in the corner, watching me like he used to do.

"Watch your back," he warns, his voice deadly serious.

Then, the phone goes dead.

31

LEVI

My trowel scraps across the wall, spreading the gray mortar across the surface. The shower tile is going in today on the Silvey house. We're down to only a few more projects to complete, then the house will be finished. I've got a few other builds starting up soon, but I won't have to be at them full time, so I'll be able to focus solely on my own house. A good chunk of the upstairs is done, but the downstairs still has quite a bit to go before it'll be ready to live in.

Making my house livable hasn't been much of a priority since I've basically moved in with Hope at this point. It's been a couple of weeks since we went to the beach, and I haven't had any desire to move back into my apartment. Hope hasn't made it seem like she wants me to leave, either, so I'm taking advantage of the extra time I get to spend with her.

We've settled into life as a couple so seamlessly, it's as if we've always been together. Hope has a huge event tonight that she's been prepping for all week. There have been some late nights at the store, but it could be huge for business. It'll get her recognition as well as potentially bring in a slew of new clients.

I wish she'd hire another part-time employee since the shop is doing so well. She's worried the income won't be there forever, which I can understand. I just don't want her to have to work so hard. It's been killing me how much time she's been putting in the last few days. I know she's exhausted. At least she's letting me help her drop off the flowers tonight instead of trying to do it all by herself.

Continuing to put the tiles against the wall, I make sure everything is as straight as possible. This is when I love my job. The moment my mind wants to start moving a million miles a minute, all I have to do is start on a project that requires my full attention.

If I didn't have to focus solely on these tiles so they're straight, I'd be thinking about everything I could screw up with Hope. I've enjoyed getting to know her on a deeper level. I know she likes to go through her bedtime routine in a certain order every single night. She knows I like to strip down to my underwear when I get home since I'm usually a mess. I know she loves to cook dinner but hates grocery shopping. All the little things in life you only learn when you get close to someone.

I wish I could help ease the tension Hope has been feeling this past week. She's been up at all hours, her anxiety not letting her sleep, and working long days at the shop to finish the arrangements for this event. It's been a lot for her. Sometimes it feels like it's more than the event that's weighing on her, but she hasn't said anything to the contrary. I've even asked her to be sure. Hopefully, once it's over, she'll be able to relax again.

Shaking my head, I focus back on my task. It's so easy to let my thoughts slide to the negative. I have to keep reminding myself that Hope and I are adults, who are fully capable of communicating any issues we have. I just have to keep trusting that she'll tell me if something isn't right so I can help her fix it.

*   *   *

I PULL into the empty parking lot of Blooming Beautiful. Hope closed the shop early today so she could focus on the event tonight instead of customer orders. I'm going to have to do my best to help her relax when we get home tonight. She's been stressed to the max and working so hard, she deserves to be pampered.

Walking into the store, I'm surprised the door is unlocked. The door doesn't chime, reminding me I need to fix it for her. It broke a few days ago, but I haven't had a chance to get to it yet. I'm early to pick her up, so maybe I can work on the door while she finishes up.

Since I don't see her out front, I head toward the back room where she has a big walk-in fridge for her extra inventory, as well as another table she uses to make arrangements when she needs more space. I finally find her sitting in her office. There's only a desk in the small room, so it's more like a closet than an office, but she likes it well enough.

"Hey, sweetheart," I say softly, making her jump a mile.

"Jesus Christ." Her hand flies to her chest as her breathing increases. It's been a long time since I've scared her like that. She must've been super into whatever she's working on.

"Sorry! I thought my days of needing to wear bells on my shoes were over." I lean down to kiss Hope's temple while squeezing her shoulders.

I watch her shake her head as she smiles at me. "I was apparently too in the zone to hear you come in." Her eyes dart to her computer, then back to me.

"The chime is still broken on your door, so that probably didn't help. If we've got some time, I can install the new one."

"We've got about thirty minutes before we need to load up the truck."

I nod at her before I lean down to press my lips against hers. Soft under mine, she lets me take over the kiss. It humbles me every time she lets me lead. Especially after everything she's been through. Having her trust me enough to let me take over is one of the best feelings.

I pull back before I get too carried away. As much as I'd like to boost her up onto her tiny desk and have my way with her, we don't have time for me to give her the attention she deserves.

Her dazed face has me grinning down at her. "The quicker we get this event done, the quicker I can get you home, so hurry it up." I wink at her, then head back to the front with the sound of her laughter following me.

The minute I'm done getting the door chime installed, Hope is ready to pack up my truck. We get everything loaded, then head to the convention center outside of town. There are about a million flowers in my back seat and truck bed, which has a top cover on it to protect my tools. Right at this moment, it's protecting flowers.

She's quieter than usual as we drive over to the center. She's been pretty quiet in general since we hung out at Natalie and Tucker's last weekend. I worried my friends overwhelmed her, but she assured me they didn't. She's been texting with the girls ever since, so I think she's being honest.

I know she's been stressed about this event, and I'm sure the anxiety of doing well has made her withdraw into herself. I just hope she hasn't built her walls back up too high. It was tough to break through them the first time, but I'll do it again. I'll do whatever it takes to prove I'm in this for the long haul, no matter how hard things may get.

"You worried about the event?" I ask, trying to pull her out of her deep thoughts.

"Not anymore. With the arrangements done, I'm feeling fine about it. Once we get everything dropped off, I'll be able to slow down again."

"Good. You've been working hard this week. It'll be nice to see you relax a little."

Hope sends me a small smile in agreement but doesn't offer much else in response. I let her have her silence instead of pushing since we're almost to the convention center.

I park in the loading area and help transfer the flowers from the back of my truck to the conference room. Then, I stand in the back, watching Hope do her thing. She places each piece in the middle of the tables, fluffing them if they were smashed in transport.

Watching her work with the flowers is mesmerizing. Every move she makes is full of confidence, knowing exactly what needs to go where to look the best. She's amazing and so fucking beautiful it's hard not to grab her around the waist and carry her home.

When the final arrangement is placed on a table, she looks up to scan the room. She suddenly freezes where she stands. Her body is so stiff, I can see it from all the way across the room. Scanning the area, I try to find what made her freak out but only see a group of employees from the convention center.

I look back at Hope right as she shakes her head and resumes scanning the rest of the room. The moment she finds me, her body relaxes as a small smile pulls at the corner of her mouth. Knowing that I can ease some of her tension just by looking at her gives me so much pride, I'm barely able to wait for her to come to me.

Again, my body is on edge, wanting to sweep her out of this place. To spend all my time worshiping her incredible body. Even though I've had her several times since our first, I can't get enough of her.

"Everything okay?" I ask when Hope gets close.

"Yeah, why?"

"I saw you freeze out there, so I wanted to make sure you were okay."

"Oh, um, I'm fine. Thought I forgot something, but I

didn't." She glances at the group of employees standing at the back of the room, then back to me.

I hesitate, knowing she's not being honest with me. Do I push her to tell me the truth or let her come to me when she's ready? Knowing the stress she's been under, I decide to let it go. "Shall we head out, then?"

"Yes. I'm sorry it took longer to get the flowers in place than I anticipated. Thank you for waiting."

I grab her hand to lead her out of the conference center. "Of course. If I'm being honest, I enjoyed watching you work."

"Really?" Hope frowns in disbelief.

I open the passenger door of my truck to help her in. "Really. It was a major turn-on, actually. You looked so confident and in control. It was hot." I grin at her look of surprise. I don't know how she doesn't see how incredible she is. I'll have to make it my mission to make sure she knows it every day.

* * *

HOPE'S moan echoes through the bathroom, going straight to my dick, which is already harder than steel.

"Levi, that feels incredible."

My hands continue digging into Hope's shoulders, her olive skin smooth under my calloused hands. With her dark hair pulled up into a messy knot on her head, I've got full access to her neck, shoulders, and back.

When we got home, we warmed up some leftovers for dinner, eating them while catching up on the rest of our day. Then, I carried Hope up the stairs to the bathroom, where I filled the tub for her to soak her tired body. She insisted I get in with her, even though the tub's not quite big enough for my frame. With my legs stretched out on each side of her,

I've been able to massage her back, working some of the tension out of her muscles.

I didn't realize how tight she'd gotten over the last week. I've been working to get rid of some of the edginess she's been carrying. I'd do anything for her to go back to her happy, relaxed self.

"I'm glad it feels good. You've been working hard this past week, so you deserve to be pampered."

Instead of responding, she turns her body so she's facing me, sliding her legs around my sides to sit on my lap. My arms naturally snake around her waist, pulling her closer to me. My cock is weeping at how close her center is, but I know the purpose of this move is not for the sexy times it's hoping for right now.

Her face is serious while her eyes are wide and vulnerable. The dark pools of her irises pull me so deep, I'd never be able to find my way out, even if I wanted to. And I definitely don't.

"Thank you for supporting me, Levi. I'll never be able to put into words how much I appreciate your ability to be by my side, helping when I need it, and letting me do it my own way. Being able to come to you, knowing you're not going to take over everything for me is something I hope to never take for granted. You're everything I've ever dreamed of and never believed I'd actually get to have."

"Oh, sweetheart." I run my thumbs across her cheeks, completely overwhelmed by my feelings for this woman. She's absolutely shattered every illusion I had of what a committed relationship would be like. She's brought so much more to my life than just companionship. My world is brighter, happier, with her in it than it ever was before.

"I need you to know how much you mean to me. I thought moving here was going to be the best decision I ever made, but saying yes to going on a date with you was much better." She pauses for a moment as a small smile begins to form. "I love you, Levi."

My chest expands with so many feelings, I have no idea how to deal with them. Instead, I push forward, taking Hope's lips in an all-consuming kiss, pouring all my love for her into this one moment. I'm overwhelmed with emotions, and the only thing I can think to do is get as close to her as possible.

It seems Hope has the same idea because she reaches down to grab my cock, guiding it to her center. She slowly lowers herself down, her tight sheath pulling me in deeper. We both groan when I'm fully seated inside her. God, she feels incredible. It was the best day when we decided to forgo the condoms. With us fully committed to each other, and Hope on birth control, it was a no-brainer.

"You're everything I've ever wanted in a partner, Hope. I never thought I would get to be with someone like this, but it turns out, I've been waiting for you to come into my life." The words are tumbling from my mouth so fast, I barely even register what I'm saying.

I think Hope likes them, though, because her hips start moving faster, grinding down on me with every pass.

"Fuck, you feel good," I growl, which only spurs Hope on more. I grab her hips, squeezing her hard while helping to guide her movements. The water is splashing everywhere, but it barely registers as I watch Hope's body writhe on mine.

Water droplets fall down her chest in a sensual glide, highlighting her round, full breasts. Leaning forward, I suck her nipple deep into my mouth, making Hope moan while her pussy tightens around me. I can tell she's getting close, pulling me along right behind her.

I gently bite down on her nipple, tugging on it. Hope throws her head back, her orgasm crashing through her as her pussy clamps down on me so tight, I have no choice but to follow her. My entire body explodes as I come harder than I ever have before. It's intense, matching the words and feelings we shared earlier.

Our breathing is heavy, the little water that's left in the tub laps at our skin. Hope's hands run across my shoulders and back while mine do the same to her. It's soothing as we both come down from our heightened states.

"I love you so much, Hope," I whisper against her lips. She gently kisses me despite the grin on her face.

"That's good because I'm not letting you go."

"Oh, yeah?" I smirk, raising my eyebrow. Hope's giggle has me melting, my smile growing even bigger.

She nods her head, happiness radiating off her in waves.

"Good because I wouldn't let you."

HOPE

I clench the sheets hard, my whole body tightening. I've never felt anything quite like this in all my life. Levi's tongue continues its devious strokes across my center. He keeps switching the speed: slow, decadent laps and sucking pulses, then fast, hard drives. It's maddening. And incredibly arousing.

"Levi, please."

"I told you I was going to draw this one out. I can't send my girl to work anxious about the day." I can barely see his wicked grin before he lowers his head back down.

"You're going to kill me, I swear it."

"Where would be the fun in that?" he whispers against my skin.

All I can do is groan and fall more in love with the crazy man, even if he is torturing me.

I think he takes pity on me when he adds his fingers into the mix, first one then another. His tongue starts a steady rhythm, making my body climb higher. I didn't think it could get any better, but somehow, Levi makes it happen.

He sucks my clit deep into his mouth, and I explode into a million pieces. Absolutely decimated by this orgasm.

I barely register Levi moving over me, kissing my stomach, my breasts, and up my neck before finally landing on my lips. His cock rubs across my wet flesh, the sensitive nerves making me moan into his mouth. When I tip my hips, Levi presses into me, his chest rumbling with a growl.

I love the sounds he makes and that I'm the one drawing them out of him. It's a powerful feeling.

Levi runs his hand up my arm, pulling my hand above my head. Instead of feeling restrained, it feels intimate as he threads his fingers through mine, connecting us on every level possible.

Hands, lips, bodies.

His thrusts begin gaining in speed as need pushes past his control.

"God, you're incredible," I moan.

"Only because of you, my love." He kisses me slowly despite the speed of his thrusts, and I crest the ridge again, pulling Levi over with me. We groan in unison, our orgasms crashing together in a spectacular wave of pleasure. Our love surrounds the room so heavily, I feel as if it'll imprint on my heart forever. No matter what happens.

Wrapping my arms around Levi, I pull him closer, hoping the moment will last longer than the few minutes it takes for our breathing to slow. I'm not ready for my brain to start working in overdrive again. That's what prompted this little session, to begin with.

After a kiss on my shoulder, Levi pulls out, and we both head into the bathroom to clean up. I wish we could stay in bed the rest of the day, hiding in our bubble so I wouldn't have to think about work or the future. Or the phone call.

I force myself to stop those thoughts in their tracks. I've gone round and round in my head to the point I don't even know what's up anymore. I have too many other things to worry about than what the phone call could possibly mean.

Today, I am interviewing candidates for a part-time position to help with the additional business I've been getting. After the function a couple of weeks ago, I've been inundated with calls for more orders than I can handle. Levi finally convinced me that hiring another person would both help the store and keep me sane. Even with adding an extra set of hands, I still won't be able to accept all the requests, but it should help when my focus needs to be on an event instead of everyday customer orders.

Levi wrapped up the Silvey project last week and is now spending all his time at his new house. He's still overseeing most of the other projects his company is working on, but he doesn't have to be on-site full time until he's done with his house.

He's getting close to being able to move in. The renovations aren't anywhere close to being fully completed, but the kitchen will be finished soon, as well as the living room, so he'll have all of the necessities to live comfortably while he renovates the rest of the rooms. Although, he hasn't mentioned anything about moving into the new house when he's able to.

We don't technically live together right now, even though a good chunk of his clothes are in my closet, and he sleeps here every night. We never talked about him officially moving in, it just sort of happened. Not that I'm complaining. I love having him here in my space. I'm not sure what I'll do if he decides he wants to move into the new house when he can.

"What are you thinking about so hard over there? I thought I sexed those worries out of you a minute ago." Levi leans into the shower, turning the water on full blast.

"Oh, you definitely did. I feel so languid, I'm worried I won't be able to make it to work." I grin at him, and he pulls me into the shower, kissing me under the warm spray.

"Good. Since I'm the cause, I'll happily help get you to work." He winks, and my knees threaten to buckle.

The wink gets me every time.

* * *

CLICKING PRINT ON THE FILE, I wait for the résumés to print out. I want to go over them one more time before the candidates arrive. I also want them handy while I conduct the interviews. I've got three lined up today, each one seemingly a good fit based on their experiences. We'll see how we mesh personality-wise when they get here. That will be my deciding factor. It's the reason I hired Claire on the spot.

"Hey, your first interview is here," Claire says, her eyebrows raised in an unreadable expression.

"Thanks, I'll come grab her." I stand from my chair, following Claire out to the front of the shop.

A woman with sleek, black hair pulled up in a chignon stands next to one of my hibiscus plants. She's in business attire—actually, she's in a full pantsuit, which feels overly formal since I'm in my work T-shirt and high-waisted shorts. I'll give her credit for effort, though.

"Hi, Theresa, I'm Hope Langley." I stretch my hand out to her when she turns. Her lips turn up in a minuscule smile, barely softening her severe features as she takes my hand. "Why don't we head back to my office so we can chat."

After leading Theresa through the back room, I gesture for her to enter my office. Her face pinches as she takes in the small space. It seems my small, cozy office doesn't appeal to her. Theresa sits down, crosses her legs, then stares at me.

I blink at her, forgetting for a moment I'm supposed to be leading this interview. She's a little intimidating, which feels weird to say when I'm the business owner.

I clear my throat and open my mouth to start when Theresa interrupts my thought. "Your hibiscus plant seemed overwatered."

I pause. That wasn't what I expected her to say. "Um, I'll

197

take a look at it later." I know for a fact I'm not drowning my plant, but I've always been a peacemaker, so I don't say anything about it.

"Anyway, can you tell me about the last store you worked for?"

Theresa begins telling me about her previous job, managing the entire store of ten employees. According to her, she ran a tight ship with no slacking and carefully structured plans for each plant on the floor. I think flower warden would've been a better description for her previous title.

She's completely overqualified for this job. And… stern.

When she finally finishes her diatribe on how plants should be cared for—with strict, regimented schedules—I let out a deep breath in an attempt to gather my thoughts.

"Wow, it seems like you have a lot of experience with a multitude of plants. Um, the thing is, I'm only looking for a floor worker. Not a manager. I feel like you're overqualified for this position."

"Hmm. That was evident when I walked in the door."

Ouch.

I clear my throat. "Right, well, thank you for coming in. It was lovely meeting you." I stand from my chair to lead Theresa back out to the main floor.

The minute the door closes, I sag against the counter.

"You okay there, boss?"

"She was a very scary lady."

Claire laughs, nudging me with her shoulder. "I wondered if the inside matched the outside. I try not to judge based on looks, but she wore her personality on her sleeve."

"That is completely accurate. My next interview should be here in twenty minutes."

"Can't wait." Claire grins. I'm more nervous about the second interview since the first one was such a disaster.

Nerves seem to be my constant companion these past few

weeks. Keeping them at bay has almost become a sport for me at this point. I almost wish Tomas had never called me in the first place. All it's done is put me on edge, constantly looking over my shoulder for the boogie man to be lurking behind me. It's exhausting. There have been many times I wish I would've told Levi the full truth of what happened to me so I could share this burden with him. That makes me feel selfish, though. All Levi's done since we got together is make me feel safe. The least I can do is not add to his already full plate.

When the door chimes, I look up to see a twenty-some-odd-year-old girl, striding into the store. She's the epitome of goth queen, hitting both the slightly scary and sort of chic look.

"Are you Anna?"

"Yep."

"Um, okay, well—"

"Yeah, so I already got a job and don't need this one anymore."

"Oh... Uh, thank you for coming in to tell me."

"Sure." She turns on her black combat boots and walks right back out the door. Silence descends on the store for a second while I stare at the now empty space Anna was previously standing in.

"Well, that was unexpected," I say, finally breaking the silence.

"I think it's the theme for the day." Claire's laughter pulls me from my stupor.

"Right? I guess I'll go work on paperwork since I've got some extra time now."

"I'll let you know when the last one arrives."

"Thanks."

Once I'm in my office, I dig into all the admin stuff I've been putting off while I wait for the next interview. Who knew finding part-time help would be so difficult? I was only nervous about asking the right questions. Not about the people interviewing.

An hour later, Claire pokes her head around the corner of my office door. "Hey, your next interview is here."

"Thanks, do you mind bringing her back?"

"Not at all." Claire's smile is mischievous, which I don't fully understand. I'll ask her about it later when the interview is over. She comes walking back around the corner, and behind her is not a girl like I thought but a teenage boy.

The résumé said Sam Waters, which made me assume they would be a woman. I was definitely wrong. Not even our emails to set up the interview tipped me off. He's maybe seventeen if a day older.

"Hi, Sam, my name is Hope Langley."

"Hi, Hope. It's nice to meet you." His smile is gentle as he shakes my hand. His curly mop of brown hair falls in his eyes as he sits in the other chair in my office. He's got on a blue button-down shirt and a pair of nice, dark jeans. I would wager a guess these are his church clothes.

"So, tell me about yourself, Sam."

"Well, I'm seventeen. Uh... I go to Sonoma High, and I play baseball."

"And tell me why you're looking for a job here."

"My mom said I had to get a job if I wanted to start driving myself places. I used to help my grandma in her flower garden." His voice grows quiet. "She passed away last fall, though, so I haven't been around flowers in a while."

Well, he's officially the cutest thing ever. His résumé was the least experienced, but he wrote his knowledge of flowers, so I knew he had some background in plant life.

"I opened this shop because of my own grandmother's love of flowers. She started my obsession, and even though she's long passed, I feel her in this store every day. Maybe you'll find the same peace, as well, Sam. I'd be honored to hire you if you're willing to learn how to make arrangements."

"I'm definitely up for learning." He grins.

We discuss the pay and hours as well as my expectations for when he's here. He's going to start this weekend to give us plenty of time to get him trained. When we're finished with all the paperwork, I lead him out of the shop. He gives Claire and me a wave before he steps out the door.

"He was the one, right?"

"Yep. He used to help his grandmother in her garden before she passed away last fall. The kid is the sweetest. I couldn't say no."

"Good. I had a feeling we'd like him."

I smile at Claire, understanding her mischievous smile now.

"Oh, I grabbed the mail earlier. Forgot to put it in the basket." She hands over a stack of envelopes I tuck under my arm to take back to my office.

I've got a new inventory magazine for clients, some bills to pay, and something else I don't recognize. The white envelope is plain with only my name handwritten on the front. My stomach drops as the cream cardstock slips from the envelope.

YOU'VE DONE WELL *for yourself, Rosemary. I should be impressed. Unfortunately for you, I'm not. You should've known better than to go against my rules. You will be punished for it. I can't wait. -A*

WITH MY HEART in my throat, I jump from my chair and race to the bathroom. The contents of my stomach spew out of me with such violence, my entire body quakes. Terror has drenched me in sweat as I continue to heave.

When there's nothing left in my stomach, I sit on the tile floor, willing my heartbeat to slow.

I never thought this could happen. I did everything I could to make sure it didn't, but it seems my efforts were futile.

He found me.

33

LEVI

My hand slides across the bed, seeking Hope's warm body. Instead, I find cool, empty sheets. As my eyes flick open, the room is still dark, the early morning light not quite bright enough to get rid of the shadows.

I stumble out of bed, rubbing the sleep out of my eyes as I make my way downstairs. A few lamps are lit, guiding me into the library, where I find Hope curled up in a chair, reading a book. Her dark hair is piled on her head, her knees tucked to her chest with my T-shirt stretched across them. I couldn't love her any more than I do right now.

"Couldn't sleep?" I ask quietly, making Hope jump a mile. Her book falls to the floor as her hand flies to her chest. "Sorry, I thought you heard me come in."

She heaves out a big breath while giving me a half smile. "Um, no. I had a nightmare, so I decided to come down and read."

I step into the room, kneeling on the floor in front of her chair. "I wish you'd have woken me up."

"I didn't want to interrupt your sleep. You've got a long day ahead of you."

"Next time, wake me up, love. I don't mind." I lean in for a kiss and get a small one in return. "I'll go make some coffee."

I walk into the kitchen, my thoughts swirling. Over the last few days, it feels as if Hope has been… regressing. She's been a lot more closed off with her emotions, as well as startling at the smallest things, even if I try to avoid it. There's even been a couple of moments where she's flinched if I moved too fast, which she hasn't done since we went to the beach.

I've tried talking to her about it, but she shrugs it off or changes the subject. I wish she'd be honest about what's going on. I just want to be there for her, help her in whatever way I can. I also know I can't push her too hard, so I'm waiting for her to come to me when she's ready.

When the coffee is done, I take two cups upstairs, having heard Hope go up a few minutes ago. I set the cup down on the bathroom counter next to her with a kiss on her cheek, then step to my sink. We both get ready for our day, the silence continuing. It's not awkward, but it is strained. I can feel the tension radiating off Hope. I wish I knew how to make it better for her.

I walk out of the bathroom and into the closet to throw on my work clothes. Hope comes in as I'm buttoning my jeans, a distant look on her face. Unable to help myself, I pull her into me, happy she comes willingly. Her forehead lands on my bare chest as she melts into my arms.

It's these moments that remind me we'll be okay. We'll figure it out because this matters. We matter.

"When you're ready, I'm here. I will always be here. No matter what," I say into her hair, pressing my lips against her head. She squeezes me tight, and I soak in the moment. "I love you, Hope."

"I love you, too, Levi." She kisses my chest, then drops her arms to finish getting ready.

* * *

"I THOUGHT my house was a mess, but you've got me beat, man," I say to Benjamin Crawford, the new veterinarian in town. He bought a disaster of an old farmhouse a few miles outside of town. He doesn't even have a working kitchen right now.

"God, I know. I don't know what I was thinking when I bought it. Mainly, get out of Mom and Dad's house, whatever it takes."

I laugh at the pained look on his face. "A little too close for comfort?"

"I love them, but, dude, I'm a grown-ass man. Having my mother smother me every day is about to kill me."

"I would never be able to move back in with my mom, so I can imagine. We'll get you fixed up in a few months, then you'll be free as a bird."

"If only that were true," he mumbles, running his hand through his blond hair. From what I've heard from the gossip hens, his move home wasn't his idea. His dad, Dr. Charles, has had some pretty serious health stuff going on, which forced him to retire as the chief vet at the Sonoma Animal Clinic. Ben moved back home to take over the clinic for his dad, and apparently, it was not his first choice.

"Give me a little bit of time, and we'll get you set up. Let's look at some of the design stuff."

He nods his head, so I lead him over to the samples I keep in the bed of my truck. We go through all the options for his kitchen since we're starting there first. Ben's ability to pick matching designs is comically horrible, so he ends up giving me free rein. I lay out the ones I like the best for his farm-house, and he gives me the go-ahead.

I won't be here for all the renovations, but it's nice to know Ben's not going to give me grief about each tiny detail. There are so many homeowners who think they need to have a say in every single aspect. It ends up becoming a hindrance, making the renovations take longer than they should.

Knowing how laid-back Ben is about all of this will speed up the process, getting him into the house faster, which is his —and my—ultimate goal.

"If you're looking for something to do, our group still gets together regularly to hang out. We'd love to have you join us sometime."

"You and your brother still hanging with Todd Montgomery?"

"Of course. We've all partnered up at this point, but we still have a good time. Natalie Carlisle and Tucker James are actually together now if you didn't know. You were in the same class as Tucker, right?"

"I was a year ahead of him, but I know who you're talking about. It would be great to hang out with people my own age again. Mom's friends are nice, but, you know..." His eyes widen as if he won't survive another dinner surrounded by a bunch of meddling women.

"I definitely know." I laugh. "We'll take care of you, man."

"God bless you."

We finish going over renovation details, and after I check in with my crew, I head over to my house. A couple of my guys are already here working, which has sped up the renovations exponentially. Another month at this pace, and it'll be finished. I haven't broached the subject of moving with Hope yet. I was going to the other day, but with the weirdness going on between us right now, I don't want to make things worse.

Right now, we're in her house, in her bed, where she has control. If I asked her to move into the house with me, it could make her feel unbalanced. Since we're already on shaky ground, there's no reason to tip the scales more than they're already tipped.

I honestly don't mind. At this point, the only thing that

matters is that she's in my life at all. As long as I have Hope, it doesn't matter where we live or what we do. She's become my home.

"Everything okay?" I ask Michael, who is working in one of the guest bathrooms upstairs.

"So far so good, boss. We're getting close to the finish line."

"Thank God." I grin at him. "Let me know if you need anything. I'll be in the library."

He nods his head, then goes back to laying tile. When I walk into the library, I make a game plan for my tasks. I'm refinishing the built-ins, sanding down the crown molding, and fixing the ladder rails. Despite being okay with not moving into the house right away, I can see Hope in here, curled up with a book in her hands. I can even see her cuddling with a little girl who looks just like her, reading story after story until she falls asleep.

It's the dream I never thought I'd get to have. A dream I can see so clearly in my mind. One day, it'll be a reality, and I'll happily wait forever for it.

After I finish in the library, I decide to knock off a little early to pick up dinner for me and Hope. I've been craving a BLT from the café all day. Plus, Hope won't have to worry about cooking tonight.

Walking my tools out to my truck, I dump them in the back. Having done this so many times in my life, it's become something I could do with my eyes closed.

"You've got a great place here," a voice calls from the sidewalk.

Turning, I find an older man looking up at my house. His salt and pepper hair is nicely styled, but his dark sunglasses hide a good chunk of his face.

"Thanks, it's coming along nicely. It was a mess before I got my hands on it."

"Are you a contractor?"

"Yeah. I'm co-owner of JM Construction."

"Do you have a business card? I recently bought a house in town and will need some help with renovations."

I walk towards the man as I pull out my wallet from my back pocket to grab a card. After I give it to him, I hold out my hand. "I'm Levi Jackson. Give me a call anytime. I'd be happy to talk with you about what you're needing."

"It's nice to meet you, Levi." He peers at me for a moment as he shakes my hand, then grins.

I nod my head.

"I'll give you a call sometime next week when I'm ready to chat."

"Sounds good, man. Have a great one." I head back up the driveway to finish packing my stuff. That was a bit of an odd encounter. People come up to our sites semi-regularly, though, so I shouldn't be surprised. The guy was just a little weird, I guess. With my tools packed up, I get in my truck to head home. As I'm driving, I see the dude walking up the sidewalk. He must live close by.

Shaking off the odd interaction, I call Hope to let her know I'm picking up dinner. She seems lighter over the phone, so hopefully, she's having a better day. I'll have to think of other ways I can keep making her day better. It is one of my favorite things to do, after all.

3 4

HOPE

Laughter filters into the kitchen as I put the final touches on the food. I'm finally hosting the dinner I dreamed about when I first moved into the house. It's still a little unfathomable that I have friends to invite over now, but I'm going with it.

"Hey, love. Are you ready to put everything on the table?" I turn at Levi's voice, his hazel eyes shining with love, as well as a little weariness. His hand lands on my hip, and I sag against him, overwhelmed with his constant support despite my inability to talk to him.

"Yes, everything is ready."

He leans down, pecking me on the lips before taking the bowl of paella to the table. I grab the carafe of wine and follow Levi into the dining room.

Max, Lucy, Cooper, and Quinn meet us at the table. Each one says something about the meal looking amazing. Of course, I beam at the praise, ecstatic my friends are happy.

I wish the others could have come, too, but they were each doing their own thing tonight. It's probably for the best with my nerves still feeling frayed beyond repair.

It's been three days since I got Antony's note, and I

haven't felt a moment of peace since. Which, I'm sure, was the point. His goal was to put me on edge, to scare me so he would have the upper hand, and I let him. I've let him scare me before, but this time, it's different.

I'm not afraid for myself. I'm afraid for Levi. My friends. There's no predicting what Antony will do when he's pissed off. And he's pissed at me. For many, many reasons. All of which he will use as justification for punishing me.

If I step out of line or tell anyone about the threat, I know he'll go after my friends. He'll use the ones closest to me since it would hurt me the most. He won't just threaten them, either. He will actually cause them harm, both physically and mentally. I can't have that on my conscience.

Going to the police is out since there's nothing they can do anyway. I don't have a restraining order in place, believing he'd be in prison for the rest of his life. He hasn't physically attacked me. I don't have proof he sent me the note since it wasn't signed, and Antony isn't stupid enough to leave prints. There's nothing anyone can do.

No one has ever been able to stop him.

If I were stronger, I'd leave. Pack up and head out of town so he'd follow me instead of harming the ones I love, but I'm not. I'm weak. I don't want to leave these people. Not when I've finally brought them into my life.

Like I said, weak.

Selfish.

All the cruel words used against me in my past are true now.

"Lucy, how are you feeling?" Quinn asks. They told everyone about the baby a few weeks ago, which, of course, caused a huge buzz of excitement in town. Everyone kept asking about it when they came into the store. I think the gossiping hens expected me to share the juicy details since I've been hanging out with the group more. They were highly disappointed that I was sticking to my predilection for being close-lipped.

"Pretty good, all things considered. I've had a little bout of morning sickness, but it hasn't been too awful. It's still early, though. I've heard it can get worse."

"I will always be in awe of a woman's ability to grow an actual human being in their bodies," Levi says, shaking his head. "I mean, us guys get off easy. We get to do all the fun stuff while the girls get the shaft."

"Glad you recognize the imbalance, Levi." Quinn laughs.

"Hey, I've always been a huge supporter of worshiping women." He winks.

"Oh, really?" I raise my eyebrow at him. "And what women are you worshiping?"

He starts sputtering. "Not, like, *all* women. You... you're fantastic."

I bust out laughing, unable to hold it in any longer. Quinn and Lucy join in on teasing Levi as he shakes his head.

"How dark is it in that hole you're digging?" Cooper teases.

Levi gently grabs the back of my neck and pulls me to him. "You're evil." He grins, then kisses me.

"You can worship me later to make up for your comments," I whisper.

His eyes heat to a molten gold. "Happily."

I turn back to my friends gathered around my table, laughing and eating the food I made, and a feeling of rightness comes over me. This is everything I've ever wanted in my life. A group of friends who unconditionally love each other and a partner who supports my dreams.

It's beautiful.

I wish I could have it forever.

* * *

"Levi," I grind out through my teeth. His answering chuckle only pushes me further to the edge. Teeth and tongue trace the skin on my inner thighs. I didn't think I could be this close to orgasming when he hasn't even touched me. He's been kissing every inch of my body since our friends left an hour ago. It's maddening.

"I'm only doing what you asked, my love."

"I said *worship*. This is torture."

A swipe of his tongue in the one spot he's not touched this whole time turns my overheated body into an inferno. The quick flicks, the smooth thrusts, it all pushes me over the edge so fast I'm barely able to hang on to his hair to keep me grounded.

Suddenly, I'm flipped over to my stomach while my hips are lifted into the air. Then Levi is filling me with a thrust so deep I can't help but call out his name. The tail end of my orgasm has me so sensitive; every push of his hips has me clenching harder around him. His loud groans surround us as we move in a frenzy. It's overwhelming, heady. Freaking scorching.

He's usually so careful with me, always in complete control, but tonight, I can feel our desperation to be closer to one another. To rebuild the bridge between us that's threatening to fall because of my omission. Every sense of uncertainty is my fault. If I would've been honest from the beginning, I could've shared my fears with Levi instead of being alone with them.

"Fuck, Hope. I'm close," he grates out. He reaches around my body to strum my clit so I'm right there with him.

"Yes, Levi."

My body tightens, the orgasm crashing through me so hard my arms collapse under me. Levi's hands clench on my hips to hold me up as he pumps twice more before groaning through his release.

He collapses on top of me, careful not to crush me. His

hands run softly across my skin, soothing my overheated body. God, I love this man.

"Sorry, I got a little rough there," Levi whispers into my hair.

"I didn't mind. In fact, I really liked it." I turn my body so I can see his face, taking in his beautiful hazel eyes that have told me I'm safe since the first time I saw them. These past few days, I've been so distracted by my fear, I forgot how safe I am when I'm with him. He's my home. My soft landing pad.

He's everything.

"I'm ready, Levi."

His eyes search mine, attempting to read my thoughts. I'm sure he's worried about what I have to say, and if it pertains to him or us. He should be worried, but not about how much I love him.

"We'll talk tomorrow. Right now, I just want to hold you for a little while longer."

"I love you so much," I whisper into his chest.

"I love you, too."

I hope our love will be enough.

3 5

———

LEVI

The garage door rattles as it closes behind me. Once it's shut, I strip down to my underwear next to the kitchen door. My clothes are always a mess after working, so I take them off before going inside to keep the mess out of the house. Plus, Hope checks me out every time I walk into the kitchen, which is a huge boost to my ego.

When I step inside, she's standing by the stove, cooking something that makes my mouth water. She turns, taking in my body as I stalk toward her. "Hi, love."

She grins. "Hi there. How was your day?"

"Not bad. I keep feeling like we're going to be done with the house soon, but then another list of projects comes up, and we're adding another week." I wrap my arms around her waist as she stirs a pot.

"That's what you get for buying a ginormous Victorian house with a million rooms."

"No kidding. What smells so good?"

"Spaghetti with homemade meatballs."

"Damn, woman. I'm going to need to marry you so you can't get away from me."

Hope tenses in my arms then huffs out a laugh. "You're funny. I'm not going anywhere."

Odd. I'm a little surprised by her reaction to me bringing up marriage. Maybe she's not ready to talk about getting married yet. It's understandable, given her history with men hasn't been great.

I decide to let it go for now since we're supposed to talk tonight about why she's been struggling the last few days. I'd prefer to have one serious conversation at a time. "How was your day?"

"Great. Our new kid, Sam, is fantastic. He's picked up on things quickly, even has a decent eye for arrangements."

"Good, maybe you can take some time for yourself now. You haven't read much in the last few weeks."

"I know. I'd like to get back to a normal schedule again."

"Maybe we can plan a trip back to the beach when you're feeling caught up."

Hope beams at me. "Yes! That would be perfect!"

We finish making dinner together, keeping up a constant stream of chatter the whole time. It feels as if things are finally getting back to normal again. We still need to talk, but for now, it's nice not to have the lingering tension.

As we set the breakfast bar to eat, my phone rings, showing *Cooper* on the caller ID.

"Hey, man, what's up?"

"Are you at home?" Cooper's terse tone has the hair on the back of my neck standing on end.

"Yeah, why?"

"If Hope's in the room, can you go somewhere else, please?"

I leave the dining room, moving out of earshot. "I'm in the library. Cooper, what's going on?"

"Look... I'm sorry, but I had a buddy of mine do some digging on Hope. I couldn't let it go, man. It was just too weird."

My blood drains as Cooper continues to tell me the sordid story.

It's so much worse than I could have even imagined.

Every word he says makes my stomach drop further until he's finally done. I hang up the phone, taking slow, deep breaths to keep from losing my mind.

When I feel like I have some semblance of control, I walk back to the kitchen where Hope is sitting at the counter, scrolling on her phone. She looks up, her eyebrows furrowed. "Everything okay?"

I shake my head. "Hope isn't your real name, is it?"

3 6

HOPE

I freeze.

He knows.

He knows everything.

I don't know how he knows or who told him, but by the look on his face, he knows my whole story.

"Answer the question, please," he says, his voice harder than I've ever heard him speak to me.

"My legal name is Hope Langley, but it used to be Rosemary Hope Malatelli."

"And why the fuck wouldn't you tell me something like that?"

Tears well in my eyes. I close them, unable to look at Levi's hurt face. "Because I didn't think you'd be safe if you knew the whole story. I thought I was protecting you."

His long, drawn-out sigh makes me open my eyes again. He's pinching the bridge of his nose, eyes closed, while defeat surrounds him. It's killing me to see him like this. All because I was too afraid to bring my truth to him. If I truly think about it, I wasn't trying to protect him. I was trying to protect myself. I thought if I told him the whole vile truth, he'd walk away. He'd find someone else who wasn't as broken or as sullied as I am.

"Tell me the story. The whole story, leaving nothing out."

"Okay," I whisper.

I follow him into the living room, leaving our dinner plates on the counter. My heart cracks when Levi sits in the chair, forcing me to sit by myself on the couch.

He sits there, looking at me, and I realize he's waiting on me to start.

"Everything I told you was true. There are only two parts of my story that I didn't tell you about: how I got to Sonoma and my relationship with Antony." I pause, hoping for something from Levi. A reassuring nod or an acknowledgment of my stress, but I don't get anything. It's not like I deserve his reassurances; I've broken his trust. Why would he feel the need to make me feel better when I haven't done anything to earn that response?

Clearing my throat, I open myself fully, telling him the entire shameful tale.

"When my dad died, I had this small glimmer of hope where I thought I was finally free. I was already paying all our expenses, and without Dad taking his gambling money, I would've had plenty to live on. I was finally going to get my dream of being on my own. But a couple of days before my dad died, Antony came to the hospital and told me about my dad's gambling debt. Everything we owned was going to Antony to pay for Dad's debt. Cars, furniture, even our apartment, which I later found out Antony owned.

"When Antony told me about how the debt was to be paid, he dropped another bomb on me. I was also a part of the deal. My dad sold me. Like a piece of property. I always knew he didn't care about me, that he was pissed about having to take care of me, but in that moment, I finally understood I was truly nothing to him."

My gaze flicks to Levi. His elbows are resting on his

knees, hands tightly fisted together. His jaw is clenched so hard I can see the strain in his temple. His entire body is rigid with anger. It's making me nervous, but I push through it so I can finish explaining.

"I tried to run. The minute I could, I tried to get out of the city, even though I only had a few thousand dollars. I knew going with Antony would be a prison sentence. But he found me. I had no idea the power Antony had back then, how large his reach truly was.

"When Antony caught me, I was more than his prisoner. I became his wife. By then, I was so defeated by my life, I just did it. I didn't have any fight left in me, so I married him.

"The first few months were okay, mostly verbal abuse and the coffee cup incident, but then I ordered the wrong kind of cigars, and Antony lost it. I'd never been beaten like that before. Afterward, I finally understood what my life was going to be like. There was no escaping my fate, so I did what I could to make the abuse better. I kept silent. I did everything perfectly. Whatever it took to keep the beatings minimal. He started raping me about a year after I moved in. Said it was my payment for all the luxuries I was afforded by being his wife.

"It didn't happen frequently, only when he felt like I was getting too comfortable in his house or a beating I took didn't satisfy him enough. Then, one day, I stumbled upon a meeting Antony was having with his associates. At that point, I still wasn't sure how he earned all of his money. I knew it wasn't legal, but I didn't know any specifics.

"This meeting was about his operation getting thwarted by the cops. Someone was leaking information to police, and his shipments kept getting seized. I later found out he was running both guns and drugs. Sometimes even humans, although I never got evidence to support that.

"I was eavesdropping, trying to learn as much as I could, when Tomas, one of Antony's associates, found me listening in on the meeting. I hightailed it out of the house before he could confront me. And even though I'd left before Antony could punish me, I knew the minute I got home I was going to die. He wouldn't have allowed me to live, knowing I had listened in on his meeting.

"Except, he didn't. Nothing happened when I got home, or even at dinner that evening. I spent three days absolutely terrified of what was going to happen. I'd even gone so far as to accept my death. After living in hell for two years, I figured death would be a welcome reprieve.

"It was only after a full week of waiting for the shoe to drop did I finally realize that Tomas didn't tell Antony anything. From then on, I did my best to keep gathering information as well as actual evidence. It wasn't easy. It took me about a year before I had enough to do anything with.

"A few days before I was going to go to the police with my information, Tomas busted into the house with a SWAT team to arrest Antony along with anyone else in the house, including me. It was a scary few days, but I was able to tell Tomas about all the evidence I had collected over that year.

"Some of it helped solidify their case, but I wasn't able to testify since I was his wife. It was probably for the best since I would've been in danger if I had. After he was sentenced, Tomas helped me change my name, get all new identification, and divorce Antony while he was in prison. Antony tried to stop it, but the courts agreed that he married me under false pretenses, so I was able to get it approved without any contingencies.

Then I hopped on a bus and made my way here. I still had the money I'd saved up before my dad's death, and I found out my grandmother had left me a small inheritance that I was able to access upon my twenty-first birthday, though my dad and Antony kept this information from me. It was enough to set up my shop and get by until I started turning a profit."

I pause but can't yet look at Levi. I can feel the anger radiating off him. I don't want to know if he's angry at me or my story. Probably both if I had to guess. I know he will definitely be angry when I tell him this next part.

"There's one more thing I need to tell you... Tomas called me a while ago to tell me Antony managed to get out of prison on a technicality... I think he's here. In Sonoma."

"Fuck!"

I flinch at Levi's outburst as he starts pacing from the living room to the kitchen, hands constantly running through his hair. I don't know what to do right now. I've never seen him so agitated or angry, and if I'm honest, I'm a little afraid of what's going to happen next.

"Levi," I whisper, needing something from him to tell me what to do.

He stops in his tracks, turning toward me. His wild eyes take me in, and it's as if a balloon pops in his chest as he deflates. He slowly makes his way back toward me, sitting next to me on the couch. He wraps his arm around my shoulder, pulling me into his strong chest.

His lips meet the top of my head, and I feel the same balloon of tension deflate in my own chest.

"I'm going to be honest, I'm super pissed at you right now. You could've trusted me with your story, and it hurts that you didn't. I can understand being scared after everything you've been through, but I thought I'd proven myself to be your safe place, Hope."

"I was going to tell you tonight. I swear. But I'm sorry I didn't trust you earlier. I was scared. I've lived almost my whole life in fear of saying the wrong thing or sharing too much of myself that will be used against me. It's a hard habit to break. I wouldn't be in your arms right now if I didn't trust you, Levi. It's going to take time for me to get used to being able to trust you all the time, no matter what."

Another kiss to the top of my head has me relaxing

further into his arms. "I'm also pissed you didn't tell me you think Antony is here. You've been living in fear these last few days all alone. I could've helped you. We need to call Cooper. Tell him what's going on."

"Fear makes you do a lot of things you wouldn't have thought you'd be capable of doing. I was afraid he'd hurt you or the others. I know he's got eyes everywhere, so he knows who to threaten to get me to do what he wants. I actually feel selfish. If I were stronger, I would've left so Antony couldn't hurt any of you."

"Absolutely not. You're not leaving, and we are telling Cooper whether you want to or not."

I sigh, happy Levi isn't running for the hills, even though he has every right to. "Okay, Levi. We can tell Cooper. Just know, there's nothing he can do. Antony has every right to be here whether we like it or not. I don't have a restraining order on him, and he's out free and clear. He can do whatever he wants."

"Not if I have anything to say about it."

37

ANTONY

That little bitch. She was the reason I went to prison?

I throw the headphones off my head, unable to stomach listening to anything else she has to say. I knew the bug Dominic put in her house last week would prove fruitful, but I had no idea exactly what I would learn from it. It's been all too easy inserting myself into her life without her knowing. Breaking into her house was simple. Having Dominic pose as a regular customer was seamless.

She's become complacent in her life here. I'm happy to remind her of my lessons in expecting the unexpected.

Apparently, I need to learn that lesson, as well. I truly believed the little snitch of a cop was the reason I was put away. I never would've guessed my little mouse would have had the balls to do it herself. I underestimated her, believing she was the meek little girl who wouldn't cause any trouble. I won't make the same mistake again.

I've righted a lot of the wrongs done to me since I've been out.

The rat cop who infiltrated my organization. *Dead.*

The bitch lawyer who couldn't keep me out of prison. *Dead.*

The men who allowed Rosemary to escape after I was sentenced. *Dead.*

And now, it's *his* turn.

He thought he could take what's mine. Taint the good girl she was, undoing all the work I put into making her the woman I wanted.

I'll take care of him. I already have the perfect plan in place. He'll have no idea what's coming, and when he figures it out, it'll be too late.

Fuck, I love revenge.

I'm saving Rosemary for last. With the information I've learned tonight, she'll be the sweetest revenge I've ever taken. I'll make sure she remembers exactly who she belongs to. She won't make the same mistake again. Neither will I. She'll be so broken, she'll have no choice but to be mine forever.

HOPE

With my heart in my throat, I step into the police station. Memories from my past threaten to overtake me as we walk down the sterile, white hallways to Cooper's office. When I did this two years ago, I never thought I'd have to do it again. I thought I was finally free from the terror of my life.

At this point, I don't think I'll ever be free of it. It will always be a part of me. The broken pieces of my soul may fuse back together over time, but the cracks will never go away. They are my story, making up the pieces of who I am. I do not have to be defined by those cracks, but I will carry them with me, knowing I survived.

Finally sharing my whole truth with Levi last night allowed me to lay down all my burdens, giving me a chance to accept the kind of love I deserve after all these years. It's finally time for me to accept who I am now, and who I want to be in the future.

Cooper is sitting behind his desk, a stack of papers on one side, a computer monitor on the other. He's bent over a folder, immersed in whatever is on the paper in front of him.

Levi lightly knocks on his door, signaling our arrival.

"Hey, guys," Cooper says, a small smile at the corner of his mouth. He stands from his chair to give Levi a hug, then steps to me and wraps his arms around my shoulders. I know my body is stiff throughout the hug, but I'm genuinely happy he hasn't started treating me differently despite knowing my history.

Levi told me last night that it was Cooper who figured out what happened to me. I haven't quite decided how I feel about everyone knowing my story. I'm sure Cooper told Quinn, and I could almost guarantee she told the rest of the girls. They share everything with each other.

"So, I'm going to be honest, I know pretty much everything about the trial as well as who you were before you came to Sonoma. I feel a little guilty about not letting you share your story with us yourself, but after what happened with Quinn last year, I couldn't take any chances."

"I totally understand. I should've been honest earlier, but living your life in fear tends to do some damage." I genuinely do understand why Cooper did what he did. Quinn was kidnapped and almost killed last year. Cooper barely found her in time, otherwise, she would have died from blood loss.

"With that in mind, you need to know that Antony is probably in town. I don't have solid proof, but I got this note from him a few days ago." I hand Cooper the note I received along with the envelope. Levi put it in a ziplock bag so we'd keep it safe. He even wore gloves while he did it.

Cooper reads the note and swears. "Why didn't you say anything before now?"

"Fear mostly. I also know there's nothing you can do other than keep an eye out. I don't have a restraining order against him. He's out of prison free and clear and has every right to be here."

"Does he know you were the one to give the police evidence?"

"No. I provided the evidence I'd collected over the years,

but being his wife, they didn't want to risk a mistrial if I testified. Seems like him going free couldn't have been avoided, apparently."

"Is there any other reason he'd be here to harm you? If he doesn't know you were the reason he went to prison, I don't understand why he'd be here in the first place."

I thought Cooper knew everything already. I guess his reports didn't mention the abuse, which makes sense. It was never a part of the trial, so there's no reason Cooper would know about it.

Levi grabs my hand, giving it a reassuring squeeze. He knows how hard it'll be for me to tell Cooper my whole story. The odd thing is, I'm not as nervous about telling him as you'd think I would be. I don't know if it's Levi's love or my healing that is making me feel like this. Probably both if I had to guess.

"Antony abused me," I say finally. "The trifecta, actually. Verbally, physically, and sexually." I manage to keep Cooper's eye contact, even though his whole demeanor goes hard in anger. His jaw clenches along with his hands. "It wasn't part of the trial because I didn't want it to be. I knew if he was brought up on domestic abuse charges, I would have had to testify in person, and I was not in a place where I could do that. I also didn't have proof of the abuse, so it likely would've ended in a he said, she said situation that I was not strong enough to deal with at the time. I knew he'd be going away for running drugs and guns, so that was enough for me. I didn't expect him to get out of prison on a technicality."

"Hope... I don't have the right words to tell you how sorry I am for what you've been through. I will never under-stand what motivates people to hurt others so sadistically." Cooper's words are quiet but vehement. His response makes me even more grateful to be able to call this man a friend.

Maybe I'll be able to build up the courage to tell the girls my story, as well.

"How can we catch this bastard?" Levi asks, attempting to move the focus away from what I went through. I squeeze his hand in thanks.

"For starters, Hope, you don't go anywhere by yourself. I want someone with you at all times."

"I can take you to and from work. Since you've got both Claire and Sam at the shop now, you should be covered until I can come pick you up," Levi offers.

I can only nod my head at the overwhelming display of protection between these two men.

"The cameras at Quinn's rental house are still up but not running, so we can start there. I'd like to set up a couple at your store, too. One covering the front door, the other covering the alleyway in the back. I can have those set up today when we get done here."

"And if he contacts her again?" Levi asks.

"The only thing we can do at this point is file for a restraining order. Other than that, Hope is right. There's not much else we can do." Cooper looks at me. "Do you have any questions or anything else we need to talk about?"

"I don't think so, but I'm also a little overwhelmed right now."

Cooper smiles at me and nods his head. He and Levi finalize the rest of the protection detail while I attempt to keep up. There are entirely too many thoughts swirling in my head right now. Both positive and negative.

I'm realizing how incredible my life has become in such a short time. I have friends, people who love me enough to want to do whatever they can to protect me. I have a boyfriend who still loves me despite my keeping a ginormous secret from him.

I also have a vindictive, psycho ex-husband out to get me.

Jesus. I was so close to having everything I've ever wanted, and Antony had to ruin it. Again.

Tuning back into the conversation, I realize they're wrapping things up. "Cooper, before we go, I need you to know, there's nothing Antony won't do to get his way. He's a sociopath capable of anything. Please keep your eyes out, and tell Quinn to be safe. I don't know what he'll do to get me back in his clutches, but I wouldn't put it past him to use those closest to me to get what he wants."

Cooper looks at me for a moment, then nods his head. "We'll find him, Hope. I promise."

Levi leads me out of Cooper's office, still holding my hand in his. Despite knowing we're doing everything we can to protect ourselves, there's still a pit in my stomach. A feeling of disquiet settles in my gut, telling me something bad is about to happen.

Something we won't see coming.

39

LEVI

The early morning light peeks through the window, slowly waking me up. The past two days have been tough. With Hope's confession and talking with Cooper, I feel mentally and emotionally drained.

I look over at Hope, who's sleeping peacefully for the first time in a week. She didn't have a single nightmare last night when most of the past week she's either been restless or waking up in a panic. I'm still hurt that she didn't trust me enough to tell me her full story. After hearing what happened to her, it makes sense, but it doesn't stop the hurt from being there.

I know I need to have patience and give her time to adjust to having a safe, loving relationship. I have to keep reminding myself it's only been a couple of months. With how fast our relationship moved forward, I forgot where we started.

And I'm willing to wait. I've always been willing to wait. I love her with everything I have.

She's it for me.

Hope starts to stir, her eyes fluttering open, vulnerability spearing me as she takes me in.

"Good morning, love."

Hope smiles, her eyes shining with love. I think this is the first time she's seemed completely open to me. As if there's nothing standing in her way anymore. Nothing blocking her from fully accepting me into her life. "Good morning."

I run my thumb across her cheek, wishing we could stay in bed for the rest of the day. "I don't want to go to work today. Can we stay right here all day instead?"

"I would love nothing more, but I have The Boys & Girls Club event to finish today."

"Damn responsibilities."

Hope grins. "You still wanna take me to the beach?"

"Fuck yes. Plus, it'll be warm enough to get you in a bikini." I smirk.

Hope laughs at me, shaking her head. "If you take me to the beach, I'll wear a bikini for you."

"On it." I lean over to grab my cell phone from the nightstand. "I've got this weekend available. Shall I book it?"

Giggling, Hope grabs my phone from my hands, then leans in for a kiss. "Crazy man. I didn't mean *this* weekend. But soon."

"Soon." I kiss her deeply. Even with the stress of Antony breathing down our necks, I know we'll be okay. Whatever comes our way, we'll figure it out in the end.

Groaning, I get out of bed to start my day with Hope following closely behind. Side-by-side, we go through our routines of getting ready. There's a deeper feeling of connection this morning than there has ever been, which makes me incredibly happy. If only this mess with Hope's ex could be sorted out, we'd be home free. I'm ready to explore what we could be without any secrets between us.

"Have I ever told you how much I love those black jeans you wear?" I ask, watching Hope go through her clothes.

"These?" She holds up the exact pair I'm talking about. She's standing in the closet in nothing but her bra and panties, and it's taking a lot of effort not to throw her on the bed and have my way with her.

"Yep. Your ass looks fantastic in them."

Hope looks at me with a raised eyebrow and a smirk. "You're sassy this morning."

"I love you this morning. I'm also having a hard time concentrating on anything else but you in your underwear right now." My gaze roams over her body for the millionth time.

"Eyes up here, mister."

"No thanks. I'm good right now."

Laughing, Hope rolls her eyes as she puts on the black jeans. Score one for me.

I can't wait to take those off her tonight.

* * *

THE SPACE I'm in is dark and small. I wasn't sure I'd be able to fit, but I squeezed my wide-ass shoulders into it for one reason only...

...And here it comes.

"Boo!"

"Fuck!" Michael shouts, tossing his paintbrush into the air.

I stumble out of my hiding place, laughing with the other guys.

"I hate you all," Michael grumbles, bending over to grab the paintbrush off the floor. "How did you even fit your fat ass in there?"

"It wasn't easy but so worth it." I wink.

"One of these days, I'm going to get you back, and you're going to be pissed."

"Nah, you shouldn't dish it out if you can't take it. Bring your A-game, bro."

Shaking his head, he goes back to work. I follow behind

him to finish installing the vanity in one of the guest bathrooms upstairs. There are so many rooms in this house, it's a bit ridiculous.

I wonder if Hope will want a big family or a small one. She may not want a family at all. We haven't talked about it. Most of our time has been spent getting comfortable with each other. Even though I know she's the one for me, I don't want to push her too quickly. I thought giving her some time to adjust to me first was the right way to start our relationship.

Since she hasn't seen the house in a while, maybe I can plan a big reveal for her, see if she'd want to move in when it's finally ready. At this point, I'd be surprised if she didn't, but you never know. She may want to keep her own space for a while longer.

With Hope firmly on my mind, I finish outfitting the bathroom, happy with the progress we've made today. Despite the never-ending list, we're in the home stretch now.

I go downstairs, where the rest of the guys are working on the kitchen. They're putting up the gray subway tile backsplash, which looks so good against the white cabinets. I double-check that the pallets of wood came in for the back deck, then after making my final rounds through the house, I tell everyone they can knock off for the day.

I send a quick text to Hope, letting her know I'll be heading her way in a little bit. The guys all head out while I finish cleaning up my tools, prepping things for tomorrow. I'm ready to get home and stay in for a while. Maybe put on a movie for the sole purpose of having a make-out session with Hope like we're teenagers.

The last couple of days have taken their toll on me. I know they've been even harder on Hope, especially knowing exactly why she's been so stressed. I might see if I can sweet talk her into another bath tonight.

A noise behind me makes me turn, thinking one of the guys forgot something.

The punch comes out of nowhere, sending me flying backward.

Fuck, that hurt.

"That was more satisfying than I expected it to be."

Despite the pain, I attempt to open my eyes to figure out who hit me. The voice sounds oddly familiar, but I can't place it. I stand while my eyes focus. The guy who stopped by the other day is standing in front of me, holding a crowbar in his hand.

"I've imagined this moment many times over the last couple of weeks. It's been incredibly difficult to wait for the right moment to enact my plan."

"Who are you?" I ask, scanning the room for any weapon of my own. He timed it perfectly so I don't have any of my tools lying out.

"Oh, right, introductions are in order. I'm Antony Malatelli, Hope's husband."

Fuck. I shook this guy's hand. I had the opportunity to end him and never even knew it.

"I believe you mean *ex*-husband."

"Not so much. You see, the divorce was contingent upon my conviction. Seeing as how I'm a free man... She's. Still. Mine."

"Fuck you." Lying asshole. There were no contingencies in the divorce; I saw the paperwork when Hope gave it all to Cooper. His lawyer probably lied to him so it wouldn't create any bigger issues. Now it's time to show Lord Fuckwad he can't have whatever he wants.

Antony's eyes harden, evil glinting bright in them. He comes at me with the crowbar, and I snatch a scrap piece of wood off the floor to use as a shield. His arm swings down, thunking against the wood so hard the vibrations move up my arm. The wood is too cumbersome to continue holding, so I throw it hard at Antony.

He stumbles backward with the weight, and I use the momentum to gain the advantage. Landing two punches to his gut, he goes down hard. I get a third punch to his face before he responds with the crowbar still in his hand.

It lands hard on my ribs with an audible crack. I grit my teeth against the pain spreading through my entire upper body. I try to take the crowbar from him before he can get any other hits in with it. We grapple across the floor, both of us trying to overpower the other.

A kick to my thigh makes me lose my footing, allowing Antony the upper hand. My fists fly in an effort to throw him off, but he still has control of the crowbar. A blow glances off my shoulder, then my rib cage again. Both effectively paralyze me.

The blows keep raining down on me until all I can see is Antony's face, contorted with a rage I've never seen on anyone before. It's demonic.

"She. Is. Mine!" he screams, striking me with each word. He hits me twice more before everything mercifully goes black.

40

HOPE

"Then you'll put a little of the greenery in at a time, layering it with the flowers so they flow cohesively." I look over at Sam's arrangement, proud of how quickly he's picked up putting bouquets together.

"Can I add some of the garden roses to this one?"

"That would look beautiful, Sam. Perfect idea."

He grabs a few stems of the pink garden roses, placing them carefully into his arrangement. He really is a natural at this. I'm so glad he's stayed on with us. Part-time employees can be a little flaky when they start working, especially teenagers. Sam has been nothing but eager to work the hours, soaking up everything I teach him like a sponge. He's surprised me at every turn. I can't wait to see what else he's able to do.

Our next task will be learning how to make floral arrangements for events, which will take a huge load off my shoulders if he can help me. Claire loves working in the shop, but making the arrangements is not her strong suit. She's my plant person, taking care of all our potted babies. She makes sure they're strong and healthy when they go to their new homes.

Sam puts the final touches on his bouquet, wrapping it in paper, then tying it with a ribbon. "What do you think?" he asks, a little hint of worry in his voice as he looks at me expectantly.

"I have thoughts, but I want to know what you think first."

He takes a moment to look at the flowers and then back at me. "I think it's a little unbalanced on this side. Next time, I'll account for the shift in movement when I tie the ribbon."

I grin at him. "I was going to say the exact same thing. Even with the shift, it's beautiful, but when you nail the movement next time, it'll be gorgeous. The fact that you noticed and identified the problem shows how incredible your eye is, Sam. You've got a gift."

A hint of pink shines in Sam's cheeks as he smiles at me.

My phone beeps on the counter, and I lean over to read what the message says.

Levi: Cleaning up now, should be on my way to you in about twenty.

Me: Perfect. I love you.

I don't immediately get a response, so I set my phone down, turning back to Sam, who is cleaning up the random leaves on the counter. "Why don't you take your arrangement home to your momma? It'll be your bonus for working so hard today."

"She'll love it. Thanks, Hope."

"Get out of here, kid. Levi will be here in a few to pick me up."

"Okay. I'll see you tomorrow."

"See you!"

I walk to the front door, turn the deadbolt, and flip the sign to say *Closed*. It's about a half hour early, but with Levi picking me up soon, I want to have time to get some paperwork finished. After the door is locked, I head back to my office and spend a few minutes cleaning up until my desk is visible again. Then I get started on ordering inventory, updating my budget spreadsheets, and any other task on my to-do list I have yet to complete. It's monotonous and a total time suck.

Coming out of the zone I'd fallen into, I realize it's been an hour since Levi texted me.

Looking through the newly made mess on my desk, I try to find my phone. It's not here, so it's probably still out on the counter in the shop. I step out of my office and directly into a wall of chest. Hands wrap around my arms to steady me before I fall over. I look up, expecting to see Levi, when steely blue eyes peer down at me.

My entire body freezes.

Antony's smile is vile, predatory, as he peers down at me. He has a black eye and a split lip, which only adds to the menacing look. "Hello, Rosemary. Did you miss me? I sure missed you despite your disobedience."

"I'm not alone. Levi will be here any minute."

"I hate to break the news to you like this, but Levi is currently indisposed. Forever."

The blood drains from my face, sheer terror hitting me for the first time since Antony grabbed hold of me. "What?" I whisper.

"Well, I couldn't let the little bastard continue breathing when he'd stolen what was mine. It's time to go now. We have places we need to be."

Levi's dead?

I don't... I can't... *No.*

"Oh, yes, he very much is, my dear. Get over it."

I didn't know I'd spoken those words out loud, but to hear them confirmed is unbearable. How can I live without the love of my life? I know with everything in me that Levi was the one for me. He was everything I've ever wanted in a partner.

Loving. Happy. Safe. There is no life without him. There's no way I can be strong enough to survive life with Antony again. Especially knowing the one person who meant everything to me is no longer in this world.

I can't do this.

It's then I notice Antony has dragged me out of my store toward a waiting car in the alleyway.

"No! I won't go with you!" I scream, dropping my body weight in an attempt to break Antony's vice grip around my arm. For a moment, his grasp slips, and I push against the car, running down the alleyway.

Hope blooms in my chest as I get further away until my hair is yanked, pulling my body backward. Antony drags me back to the car by my hair. I have to hold on to the strands to alleviate the pain. I'm unceremoniously thrown into the back seat of the car, then tied to the passenger seat headrest by my hands. The zip ties are entirely too tight, cutting off the circulation in my hands quickly.

Antony gets into the driver's seat, taking a moment to compose himself. "We will discuss your insolent behavior when we reach our destination. Until then, I don't want to hear a sound out of your bitch mouth. Understand?"

I remain silent, knowing it's the only answer he wants. He nods when my silence continues, then starts the car. We drive for several minutes before pulling into the driveway of a house I've never seen before. I have no idea where we are, only that we're on the edge of Sonoma.

In the span of about ten minutes, Antony is out of the car, in the house, and back again with a duffle bag in hand. When he throws the bag in the trunk, I fully understand the seriousness of the situation. We aren't staying in Sonoma. He'll take me as far away as possible so there will be no possibility for me to escape.

I will be a prisoner for the rest of my life if I don't fight him.

But what's the point of fighting for my life if the one I love can't share it with me?

No.

Levi would yell at me for those thoughts.

He wouldn't allow me to become a shell of myself again, even if he's not here to see it.

When Antony climbs back into the driver's seat, he doesn't even spare me a glance. It's disconcerting knowing exactly how angry he is with me. His body is rippling with it. I've never seen him quite at this level before. What's worse is if he succeeds in taking me away, he will do everything it takes to break me. I know it deep within my soul.

If we get to where we're going, I will not survive this.

We back out of the driveway, taking roads that lead us to the highway. My mind is swirling with thoughts of what's going to happen next. I have no idea what to do or how to get out of this situation. All I know is if we make it to our final destination, I will die there.

The silence stretches out as we get onto the highway, my fear ratcheting up higher the further we get away from Sonoma. I'm going to have to do something soon if I want to survive.

Antony's phone rings, disrupting the rising tension. When he answers, I let out a deep breath, feeling like I can relax for a minute while he's distracted by his conversation. I don't even listen to what he's saying. It doesn't matter at this point.

I look down at my aching hands, already white from lack of blood flow, and notice the headrest has been lifted to its highest setting. If I can lift the bar a smidge further, I could pop the headrest out of its track, freeing my hands from being immobile.

I quickly glance at Antony, his right hand is holding his phone to his ear, blocking his peripheral vision. Looking back at my hands, I slowly shift so I can push the button to lift the headrest.

My heart is pounding in my ears, and I do my best not to hurry. I don't want to draw attention, but I also have no idea how long his conversation will last. Despite having limited range, I'm able to squeeze the bar in between my thumb and forefinger, pulling up until the end of the headrest comes out of the track.

I freeze. If I move too quickly, Antony will notice what I'm doing, phone call or not. Silently, I take another breath, forcing myself to listen to the call. If he's close to being done, I will either need to move lightning fast or wait for the right moment.

"I don't give a fuck what happened, Dominic. Fix it."

I wait, hands throbbing from the tension they're under.

The silence continues as Antony listens to the other person on the phone.

"I want to know the minute it's done." A pause. "What are you doing about the brother?"

With confirmation his conversation isn't ending, I slowly move the headrest high enough for the zip tie to slide underneath. It's excruciating as my hands contort, moving as slowly as possible to not draw attention to myself. I can't risk being caught. There's too much at stake for the pain to even matter right now.

The tie clears the bar, and I grit my teeth to keep from cheering out loud. My gaze flicks to Antony; his phone call is wrapping up now. I'm not sure what my plan is since my hands are still bound together, but with them free of the headrest, I've got a better shot at escaping.

I keep my hands around the headrest to make it seem as if

they're still attached. I need a minute to figure out what to do next.

Antony ends his call, placing the phone in the cupholder. "Incompetent idiots. I swear they would be in jail without me telling them what to do." Antony continues venting his annoyance with his minions, lamenting about how the men he trusted were all in prison now.

While he rants, I take in my surroundings. Fields are on either side of the highway, and there are very few cars on the road. I could grab the steering wheel, but the potential for Antony to overpower me before the car stops is high. I don't have a seatbelt on, so no matter what I do, I'll likely be injured beyond repair. In the end, it would be better than what Antony is capable of doing to me.

He's finally silent, visibly relaxing into his seat as he settles in for the drive. The movement has an idea forming in my head.

It's insane.

Probably deadly.

But it's the only choice I have that gives me any chance to survive.

I can do this.

Taking a deep breath, I spring over the console to grab the e-brake, pulling back as hard as I can. The abrupt movement causes Antony to flinch. The second he releases the steering wheel, the car goes sideways, flipping over the guardrail.

My body flies into the ceiling with a sickening crunch, then lands on the floorboard of the back seat. Fire races down my arms, into my shoulder, and through my chest. With my hands still hooked around the handle of the e-brake, my chest is stretched across the center console, pulling my shoulders further out of place.

Disoriented, I attempt to plant my feet on the floor of the car. Everything screams at me to stop moving, but I don't have a choice. I have to get out of here. Antony hasn't made a noise since we crashed. I don't know if he's dead or just knocked out. I'm not going to take any chances of him waking up and finding me here.

I grit my teeth, lifting my arms over the handle of the e-brake. Blackness swirls in my vision as pain screams through me.

Push through it, Hope. You can do this.

Once my arms are clear, I open the door, pushing myself out of the car. I stumble to the ground, the tall weeds in the ditch surrounding my body. I don't think I can get up. My entire body feels broken.

You can't stay here.

Growling, I force my body to move. I get to my knees, holding my bound hands to my chest in an effort to contain the pain. When I plant my foot on the ground, I push my weight up to stand.

My vision swims, making it seem as if a passing car has stopped. The road is so far away. *I'll never make it.*

I'm sorry, Levi. I tried. I tried so fucking hard to survive. To be strong. For you.

I love you.

41

HOPE

Pain.

It's the only thing I can feel at this point. My entire body is burning with it.

Instead of dying on the side of the road, I was brought to the hospital. Turns out, I wasn't hallucinating the car on the side of the road like I thought.

A man saw the crash and pulled over to help. The nurse told me I was rushed to the hospital, taken for scans, then immediately went into surgery when my lung collapsed.

That was four days ago.

Since surgery, I've been in and out of consciousness because of the pain. They've been heavily sedating me so I can heal. I've got cracked ribs, a fractured spine, faulty lungs, a broken collarbone, and a shoulder squarely back in place now.

My lungs have finally stabilized, so they're working on reducing my pain medication. They need me to be lucid so I can answer some questions. I guess they called the police because my hands were zip-tied together, but I haven't been awake long enough to give them any sort of information about what happened.

"Hope, the police are here. Are you ready to answer some questions?" my nurse, Jennifer, asks as she checks my blood pressure.

"I guess so. How much longer until my next round of meds?"

"About fifteen minutes."

I groan. Fifteen minutes is going to feel like a year with how bad my body hurts.

Jennifer gently pats my arm. "I'll send the officers in."

About thirty seconds after she leaves, Cooper bursts into my room with another officer hot on his heels, their navy blue uniforms looking very official. "Fuck, Hope. Are you okay? I've been trying to get in to see you for days, but since I'm not family, they wouldn't let me."

Looking at Cooper is almost as painful as my physical injuries. He looks so much like Levi. God, what am I going to do without him?

Tears form in my eyes. I have to close them so they don't fall. I can't afford to fall apart right now. There are too many things I need to do before I'm allowed to break.

"What happened?" Cooper's voice makes me open my eyes again, but I don't look at him. I can't.

Keeping my eyes on the sheets covering my body, I tell Cooper what I can remember. "I was waiting on..." My words freeze in my throat. I can't even say his name. "I was waiting to be picked up from the shop when Antony grabbed me. He forced me out the back door and to the car waiting in the alleyway." Cooper grabs the chair in my room and sits. The other officer remains standing by the door.

"I tried to run, but he caught me and dragged me back to the car by my hair. When he shoved me in the backseat, he tied my hands to the headrest with zip ties. We drove to a house on the edge of town, where he packed up his stuff. He was only gone for maybe ten minutes, then we got on the highway.

"I had no idea where we were going, Antony didn't say much to me after he grabbed me, but I knew I wouldn't survive if we made it to the destination. He got a phone call while he was driving, which was enough of a distraction for me to release the zip tie from the headrest. Once my hands were free, I grabbed the emergency brake, which made Antony lose control of the car.

"I don't remember much after that other than falling from the car once it had stopped moving. Then I woke up here."

"Jesus, Hope." I glance at Cooper as he runs his hands down his face. "I'm so sorry this happened to you."

I stay silent. I should be used to life constantly letting me down at this point. It's never once been kind to me.

"Antony survived the crash. He's here in the hospital, healing before he goes to trial. We'll try him for kidnapping and aggravated assault."

"Will I have to testify?"

"More than likely, yes. Will that be okay?"

"Sure. Maybe this time, he'll stay in prison."

"I'll make sure of it." Steel laces through Cooper's words.

Jennifer flounces into the room, her blonde ponytail bouncing around. She gives a quick glance to Cooper and the other officer whose name I never got, then turns to me. "Okay, Hope. Time for meds. You've also got a waiting room full of visitors here. Would it be okay if they came to say hello?"

"Sure," I whisper as she finally administers my next dose. I don't care who comes into my room at this point as long as the pain goes away. I close my eyes, hoping for the meds to kick in quickly. My hand is squeezed, then footsteps tap across the room.

Finally, silence.

As the meds kick in, my body relaxes, allowing me to drift off to sleep.

My dreams are almost as torturous as being awake.

Levi's scent of cinnamon and home floats through my senses.

His voice echoes through my mind with words of love and apologies.

It's almost unbearable because I know when I wake up, he won't actually be here.

* * *

MY EYES FLICKER OPEN, and Jennifer's smiling face comes into view. "Hey, sunshine."

Her cheery demeanor has a small smile curling at my lips. I go to move my hand when I realize it's being held. I look over and blink several times. "Jennifer, am I asleep? Am I really seeing who I think I'm seeing?"

"Oh, honey, he's real. And I'm *real* jealous."

Levi's grin is a little lopsided with his swollen face. He's sitting right next to me, clear as day, holding my hand.

"Hi, love."

Tears fall so fast, I can barely see Levi anymore. "You're alive?"

"Of course, I'm alive. I couldn't let that bastard keep us apart."

It's then that I finally break.

Every fear, hurt, and heartbreak come pouring out as Levi's arms wrap around me, pulling me into his hard chest. Surrounded by his strength, I let all my pieces fall. The ones I've been holding on to so tightly, afraid they'd shatter beyond repair if I let them go. I give them all to Levi as he holds me in his arms.

"You're safe now. I'll always keep you safe," he whispers into my hair.

I'm not sure how long we stay embraced, it could've been minutes or hours, but eventually, I get myself together. Levi grabs the box of Kleenex on the rolling tray in my room,

247

tipping it toward me. When I mop up my face, I groan at the aches in my body. While the prolonged hug was necessary for my mental health, it was not so great for my bruised and battered body.

"What happened to you? Antony told me you died."

"He was definitely angry enough to kill me but obviously didn't succeed. He beat the shit out of me with a crowbar. Broke several ribs, gave me a concussion, and broke my leg." He holds up his leg encased in a cast. "Michael ended up finding me passed out on the floor. He'd left his phone at the house and called an ambulance when he realized what happened. If I had to guess, Antony's goal was not to actually kill me but to make sure I was incapacitated so he'd have time to get you out of Sonoma. I don't think he planned on anyone finding me until morning."

"But you're okay? You're going to be okay?"

"Yes, love." He kisses me again, settling the panic in my gut.

"I thought my world was going to end when he told me he killed you. I knew what evil he was capable of, so I believed him. There was a moment, in the car, when I thought it would be easier to give up. To let Antony do whatever he wanted to me because the love of my life was gone. I knew I would never find another person to share my life with because the one I wanted had died.

"Then a voice in my head said you'd be pissed at me for thinking that way, for being okay with giving up. That's when I started planning my escape."

"Fuck, Hope. You're amazing. And I definitely would've been pissed at you." Levi presses his forehead to mine. "You're the strongest person I've ever met. I will forever be in awe of the incredible woman you are."

A knock on the door interrupts our moment as a whole slew of people come into my room. Alice and Rob, as well as

Quinn, Lucy, Sara, Natalie, and Megan. The girls crowd around my bed as Alice comes to my other side.

"Oh, my darling Hope. I'm so glad you're okay." She tucks a piece of my hair behind my ear, then gently squeezes my hand. Her fussing over me has tears burning behind my eyes. It's been a long time since I was mothered.

"Not sure how long you're going to be here, but I brought you one of my favorites just in case it takes a few days." Sara grins, holding up a paperback book. Based on the handsome face on the cover, I think I'll like it just fine.

They all want updates on how I'm doing and what happened with Antony. It sounds like Cooper filled them in on some of it but not everything. Their questions are overwhelming, but it's surprisingly nice to have people worrying over me. I've been looking out for myself for so long that I forgot what this feels like.

When I start to get tired, Levi kicks everyone out of the room so I can rest. They all assure me they'll be back tomorrow and that everything at the shop is being handled by Claire, Sam, and Alice. I'm more grateful for these people than I ever thought possible.

The minute the door closes, Levi presses his lips against mine in a beautifully tender kiss. All the tension of the past several days melts from my body. I didn't think I'd ever get to have this again. This feeling of utter contentment. Now that I have it back, I'm determined to do whatever it takes to keep it.

Because I deserve this feeling. After everything, I deserve an all-consuming love. One where my partner is my equal, my confidant, and my best friend.

And Levi is all three.

LEVI

"I'm starving," Hope groans from my right. My stomach rumbles right after, which makes us both laugh.

"Apparently, I am, too." I reach out for her hand. We're cuddled up on the couch at her house, watching mindless tv. "Should we go find something to eat?"

"Yeah. I haven't eaten anything all day. I'm going to get hangry in a minute."

We both continue sitting on the couch, not moving.

"Well, we're getting nowhere fast," I huff, glancing over at Hope.

"I don't think I can move. We've been sitting for too long, and now, I'm stiff."

"You always make me stiff." I wink.

Hope's laughter fills me with so much love. It took three days after I was allowed to see her before she was discharged from the hospital. And while being home has been great, we've had a rough week all around. Both of us are still laid up from our injuries, more her than me, now. The only thing keeping me down is my broken leg. My cast goes all the way up to my thigh, making my coordination non-existent.

Hope has been battling her nightmares again. Waking up

screaming, fighting the ghosts of her past, while her body is pushed past its limits. She wakes up exhausted, unable to go back to sleep because she's in so much pain. Healing has been rough in both mind and body.

It's been torture watching her struggle night after night. I've even sat in on some of her therapy sessions to learn what I can do to help her move forward. At this point, it's just going to take time. Time for her mind to understand she's no longer in danger. That she's safe here with me.

Groaning, I sit up to kiss Hope on the forehead, then move to stand. "Stay there, love. I'll scrounge us up some snacks."

Using my crutches, I hobble into the kitchen. Balancing on one leg, I pull together some fruit, crackers, and pre-sliced cheese. Then, finding some salami, I add it to the tray, still in the package. There's no way I'm opening that beast of a package while trying to balance on one foot.

"Shit."

"What? What's wrong?" Hope calls from the living room.

"I made a fucking amazing snack, but I'm just now realizing, I can't carry it into the living room."

The tinkle of Hope's laugh has me turning around. Despite the dark circles, she's radiant right now with a wide grin lighting up her dark eyes. It's in these moments I know we'll be okay. One day, this horrible nightmare will be behind us.

Before I can say anything else, my phone starts ringing on the counter. I'm glad I'm already up, otherwise, I wouldn't have answered it.

"Hello."

"Hey, Levi! You guys up and moving okay today?" Cooper asks. He and Quinn have been checking on us regularly. Between them and Mom, we'll have frozen meals for the next six months.

"Yeah, we're doing okay today."

"Good. I have a surprise for you. Think you guys are up for a field trip?"

"Let me ask Hope." I mute the phone, then look at Hope. She's already waiting for me to ask. "Cooper wants to know if you're up for a field trip. He said they have a surprise for us."

"I could use some fresh air."

I smile, knowing that if she's ready to leave the house, we've taken another step in the right direction of healing. Right after she got out of the hospital, she couldn't even stand to go out on the patio. Luckily, Mom, Claire, and Sam have kept up with the shop so Hope hasn't had to worry about it. Even the girls have helped out some despite being horrible at creating arrangements. Quinn sent me the photo evidence, which ended up giving Hope a good laugh.

I unmute the phone to tell Cooper we're up for whatever it is they've got planned. After I hang up, I crutch my way back to the living room. When I sit down, I turn to Hope. "They'll be here in an hour. Want to go eat the snack I made and then get dressed?"

"Sure."

I lean in closer to Hope, needing the connection. I almost lost her. She could've been killed, and I have no idea what I would've done. She's everything I've ever wanted. And I could've lost her.

Cupping the back of her head, I pull her closer to me so our foreheads touch. "I love you so much, Hope. You have every part of me in your hands. I want nothing more than to give you my everything, forever."

"Levi," she whispers. My lips cover hers before she can say anything else. Our kisses are slow, loving. Building our foundation again after it's been cracked. Strengthening our love so we can move forward. It's creating something new from the broken pieces, something beautiful.

When we pull back, I see all the love in my eyes reflecting back at me. Despite the darkness we've had to face, we've made it through. Together.

HOPE

Quinn's car pulls into the driveway exactly an hour after Cooper called. Nerves pull at my muscles, making me clench my fists to keep them from shaking. This is the first time I'll be leaving the safety of the house since I got out of the hospital a week ago.

I feel like a coward. It's infuriating how much Antony's attack truly affected me. I was so close to being the happy, carefree woman I've always wanted to be. Now, it feels as if I've gone so far backward, I'll never be able to catch up again.

Levi says he's seen so much growth in me in these past few days alone. I guess I should trust him when he says I'll get there. It's hard to see so far ahead when you're stuck in the muck and mire of your trauma.

"Ready, love?" Levi asks from beside me.

I nod my head, knowing the words won't move past the lump of fear in my throat. Levi holds his hand out to me, and I gladly take his offered comfort. He's the best man I've ever known. I'm so grateful for his patience and constant love.

He lets go to crutch his way out the front door. I follow close behind, worried he's going to fall over. The entire time he's had these crutches, I've worried about him hurting himself even more. He has no patience for how slow he has to move with them, which usually leads to him pushing himself to do things he shouldn't do. Like putting weight on his leg when he gets annoyed about holding the crutch.

"Hi, guys!" Quinn smiles big at me. The glint in her eyes has me frowning. Levi said they have a surprise for us, but I have no idea what it could possibly be.

"Hey, sis," Levi says, leaning in to kiss Quinn on the cheek. I help Levi into the car, a scowl on his face the entire time. He hates needing my help to do things. Says he wants to be the one helping me instead. I usually kiss the scowl off his face, which always makes him smile.

Once I'm also in the car, Cooper drives us through town. It's a beautiful, sunny day, the warm sunshine reminding me of all the life surrounding me. As we drive down Main Street, I vow to start living my life again. Even when I'm scared or my anxiety is overwhelming me, I want to remember how beautiful this life I've built for myself truly is.

"Why are we going to the house? I'm not going to be able to get around all the shit on the floor," Levi grumps. That's been another thing he's struggled to deal with. He hasn't been able to work on the house or any other project his company has lined up right now. It'll be several more weeks before he'll be able to get back to work, which is going to be interesting.

"Untwist your panties; you'll be fine," Cooper says. He pulls into the driveway of Levi's beautiful Victorian home. I love this place. It's everything I've ever dreamed a home could be. I've secretly been dreaming of living in this house with Levi. Maybe even having a family here one day.

Everyone gets out of the car, Cooper helping Levi with his crutches. We walk up the sidewalk to the front door, Levi's grumpy face in full force as he struggles up the front steps. He's so freaking cute.

I try to hide my smile when he glances at me, but it's too

big to conceal. His scowl melts to a fake one as he glares at me.

"Are you laughing at your struggling boyfriend?"

"No," I say innocently. "I'm laughing at your adorable scowling face."

Levi's laugh booms from his chest. Being the one to turn his annoyance into happiness makes me want to dance. I love getting to do those things for him. Even though they're small, I feel as if it's my way of thanking him for all the things he's done for me.

Cooper opens the front door, then gestures for us to enter before him. The minute Levi and I step over the threshold, I gasp. I knew Levi was getting close to being done, but I had no idea it was finished.

I look over at Levi, who seems just as surprised as I am. "What the shit?"

Laughing, I take in the entire space. Glass French doors encase the office to the left and another set of French doors leads to the office on the right in the turret. The rest of the house is wide open to the family room, kitchen, and dining room. The whole place is gleaming with new paint, shiny wood floors, and beautiful light fixtures.

"With both of you laid up, we got your crew together and knocked out the remaining things on your list," Cooper explains. "The whole company pulled together to get it all done in a week. It was crazy how many of your guys wanted to help. We ended up having to make a schedule because there would've been too many people here at the same time."

Levi crutches his way across the room, staring at all the finished rooms. "I don't even know what to say," he whispers.

"I know you would have preferred to finish it yourself, but knowing it was going to be weeks before you could get back here, we thought you'd rather it be finished."

"Thanks, man," Levi says to Cooper. They awkwardly hug around Levi's crutches.

"I brought books for you to order furniture. We thought you guys would like to pick everything out yourself." Quinn pulls several magazines from her purse.

"Give those to Hope so she can start picking out what she wants," Levi says, looking at me with so many emotions.

"You want me to pick out the furniture?" I ask incredulously.

"Well, this will be your home, too, so yeah, you need to pick out what you want."

"You want me to move in with you?" My voice is turning hysterical. I don't even understand why. We've been living together for the past month, so it wouldn't be any different. But this house was Levi's dream. It's a home for a family—his family. I may have fantasized about living here with him, but I never believed he'd actually want me to.

Levi steps toward me, his hand stroking down my face so lovingly and tender. "Of course, I want you to move in here with me. I want a future with you. A life, a family, everything, here, in the house we designed together."

Tears stream down my face. "I want that, too, Levi. So, so much."

"Good." He leans in and whispers a kiss across my lips.

My whole life has been one heartbreak after another. I've never once felt like I was meant for anything more than surviving day-to-day.

Until I met Levi.

He's shown me what it's like to be loved unconditionally. What it's like to feel as if I'm worth more than the nothing I've always been made to believe I am. He's helped me see how much strength I hold on my own and how much stronger I am with people who love me standing by my side.

I'll never be able to thank him for everything he's done. All my previously held beliefs were shattered by his smile, his joy, and his love.

All I can do is love him with everything I have and hope
it's enough to show him how much he means to me.

44

HOPE

A calmness settles over me as I sit on the wooden bench, watching the trial play out in front of me. I thought I would be racked with nerves today. It would be natural for me to be worried about what's about to happen. Instead, I feel a cold sense of justice steeling my spine. With Levi's hand in mine, I feel stronger than ever.

These past several months have been met with incredible happiness, as well as crushing setbacks. It's been hard not to let myself wallow in the hardships. Some days, it feels as if I'll never be normal. Maybe I won't. Maybe there will always be a reactionary part of me who flinches when someone moves too fast.

For so long, my life was a living hell, and even though I am no longer living in it, I will always be afraid of going back there. But, I think it's okay. It's a reminder of where I've been and how far I've come.

Now, as I sit in the drafty courthouse, listening to the judge speak about the case, a sense of peace settles over me.

In a few short minutes, the nightmare will officially be over. The black cloud hanging over my head will dissipate, finally bringing the sunshine. I can feel eyes on me across the room, hatred seeping out like a black mist. I won't dignify the bastard with my attention. He doesn't deserve it.

I can still see the look on his face when I took the stand to testify.

I ALWAYS THOUGHT Antony was the epitome of the devil. He's got the looks, the charm, and the evil lurking right under the surface. He did a great job of hiding that evil from those he needed to persuade, but I saw it.

Today, sitting across the room in an orange jumpsuit, hands shackled together, the devil inside him is no longer hiding. He looks like pure evil, and I know if we were anywhere else besides a courtroom, he would kill me. That's how much hatred is pouring off him.

"Hope Langley, please take the stand," the judge calls from his bench. Levi squeezes my leg, offering his silent support. He testified this morning, which gave me an idea of what it would be like.

With shaking hands, I stand from the audience and make my way to the front of the courtroom. After I sit down on the stand, the judge swears me in, his tone serious. My chest tightens, making it hard to breathe. For a minute, I start to panic. What if I can't get through this? What if I mess it up and Antony walks because of me?

Through my panic, my gaze lands on Levi sitting in the front row. Noticing my distress, he exaggerates a deep breath, and I unconsciously mimic his action. The tightness in my chest eases as we breathe together until I'm able to focus on the prosecutor walking across the room.

"Are you okay, Hope?" he asks, concern clear on his face.

"Yes, I'm okay."

He nods his head, then begins to ask me questions. He gives me softballs at first to ease me into the rhythm of his questioning.

"Tell me about the night the defendant kidnapped you."

Keeping my eyes on Levi, I tell the whole courtroom what happened. How Antony forced me into the car, how I caused the wreck to escape his capture. Everything. The prosecutor also asks about my previous history with Antony. How I became his wife, the assault, and my involvement in providing the police with evidence. I'm not pressing charges for the sexual assault, but the prosecutor wanted to establish a behavior pattern and prove Antony had a reason to kidnap me.

At the end of my story, it feels like the elephant sitting on my chest has walked away, leaving a sense of peace in its place. It wasn't easy to share my history with a room full of people, but I'm starting to accept it as a part of me without letting it rule my life anymore.

When the prosecutor ends his questioning, my nerves ramp back up. I know the defense is going to try to discredit my statement. The prosecutor prepared me for this moment, but I'm still worried I'm going to mess it up, allowing Antony to go free.

"You said Antony forced you into the car, but that's not entirely true. You let him lead you to the car, didn't you?" the defense attorney asks.

"Antony told me he'd killed my boyfriend. I was lost in the grief of hearing that the one I love was no longer alive. Then, when I realized he was going to put me in the car, I ran."

The defense attorney keeps coming at me, trying to make me change my statement, but strength flows through me as I repeat my story. Never once wavering on the details because they are etched so deeply into my brain, I know I won't mess them up.

Finally, the judge tells me I can step down from the stand. Knowing I did everything I could to put Antony away helps me stand tall as I walk across the floor. I don't even look at Antony as I pass by, even though I can feel him glaring at me.

When I sit next to Levi, his arm wraps around my shoulders, sending all the tension from testifying flowing out of my body. After everything, I can finally relax.

. . .

THE JUDGE'S voice pulls me back from my memory, and I wait with bated breath to hear the jury's final decision.

"Has the jury reached a verdict?"

"We have, Your Honor. For the charge of kidnapping in the first degree, we, the jury, find the defendant, guilty. For the charge of aggravated assault in the first degree, we, the jury, find the defendant, guilty. For the charge of murder in the first degree, we the jury, find the defendant, guilty."

The foreperson goes through the rest of the charges one by one. As each guilty verdict is announced, another weight on my shoulders is lifted. With mine and Levi's testimonies, there was very little standing in the way of a guilty charge, but with Antony's henchman providing evidence for the murders of Tomas, the lawyer, and some of his henchmen in exchange for a lesser sentence, Antony will be out of our lives for good.

He will never see the light of day again, no matter what happens. Adding up the minimum sentences for each charge, he'll die in prison. There will be no more appeals because of mishandled evidence, especially with proof that Antony bribed an officer to falsify the documents.

It's over.

After the final guilty charge is read, the judge orders Antony to be remanded into custody until sentencing. A deep breath falls from my chest that I wasn't even aware I was holding. Levi's arm around my shoulders shakes me from my relieved stupor. He pulls me into his chest, wrapping me up in his love.

"It's over," he whispers into my hair, echoing my thoughts. All I can do is nod. I know if I say anything right now, I'll break down. I refuse to do that until we're home. Until I'm safe from prying eyes.

This case garnered a lot of media attention the first time Antony was tried; going through it all again has blown it up even bigger. I was sucked into the frenzy because of my testimony, which has made things difficult over the past several months. I'm hoping it'll die down when his sentencing is complete.

Levi holds my hand, leading me out of the courtroom. The journalists all try to ask us questions as we leave. Some of them have been super nice, while others feel a little like sharks, lurking in the shallow end for blood.

When we make it to the car, Levi and I both exhale. He grabs my hand, holding it on his lap as usual while he drives us home.

The silence in the car is almost unbearable, but I'm not ready to speak. When we're home, and I'm safe, I'll be ready to break down. To finally purge the last of my anxieties over Antony getting released and of him finding a way to try to kill me or Levi. To move on from the nightmare of my past.

I'm ready to live in the present, looking toward my future with the knowledge that we've made it through the darkest of the dark. All that's left to do now is be happy.

* * *

"HEY, Hope, can you come look at something really quick?" Levi calls from the back door.

I finish stirring the chili simmering on the stove, then slip my coat on to see what Levi wants. The cool fall weather has finally set in, bringing with it the beautiful colors I love. We moved into the Victorian house a few weeks after Cooper and Quinn surprised us with the finished remodel. We had to wait for both our furniture to arrive and our injuries to heal.

We've slowly made it into our home, combining our styles and creating a space so perfect I sometimes have a hard time believing it's mine.

Stepping out onto the patio, I look around the yard only to see Levi standing by the arbor at the back of our property. Confused as to what he would need my help with back there,

I make my way to him only to stop a few feet away when he turns with a bouquet of tulips and white orchids in his hand.

"Come here, love," he says, holding out his hand. Walking the final steps, I grab it, seriously unsure of what's happening.

"What's going on?"

He hands me the flowers, reminiscent of the first time he gave me a similar bouquet. "I have something important I want to talk with you about."

My brows furrow. "Okay?"

"Over the past few months, we've settled into our new life in our beautiful home. It's been amazing, but there's one thing we still need to complete."

I wait, wondering what the heck he's talking about. There are no more renovations left to finish. We've painted every-thing, and the guest rooms are done, so I have no idea what we still have left to complete.

Then suddenly, he's kneeling in front of me. The flowers fall to the ground as my hands fly to my mouth in surprise.

"I love you, Hope. I knew you were the one for me when you thought there was something wrong with the flowers I was giving you instead of realizing they were *for* you." He grins. I'd laugh with him since I was an idiot, but I'm strug-gling to get past my shock. "You're everything I've ever wanted in a partner, everything I've ever dreamed of, and I would love it if you'd do me the honor of becoming my wife."

I launch myself at him, knocking him to the ground. Laughing, he wraps his arms around me to pull me even closer. "Is that a yes?"

"Yes! Oh, my god, Levi. Yes!"

I slam my mouth to his, overwhelmed with how much love I feel for this incredible man. He's my entire world. Everything I've always dreamed of having but never thought I'd truly get to experience.

Levi groans when my tongue wraps around his, pushing

the kiss from loving to passionate. I frown when he pulls away, our breaths coming out in pants. "If you keep kissing me like that, I'm going to take you right here in the grass, and despite how much I want you, I'd rather not freeze my ass off."

Laughing, I lift myself off Levi, and he quickly stands, adjusting himself before pulling me back into his arms. "You're really going to be my wife?"

"I really am." I grin.

"Thank fuck." He picks me up in his arms, carries me across the yard, then into the house. Before he gets to the stairs, I stop him. "Wait. I need to turn off the chili."

"Good thinking. I'd rather not burn dinner," he says, heading toward the kitchen.

"Or the house down." I huff out a laugh.

"Your belief in my stamina is amazing, my love." Levi's grin is wicked. "And I look forward to meeting your expectations."

When we make it to our bedroom, he finally sets me down, stripping me of my clothes, as well as his. He shows me how much he loves me with every kiss, touch, and stroke. Proving he will always love me unconditionally.

This man gave me strength when I needed it most and the space to realize I could be strong on my own. Who showed me what true love looks like and will be there by my side through it all.

He's my best friend, the love of my life, my everything.

Forever.

EPILOGUE

HOPE

Screaming giggles filter up the stairs and into the library, disrupting the quiet moment I was enjoying. There are times when I miss getting to read for hours on a Saturday with no interruptions, but hearing those giggles makes the interrupted time completely worth it.

I look over at our oldest, Ryan, who sits in one of the wingback chairs next to mine. He grins at me when he hears his dad growling like a monster. He looks just like Levi with his light brown hair and hazel eyes, but he shares my personality. At six, he already enjoys reading with me, much to the annoyance of our youngest, Adalaide. She's only four and is all Levi. An utter wild child who can make me laugh harder than her father sometimes.

"Should we go see what they're up to?" I ask.

He nods his head, then puts his book on the table next to his chair so he can come back later. I do the same, then follow him out of the room to head downstairs.

We walk into utter chaos. Pillows are on the floor of the living room, dining room chairs are placed sporadically around the couch, and Addie is jumping from pillow to pillow screaming, "You won't catch me, dragon!" Her brown, kinky curled hair bounces around her shoulders with each jump, making me laugh.

"What in the world is going on here?"

"Mommy! Daddy's trying to eat me. If we step in the lava, we die!"

"Ooo. What have we here, more people to snack on?" Levi growls, turning toward Ryan.

"Run, Ry!" Addie screams, which makes Ryan jump into the fray before Levi can catch him.

Then Levi turns his attention to me. "Hmm. I see a delicious-looking mommy over there." He wiggles his eyebrows, a salacious grin on his face saying he meant that to be dirty.

"Hurry, Mom! Before he catches you," Ryan calls from his place on the couch. When Levi lunges, I jump onto the nearest pillow, hopping toward the kids. Levi attempts to catch us, sometimes pretending to miss the kids when they sneak by, other times, snatching them off the ground, blowing raspberries into their necks.

He catches me around the waist, biting into my neck as if he's trying to eat me. It makes the kids laugh hysterically every time. When we're all panting and exhausted, we fall to the floor on top of the pile of pillows to catch our breath.

"I need a drink of water," Ryan says, jumping up from the floor and heading into the kitchen.

"Me, too!" Addie follows like she always does, leaving me and Levi lying next to each other.

Levi turns toward me. "Was that just a lot of exercise, or are we getting old?"

"Both."

His look of indignation makes me laugh. I scoot closer to kiss him soundly. He's still everything I ever wanted in a partner. He's constantly showing me how much he loves me, and watching him be a dad is one of the greatest things I've ever experienced.

Over the last ten years, we've come a long way in our

relationship. My trauma rarely rears its ugly head, but when it does, Levi still loves me through the panic. We've filled our beautiful Victorian home with so much love and laughter, I'm not sure it'll hold it all sometimes. Our life is everything we ever dreamed it to be.

"What do you say, want to add to the brood?" he teases.

When I raise my eyebrows, a smile playing at my lips, his face drops in surprise. "I don't think we have a choice this time."

"Seriously?" He reaches out to place his hand on my stomach. "Are you really pregnant?"

The awe on his face has tears swimming in my eyes. All I can do is nod in confirmation.

Levi smashes his lips to mine, showing me how happy this news makes him.

"They're doing it again!" Ryan grouses, his hands on his hips.

Levi and I both laugh at his annoyance. "And I'll never stop, son, so you better get used to it."

When he kisses me again, happiness fills my heart so full that it feels as if it will burst. I got incredibly lucky to find the one man willing to love me through my broken pieces. Through his love, I've found a strength in me I never knew I had. And with him by my side, I'll never be stronger.

THE END

ACKNOWLEDGMENTS

To you, amazing reader, for reading this series and sticking by me as I continue on this journey.

To my husband for dealing with my neurosis while I wrote this book. There were some really intense days and I wouldn't have been able to do this without him.

To my family for their never-ending belief in my abilities. Your constant support has carried me this far and I love you all so much.

To Jaime Ryter for being one hell of an editor. You were the key to making this book what it is and I love ya for it.

To Clarise at CT Cover Creations for bringing to life these two characters so beautifully.

To Tina, Robin, Emily, and Isa for taking the time to help me shape this story into a beautiful representation of how strong love can be. This book wouldn't be what it is without your help.

To the RWR group for their constant support and witty humor when I needed it the most.

ABOUT THE AUTHOR

Shelby Gunter is a romance suspense author who loves to write twisted endings you'll never see coming. She lives in Kansas City with her husband and fur baby, and is either writing, reading, or drinking coffee. Sometimes all three at the same time.

You can find Shelby on all social media sites, including Facebook, Instagram, and TikTok. You can also join the fun and grab exclusive content through her Facebook reader group, Shelby's Bookshelf Besties.

Visit authorshelbygunter.com for more info!